First Monday Murder

A Jimmie Rae Flea Market Mystery

Lisa Love Harris

Published by Lisa Love Harris

Cover design by Red Bike Studios
ISBN-10: 1470102730
ISBN-13: 978-1470102739

In loving memory of Grandma & Pappy

Acknowledgments

When I was diagnosed with breast cancer nine years ago, my busy life came to a screeching halt—if only for a moment. It was stage one cancer, but aggressive. While undergoing treatment that long summer, I read and wrote, and wrote some more. And yes, I junked! I junked with a bright bandana wrapped around my bald head. I smiled, forged ahead, and JUNKED!

During this time at the doorstep of middle age, it became all too apparent life is short and there would never be a perfect time to do all the things I once dreamed of. With nothing but time to lose, I became determined to rediscover my dreams. I like to say cancer gave me the courage to be brave and take risks. Whether that's true or not, *First Monday Murder* is the result of that summer of chemo and contemplation.

As I recovered from numerous reconstructive surgeries, I discovered a passion for wearing turquoise jewelry, cowboy boots, and listening to endless hours of Bob Wills, Lucinda Williams, and Stevie Ray Vaughn. I enjoyed hopping into my red Ford F-250, Jessie, and hitting the Texas back roads often finding new friends, awesome road food, and funky old stuff. I also realized how deep my seventh generation Texas roots run.

This joyful life journey has led me to a community of incredibly talented friends, as well as a continuous junkin' trail full of vintage, glitter, and rust.

To every vendor, dealer, road-tripper, gypsy, dreamer, artist, picker, and junker—THANK YOU! Y'all make it a true joy to be a part of something so organic, authentic, unique, eclectic, and fabulous.

To my muses, the incredible Junk Gypsies, Janie, Amie and Jolie, thank you for your generous loving spirit and makin' junkin' cool. "Well behaved women rarely make history," continues to be one of my favorite sayings. Thanks y'all.

Thank you to all my friends in the Great Pacific Northwest. You have opened my eyes to a whole new level of creative energy. My list of NW junkin' buddies is blessedly extensive.

I'd especially like to thank Pam of Bugaboo Vintage Design for sharing a booth and lots of laughs; Leslie for welcoming me to your charming Clayson Farm Antique Show; and the 2nd Saturdayz Junk Tribe for the opportunity to be a part of your wonderful Vintage Market.

Many thanks also go to Dixie and Linda, The Funky Junk Sisters, for your energetic entrepreneurial spirit, love of junk, and making Junk Salvation a happy reality.

In addition, sincere thanks go to Pam of One Gal's Trash and Plucky Maidens for your enthusiasm for all things vintage, soulful encouragement, and genuine kindness.

And now, a shout-out to my Texas junkin' buddies, especially my BFF, Tracey Jane of Diggin' It. Thanks girl for dragging me along every weekend and encouraging me to start Garden Cat sixteen years ago. Just so you know, "Junkin' has saved my life many times!" Love ya.

To my dear friends The Rodeo Queens of Petticoats on the Prairie, especially Janie of Flutter, thank you for stopping by Garden Cat at Junk Salvation. You ladies reflect all the best characteristics of Texan womanhood, and I'm so happy to call y'all friends.

A big ole, "Hey, y'all!" to all my sweet Lone Star junkin' buddies— I can't wait to catch up with y'all down the blacktop.

To Cath, thank you for living in McKinney and being from Seattle. Thanks for being a blessing in my life.

To my dear friend, Janet, for inspiring me every day with your faith and courage, and for loving Coleman Cottage as much as I do. Love you, sweet friend.

To ALL my friends at St. Peter's, MISD Orchestra, Jazzercise, McKinney Garden Club, and Antique Company Mall thanks to each of you for your friendship, prayers, love, confidence, encouragement, and laughs. McKinney will always be special to me because of each one of you.

A heartfelt "thanks" especially to Sara, Michele, Lynne, Chris, and Christine for your smiles, hugs, and encouraging words through all of life's little struggles.

A special thanks to Jayne whose incomparable faith in Jesus, and extreme Texas sass in the face of cancer continues to bless me each day. Rest in peace, sweet lady.

To Sonja, Kristi, Liz, and Lisa thanks to each of you for taking the time to assist with this manuscript. I truly appreciate your suggestions and comments.

Thanks to my dear La Petites, Susan and Jessica, for your detailed critiques and priceless honesty. Also to Susan, a special thanks for sharing your sage wisdom, getting me back on track, and for cutting the path to this new adventure.

Thanks to Sisters in Crime Guppies Chapter. Y'all are a great school to swim with!

Thank you to my fabulous copy editor, Lisa, for your expertise, assistance, and invaluable advice.

Thank you to my supportive parents for teaching me the importance of taking the road less traveled, chocolate pie, and books. I love you both always.

Thank you to our children for putting up with endless days of my junking, writing, and editing. You make me proud, and I love you both so very much.

For my high school sweetheart and the love of my life, Shaun Lee, thank you for being my partner on this sweet, slow dance of life. Love you forever.

Thank you, Lord for your abundant blessings.

Peace, love, and all the good stuff, y'all.

This is a work of fiction and while (thankfully) First Monday Trade Days does exist in Canton, TX, as does the Armstrong Browning Library in Waco, TX, Niceton, TX does not. Niceton is an imaginary place created as a compilation of all my favorite Texas towns. So don't look for it on any Texas map. In addition, as a work of fiction, names, characters, places, and incidents are pure products of my imagination or are used fictitiously and are not to be construed as nonfiction. Any similarities to actual events, locales, organizations, or persons, living or dead, are pure coincidence.

- Lisa Love Harris

Chapter One

"If we don't have it at Cowboy's Antiques and Gas Emporium you plumb don't need it! Up ahead two miles. Come see us, y'all!"

A dog shot across the road shocking my senses back to the reality of driving. I swerved and missed him only to realize the fuel gauge on my '53 Ford truck, Old Blue, was setting on empty and my bladder was sitting on full. Grandma Star's practical wisdom resonated in my head. "Jimmie Rae Murphy, never pass up a chance to use the indoor plumbing. You never know what's down the blacktop."

So when I drove around the next bend on the drowsy two-lane Texas highway and saw the painted plywood sign I knew relief was near. The funny thing was I didn't remember that place being there when I last drove this desolate road on my way to the monthly flea market.

I steered Old Blue off the two-lane toward the gravel driveway and killed the engine. Cowboy's Antiques and Gas Emporium looked to be an original 1950s style gas station. The building was wood frame with flaky white paint. Although I loved the look on Shabby Chic furniture, it looked plain tacky on this old building. Faded vintage metal motel lawn chairs lined up under the long stretch of covered front porch.

A large man with a fiery red beard and scraggly ponytail appeared at the building's double front-screened doors. Dressed in baggy blue jeans and an untucked denim shirt with "Lonnie" embroidered across the upper left-hand side, his heavily inked arms looked like the Sunday edition cartoon pages. Most of his head was pierced – from his right eyebrow to his ears, down to the small gold ring in his left nostril, barely visible through the red and gray whiskers on his upper lip.

Instinct told me to haul booty out of the gravel driveway. Nature's call overruled as I jumped from Old Blue and banged the door shut.

"Hey, little girl, what's up?" he said. He walked toward me wiping his hands on a rag and stuffing it into his back pocket. His smooth voice reminded me of the legendary radio disc jockey, Wolfman Jack, with a Texas twist.

I wanted to set this bubba straight from the git-go. *Name's Jimmie Rae, imbecile!* I let my thoughts scream. With my almost ex-husband acting like such a jerk lately, I was pretty fed up with males in general. However, since I was in the middle of nowhere Texas and late meeting up with my friends to hit First Monday, I let 'little girl' blow past me like a semi on the interstate.

"Just need a fill up and a ladies room, please." Instinct continued to pulse chills down my spine despite the warm May morning.

"What a beaut she is," he said patting Old Blue on her side as he opened her gas tank.

I didn't like the way he touched my truck, his big rough hands running along Blue's shiny paint job. "Uh, be careful. The cap's tricky."

"Oh, don't worry, I got it. You go on. The facilities are inside, toward the back, last door on the left. I'll get this old gal filled up."

"Okay. I didn't know full service was still available anywhere," I said.

"Ah, well, we do that for our special customers," he said with a wink.

Ick, creepy guy winking at me.

"There's more junk inside too if you don't have enough already," Lonnie said pointing to a few items I had in the back of my truck.

That yard sale a few miles ago had set me back a few minutes from meeting my friends, but it had been worth it. I'd scored some old windows, and even a funky seahorse birdbath.

"Can a girl ever have too much?" I wasn't flirting with the guy, but I'd learned years ago when I was first on my own it was just easier to go along with a man's smart-ass comment and be sassy back than to be argumentative or defensive. I wasn't sure if this was a Texas thing or a Southern one. However, I was pretty sure my sisters on either coast would balk at this tidbit of womanly advice. All I knew was it worked and since I was out in the middle of nowhere and had to pee right now, it was my best strategy.

I hitched my leather messenger bag a little higher on my shoulder and walked toward the building feeling his eyes sear through my backside. *Creep!* I tugged open one of the faded red double screen-doors and stepped inside before it slammed shut. Although it was almost hot outside, the inside of the old building was surprisingly cool with a frame window open and a vintage silver oscillating fan blowing back and forth. My feet followed dirty mid-century pink tiles past dusty decades-old knick-knacks, collectibles, and plain old junk to the ladies room. *What a dump*!

Discovering the gender appropriate restroom, I shut the heavy wooden door behind me and slipped the metal clasp across, locking it. Void of charm and cleanliness, the dated facilities were just a notch above porta-potty quality. I looked away avoiding my reflection in the dirty mirror, not wanting to see my unruly brown hair, tired green eyes, and sallow complexion. The past month had aged me in ways I hadn't anticipated. I knew I looked and felt every second of my thirty-seven years. Worse, I didn't even care.

A year ago when Joe first left I felt abandoned. Six months and numerous court hearings later, I knew it was a matter of days until the divorce would be final. I tried to shake off the familiar reminder of pain and failure. But today was all about leaving that crap in my life behind and hanging out at the flea market with my friends. It was just the cheering up I needed. A quick check of my cell phone for the time indicated I was already running more than a little late to meet them. I sure didn't want to have to explain to them that I'd stopped at a yard sale. I had to get my business done and get back on the road.

In addition to the usual porcelain facilities, there was a plastic shelf unit full of medium-sized cardboard boxes. A slim, rectangular box leaned against the commode. I reached over to move it. Surprised by its weight, I shook it slightly. It made no sound. My grandma says I've always had an impulsive curiosity—one that made Christmases and birthday surprises nearly impossible. I shrugged my shoulders and impulsively slit the seal of slick mail tape with my truck key.

Pulling a layer of tissue paper away revealed a man's portrait staring back at me. Shock registered from my brain to my fingertips. I readjusted my grasp on the portrait to keep from dropping it. I knew this painting well. What might look like an aged oil painting to the average person was actually the focus of the last seven years of my life employed at Baylor University's Armstrong Browning Library. My hands shook as I touched the frame. Browning's friend, Sir William Blake, captured the English poet's contemplative expression more than a hundred years ago following the death of his beloved wife, Elizabeth. I'd never held any Browning artifact without white cotton gloves and then, only in the Library's acquisition room. To now hold it in my bare hands in a public bathroom was plain wrong on so many levels. *So how did Robert Browning's portrait get here of all places?*

Once again Grandma Star's voice caught me like a line-drive upside the head. "Girl, between your cat-killing curiosity and junk obsession, mark my words someday you'll find yourself in whole heap of trouble." Today of all days seemed to be the day those words I'd heard my entire life chose to crash together in this ladies room off a lonely piece of Texas highway.

As I took the portrait from the box, a manila envelope fell to the floor. I sat the portrait on a rickety white side table and retrieved the envelope. My heart raced as the open envelope revealed what appeared to be three Elizabeth Barrett Browning letters to her beloved Robert prior to their elopement to Italy– their fragility and priceless historic value lost in this dingy bathroom. Unease burdened my shoulders like red clay bricks.

I sat the manila envelope on top of the portrait and took care of my business. As I washed my hands, a loud knock startled me.

"Hey, what's going on in there?" Lonnie's impatient tone told me I might be stretching his hospitality a bit thin. With no paper towels in sight, I slapped my wet hands on my denim skirt and considered my bizarre circumstances.

"Oh, now, you know a lady never tells." I decided what to do as I looked at the portrait and letters. My timing had to be just right. I took a deep breath and flushed. While the decades old toilet whirled, I worked. I placed the empty envelope around the portrait. There was no time to wrap it properly as I had only a few days ago when I'd prepared it to be shipped for a nineteenth-century poets' exhibit. I closed the box and mashed the tape down as well as I could. Leaning it against the wall, I opened my messenger bag to stash the yellowed letters.

He knocked again. Louder. "Hold your horses, mister! I'll be right out! Good grief!" My brain was still trying to process finding the Browning items here. It seemed I should at least take the letters as proof there was something bizarre going on here.

There was no time to place the letters in my bag without rearranging my extra clothes and other flea market necessities. Plan B sprang into action. I gingerly tucked them beneath the band of my sports bra and pulled my t-shirt down over them. After I got out of here, I would call the Library's director and ask if there were any items missing from the collection. I wasn't even sure if the letters were real or really good fakes. Regardless, my pulse raced and the sensation of opening a Pandora's Box with all its consequences was suddenly quite real.

I grabbed the sliver of Ivory soap, quickly washing my hands again. No telling how many germs were in this place. I opened the door to find Lonnie leaning a little too close to my personal space. This guy was really beginning to tick me off.

"Is there some problem, buddy? Gee, can't a lady take care of business in peace?" I said glaring him in the face. If I could stare down a room of college kids, this guy was nothing. Who cared that I had to look up to make eye contact with his six-foot-four-inch frame? I'd been through too much lately to let that slow me down. I stood tall in my favorite slightly scuffed thrift store cowboy boots and dared him to get ugly with me.

My non-verbal stance got my point across. He met my stare and offered a tension-breaking smile. "Uh, sorry. I just remembered all those boxes in there."

"Oh, those boxes?" I said pointing to the shelves. "I didn't pay any attention to them." I said in a bluff. I readjusted my messenger bag and crossed my arms across my chest, the pressure pressing the old letters solidly against my flesh. I just prayed I wasn't sweating enough to harm them. "Should I have?" I said in a challenging tone.

"Uh, no. It's just some supplies we store in there since we don't get many lady folks stopping by."

"Say, this other stuff is for sale isn't it?" I walked past him toward the junky aisles hoping he wouldn't figure out that I knew what "supplies" those boxes in the ladies room really held.

He returned the smile and quickly looked into the ladies room. Apparently, satisfied with what he saw, or rather what he *didn't* see, he moved toward a tall glass half full of (presumably) ice tea sweating on the front oak counter.

"Sure," he said. He took a long drink.

One whiff as I walked past informed me the amber liquid wasn't iced tea.

"Hey, Lonnie, get your big ass out here now!" a man's voice spewed through the round speaker hanging between an industrial sized clock and a velvet painting of the "Last Supper."

"Ma'am, forgive my brother's rudeness," Lonnie said as he went through the grimy Dutch door into the garage bay area. "You just look around and I'll be right back, 'kay?"

"Sure," I said.

Attached to the main building, the garage consisted of four bays. With the left two doors pulled down, the scent of oil, sweat, and dirt escaped from the garage bays into the building's "antiques emporium" area permeating a rancid smell. A country radio station played over plastic speakers dotting the spider-webbed ceiling.

The sound of a large metal wrench slamming to the concrete floor followed by loud curse words grabbed my attention. I peeked through the open part of the Dutch door where I caught sight of a man taller and even more muscular than "Wolfman" Lonnie in a high dollar black cowboy hat–presumably the "Cowboy" of the operation. But not like any of the cowboys I'd ever met before. A dark, thick crocheted brow shadowed his narrow eyes and crooked nose. Deep scars careened down his left jaw pulling his small, tight lips slightly to one side. Even in the light of day, darkness seemed to consume him. An unexplained evil.

Dressed in sharply creased Wranglers, a tooled leather belt with a large silver buckle, and a freshly pressed denim Western shirt, he was focused on screaming obscenities into a tiny black cell phone. It was one of those weird moments produced by modern technology. As a teacher and student of literature I was trained to find and appreciate moments of irony such as this. However, this was no time for ironic analysis. There was definitely something strange going on at this hole in the road. My brain juggled the increasing desire to contact the police with my urgency to get the heck out of Dodge and forget these creeps and this placc. I checked the time on my phone again. Crap, now I was really late!

Although I loved Miranda Lambert, now was not the time to hear her belting out "Crazy Ex-girlfriend" through the speaker just above the door. I strained to hear what Cowboy was yelling into his phone. I didn't have to strain too much to catch his extra loud, "What the hell were you thinking?" as it exploded through the garage. I tried to hear Lonnie's reply. Instead, Cowboy's voice boomed again. "You'd better find a way to shut her up or the whole gig will be over before it begins!" he said spinning around to shake a fist in Lonnie's face.

"Wait a ding damn minute!" Cowboy fumed walking over to the open garage door. He spit on the driveway and turned back around to face his brother. "Uh, Lonnie, whose damn jalopy is out there? Don't even tell me you're stupid enough to leave someone in there to snoop around."

Lonnie's garbled answer was too low to be heard over the loud radio. It must have made Cowboy madder though because the next thing I knew, he let go of a string of words that would have made a sailor blush. The expletives were punctuated with him throwing a big, metal mallet through the thick air. My eyes followed the mallet as it shot across the garage at full force. I did an involuntary jump as it hit the metal siding and ricocheted sound through the building. It landed at the far bay next to a 1970s Mary Kay pink Cadillac. I stood motionless at the sight of the car. Seeing it taunted my cranial frantic button as I fought another impulsive urge to beat feet out of this rat hole.

I recognized the car. It looked just like Maxine's. Finding my best friend's Caddy here of all places, was as wacky as finding the Browning artifacts in the ladies room. My feet sashayed away from the door while my brain weighed my chances of escaping to Old Blue and peeling out to the Texas blacktop that had led me here. I'd just let the police figure out what was going on at Cowboy's. *But wait a darn minute.* I still had to pay for the stupid gas Lonnie already pumped into Old Blue. Otherwise it would be *me* the police would be after. Darn.

I pretended to be interested in some old rose covered dishes as my hands fumbled getting my cell phone out my front pocket. I should call the police, but I wasn't sure what to report. I had no concrete evidence anything was going on. Just a hunch. And from what little I knew about it, I was pretty sure the police weren't in the hunch business. Instead, I called Maxine to tell her I was running late.

She caught my call on the first ring. "You're late! Where are you? I've been trying to call you. I'll kick your butt if you're at a yard sale or something. You were supposed to be here already," Max said in an impatient whisper. "I'm sitting here making small talk with Miss

Evelyn and Daryl Ann, but they're getting fidgety and ready to head on to First Monday. We can't let them get there before us. They'll get all the good stuff!"

"Maxine, slow down. I'm almost there," I said cutting her off. "Maybe another twenty or thirty minutes tops. That's why I'm calling. I'm at some junk-store-gas-station in the middle of nowhere and saw your car. At least I think it's your car."

"Jimmie, girl, my car was stolen a couple of days ago." *Oh, great.* "You'd better high tail it out of there. Be careful and hurry up!" Her voice faded.

"Max? Maxine, are you there? Can you hear me?" I pulled the phone away from my ear and saw the dreaded words, "No Signal." Great. I just loved modern technology. Time to get out of here before the bubba brothers decided I'd seen something they didn't want seen.

I peeked out the door again. Near the middle garage bay, Lonnie leaned against the workbench smoking a cigarette and holding his "tea" glass looking perplexed.

Cowboy's attention turned to Lonnie. "Get rid of her, you idiot!" Then they both looked my way.

I seized the moment. "Hey fellas! Nice joint you've got here. Just love that pink Caddie over there! My friend has one just like it – where'd you fellas find that one?" I fibbed from the open Dutch door, the blood pulsing through my veins. I flashed a brilliant Miss America smile, and even threw Lonnie a quick wink. I figured these two knuckleheads were all badass but wouldn't actually dare harm an innocent customer. I prayed I'd figured them correctly. An incorrect guess could mean they'd have no problems shutting me up…out here…in the middle of freakin' nowhere.

"Why you so interested?" Cowboy said as he calmly placed his cell phone in his shirt pocket. "You want to trade your crappy hunk-of-junk for a truly classy ride, girlie?"

His tone was light. Light with a hint of malice. Okay, more than a hint of malice. Maybe more like malice sprinkled with a violent tendency. His sinister tone and loud body language told me he'd have no problem committing a violent act against my person and leaving me to rot. Forget that! My pride overshadowed his threatening tone. Nobody insults Old Blue to my face.

I dropped the smile. "No reason to be an ass about it. You just don't see old Mary Kay pink Caddies everyday, mister." I kicked the closed part of the Dutch door with my boot. The action caused my oversized bag to hit the shelf behind my shoulder and knock a few Muppet Show cartoon glasses to the dirty concrete floor. Crashing glassware rang out over Tim McGraw's mellow, sexy voice. I backed away from the mess. Now there was a nice barrier of broken glass between the boys and me. "Oh, darn. Sorry 'bout that. I'm kinda in a hurry. How much do I owe for the gas?"

Cowboy walked over and looked over the Dutch door to the shards of glass. His blue eyes were full of anger. He took a cigarette from his other shirt pocket and placed it between his lips. "Hon, now you're going to have to pay for those glasses too. Shouldn't be so damn klutzy."

I looked to the floor then stared him down. "Umm, no. I don't think so, mister. Seems to me you shouldn't have stacked them so close to the doorway. The fault seems to be with your inability to display your merchandise in a safe manner." I held his glare and flipped my large bag to the other shoulder, knocking off the remaining glasses. I raised my eyebrows and smiled again.

Lonnie quickly smashed his cigarette out and pushed Cowboy aside. "Well now, accidents do happen, don't they? It's no problem miss. Just some dumb old glasses our momma bought at some damn auction. Let's get you rung up for the fuel so you can be on your way." As the two big thugs stared at one another, neither moving,

Cowboy's phone lit up again in his front pocket. He pulled a lighter from his jeans pocket, shoved his brother back, lit his cigarette, and walked toward the rear of the garage to answer his phone.

Lonnie looked over the door at the broken shards. "I'd better just go around. I'll be right there, miss."

As Lonnie walked from the garage bay around to the front door, I took the opportunity to shift Elizabeth's letters back up. I had the unsettling feeling they were slipping beneath my t-shirt. I sure didn't want to lose them now.

I busied myself looking at some Homer Laughlin dishes. The prices were cheap, a dollar each. I carried two and moved toward the vintage flowerpots displayed like a ceramic rainbow on a dusty white wooden tiered plant stand in the front window. They were priced right for resale. I selected a small aqua one marked eight dollars, fifty cents.

The front screen-door squeaked as it was pulled open replying with a loud slam announcing Lonnie's return to his torn vinyl barstool behind the cash register. I touched the front pocket of my jean skirt and hoped I still had some cash. It was past time to walk my boots right out those doors and get out of there. What a creepy place Cowboy's Antiques and Gas Emporium had turned out to be. A creepy place with a couple of sketchy characters and what appeared to be lots of stolen loot.

Lonnie cleared his throat and took another big gulp of his drink. "Sorry about that. My brother has some what do ya call it? Oh, yeah, anger issues. So, y'all set then, miss? It looks like you found a couple of things too. Let's see— The dishes total ten fifty. Oh, yeah, the gas came up to thirty-six dollars and eighty-seven cents." Lonnie pushed a few buttons on his black hand-held calculator. "With tax, that's a total of fifty-one dollars and twenty-seven cents, miss," he said as he looked out the door toward my truck. "You a dealer?" he asked.

I'd learned antique dealers could often sniff each other out. "Yeah, you know how it is. I buy what I like, but have to sell some of it so I can buy more. It's really kind of an obsession."

"Yes, ma'am," he said taking my money. He pushed hard on a stubborn key on the antique register. The cash drawer ran out in response. He tucked my bills in and took out the change. "Believe you me, I know all about the junkin' obsession. This here was momma's stuff." He stopped to cross himself. "'Tween you and me, she kinda got in over her head before her passing last fall. This is just part of her stuff. We've got a barn full. Thing is, she never bothered with the business end. Bill collectors are a far cry from antique collectors. They're just not interested in this kind of stuff. My brother has it worked out though." He winked at me and said, "He's the smart one. I'm just the good lookin' one," he said as he unsheathed a knife and began sharpening it on a whetstone.

A glance up at Lonnie sharpening his Bowie knife told me it was definitely time to beat feet out of there. Both the Browning items and Maxine's car would have to wait for the authorities to investigate. I had the feeling these boys might invite me to hang around because maybe I'd seen too much. The spidery feeling of fear crawled up my spine as visions of "Texas Chainsaw Massacre" began doing back-flips across my mind.

I adjusted the strap of my messenger bag across my body, took the plastic bag he handed me, and crammed the change in my front pocket. "Well then, thanks!"

Before I could open the screen door to escape, Cowboy entered. He leaned on the doorframe, lit a cigarette, inhaled deeply, and let out a massive plume of smoke. "What's your rush, girlie? What the hell you got in there anyway?" He pointed to my bag.

My chest tightened as my stomach threatened reversing breakfast. I could feel my entire body get tense. I hated the word "girlie." I had a Tai Kwon Do black belt and although I couldn't take both of these jerks, I could make them walk funny for a long time. Still, I erred on the cautious side. I didn't need any more drama today.

"Only the necessities and a couple of books," I said. "Now look, it's been fun and all, but I've got to get going." I walked to the door, held my breath near Cowboy as he exhaled cigarette smoke on me, and opened the door. He pulled the messenger bag strap off my shoulder.

"Not so fast, girlie. We reserve right to check all bags."

Chapter Two

"Don't miss Canton's world famous First Monday Trade Days! With more than 3,000 vendors spread out over six acres this market dating back to 1850, offers shoppers every variety of household products, clothing, furniture, home décor, antiques, and collectibles. Come on by and see what all the fuss is about!"

"That's no way to win repeat customers," I said as I opened my bag exposing feminine hygiene products, lacy under-things, and a change of clothes. Cowboy stepped back releasing the strap like it was on fire.

"I don't know what you're looking for mister, but I dare say, it's not in my bag. Now gentlemen, if you'll excuse me, the open road is calling my name." I pushed the screen door open and walked confidently toward Old Blue.

As I headed to Old Blue, I heard Lonnie call out. "Okay, miss. You just promise to come back and see us, you hear?"

As I approached Old Blue with my back to the bubba-brothers, I smiled facetiously. *Sure, and I've got some pigs that soar through the air, too.* I had perfected the hop-in-the-door-and-turn-the-ignition-on-at-the-same-time-move during a few bad choices with some unsavory characters at a bar near Kerrville. The move didn't fail me now as I spun out, kicking up gravel and dirt and pushed Old Blue as fast as I could.

In the last twenty minutes, I learned more than I needed to know about the likes of Lonnie and Cowboy. I accelerated Old Blue onto the blacktop ribbon road. Was that Max's car in the garage? And why were priceless letters from the Armstrong Browning Library now lying on the seat beside my leather messenger bag?

Almost half an hour later I was stabbing a fork into the fleshy part of an oozing cinnamon roll at the Piney Woods Café; the usual spot where I caught up with Maxine and the others. I pressed number four on my phone and called Dr. Eva Gifford, the Library's director, to leave a rather cryptic message. In the meantime, while I waited to hear from Dr. Gifford, Maxine and I would still have plenty of time to shop at First Monday, and hopefully I would get the potential Browning issue straightened out later this afternoon.

Miss Evelyn Sue Dinsmore's famous white beehive hairdo stood tall like a beacon in the crowded café. She and Daryl Ann Sumner, who was Evelyn Sue's peer, but kept her meticulously bobbed hair colored blonde with frosted highlights, were discussing the upcoming fundraiser for our hometown's animal shelter at other end of the table.

Max sat across from me near the window. Her long, silky red hair gleamed in the sunlight. She wore her favorite flea market uniform—espresso colored cargos rolled up, a white cotton v-necked T-shirt, and her red Converse high-tops. Her olive "Junk Gypsy" canvas bag hung on the ladder back chair. Max stared into her empty coffee cup as if there were some inscription there. Normally the center of every conversation, Max was unusually quiet.

I cleared my throat and said in a low tone, "Max, I think I saw your car."

She looked up at me and raised her eyebrows. "Why are you whispering, Jimmie? Where were you anyway?"

"Gee, you're testy today. I was at some junk shop called Cowboy's Antiques and Gas Emporium back on Highway 36."

"Where's that?"

"It's back toward I-45 somewhere," I said pointing toward the red striped curtained window. "I'd never seen it before or at least I never noticed it before this morning. Never mind all that, it's what I found there that's so weird."

"Yeah, I know—You think you saw my old Cadillac. I'd like to believe my car is there." Max tilted her head to one side motioning me to move closer to her, she lowered her voice. "It's such a pain to get around like today for example, depending on Daryl Ann for a ride. Do you know she made me remove my high-top sneakers inside her precious car? She's so dang picky about everything!" She rolled her eyes. Her expression softened. "Hey, maybe we should go back there and check it out."

"You mean instead of going to First Monday?" I didn't like the idea of going back to Cowboy's. I felt lucky to get out of there when I did and somehow I didn't think they'd be too friendly to me if I showed up again this morning. Besides by now they probably realized I had taken the letters and I wanted to get the police involved before I stepped a foot back into that place.

"Yes, silly. You said they had some stuff to sell, right?"

"Yeah, but they weren't too friendly, Maxine. In fact, they were downright creepy. Besides, I don't think they'd take kindly to us snooping around. It could have been just another 1970s pink Cadillac, I guess. I couldn't really see it too well. Tell you what, as soon as we get on the road we'll call the police and report it, okay?"

"Sure. You're probably right; we're a good sixty miles from Niceton. My car's probably already across the border or it's been stripped to nothing by now. I'm not sure it's even worth calling the police again. Last week they didn't seem too excited to look for an old pink Cadillac when I called it in," Max said in a forlorn voice. "They told me they had real cases to solve first."

"Well, besides the car, I found a lot of other stuff there."

"Really, Jimmie Rae, can't you just hold your horses until we get up to Canton? It's like you're afraid you're going to miss out on a piece of junk or two," Maxine said. "You've gotten so obsessed with this gig. There'll be plenty of stuff out at the First Monday, you know."

My reply to Max's speech was interrupted by her cell phone's ring-tone. Before I could explain about the Browning letters or portrait, she pushed "Talk" on her purple cell phone, rose from her chair, and headed toward the door. She held up an index finger indicating "wait a moment" and stepped outside the café. I sighed and took another bite of cinnamon roll and a sip of coffee.

"It's a disgrace how cell phones interrupt civilized conversation these days," Evelyn Sue Dinsmore said from across the table.

I looked up to catch her disapproving expression. Miss Evelyn Sue was a small woman with a Texas-sized hairdo all right. It was probably one of the best-preserved vintage things in our Niceton antique mall. Years of Stay Put Hairspray shellacked each silver strand of hair in place and kept her beehive unnaturally upright. Perhaps that could account for a ragged tear or two in the ozone over the central Texas prairie.

Daryl Ann Sumners cleared her throat and patted Evelyn Sue's hand. "That's funny, Miss Evelyn. Will you two excuse me? I'm going to dash to the little girl's room then we ought to get on the road. Do you need to go too,

Miss Evelyn?" Daryl Ann Sumner said in her most condescending, loud voice.

"Oh, fiddle. Stop with that silly "Miss Evelyn" stuff, Daryl Ann. You've known me for over forty years now," Evelyn Sue said, her southern genteel voice spiked with irritation. "I'm not that much older than you, by the way, remember?"

"Now, now, Miss Evelyn," Daryl Ann said looking at me and smoothing her perfectly straight blond bobbed hair. "You know that couldn't be true, since I'm not a day over forty-nine."

As an uncontrollable chuckle threatened to escape my lips I turned and focused my attention on my coffee and the barn painting behind me.

"I heard that Jimmie Rae Murphy! Didn't your Grandma Star teach you any manners?"

I turned back to face them. With her hands on her hips Daryl Ann was standing, giving me a wicked stare. I smiled back at her. She grabbed her Chanel shoulder bag off the table, gave a huff, and trudged toward the restrooms.

After Daryl Ann left, Evelyn Sue rolled her eyes. "If she's not a day over forty-nine, I've got oceanfront property over in Midland," she said in a low voice directed toward her friend. At her observation about Daryl Ann I freely laughed out loud. Evelyn Sue chuckled too then continued. "She's been acting extra strange since we left Niceton. If I didn't know her better, I'd think she was up to something." She reached into her vanilla canvas tote and pulled out a gold mesh makeup bag, every bit vintage 1940s. From its shimmering insides, she withdrew a gold lipstick tube and applied a fresh coat of Real Pink Rose.

It was so good to see Miss Evelyn feeling well again, even spunky. She had fallen a few months ago and we'd worried she might not fully recover. But here she was at the tender age of 84 dressed in perfectly coordinated mint green cotton slacks and a white blouse with appliquéd mint green flowers. Tiny gold sequined sandals embraced her dainty, carefully pedicured toes. Not necessarily a practical shoe choice for walking all day at the flea market. She wore her requisite classic gold 1950s wristwatch, a simple gold bangle, and a large ruby ring on her right pinky finger. There was no wedding band on her left hand since Miss Evelyn Sue had never married.

Despite the lack of nuptials, Evelyn Sue had a full life and loved having a good time. A retired elementary teacher, she was still light on her feet over at Floyd's Filler-Up and Opry on the occasional Saturday night, and continued to volunteer for everything including English as a Second Language Classes down at the Niceton Public Library on Thursday evenings. Although tonight might be the exception since she wouldn't get back home to Niceton until well after dark.

In her spare time, like the rest of us, Evelyn Sue had a booth at Blessings From the Past Antique Mall. She had moved in last year when she began downsizing the houseful of antiques and collectibles accumulated from previous generations in her historic home, Yellow Rose Hill, on the outskirts of Niceton. Now, she enjoyed shopping for unusual Victorian antiques and Texanna primitives for her booth.

"So, how's life treating you, Jimmie?" Evelyn Sue asked, her alert hazel eyes watching me as she placed her lipstick back into the gold mesh bag.

"Not as well as I had hoped," I said. "Joe's been such a jerk lately. I expect our divorce will be finalized any day. We've still got the house to get rid of, so I still have to see him on occasion—and it's never very congenial. I guess it's just good thing we hadn't started a family yet."

"Well, I'm sorry to hear that. But I have to tell you I wasn't ever too crazy about that young man. He seemed conceited and full of himself."

"Pardon my French, Miss Evelyn, but Joseph Trent Murphy is just plain full of crap a good part of the time." We paused for a chuckle at Joe's expense. "Now I'm just subbing the occasional English Comp class and still working at the Armstrong Browning Library. I'm loving that."

Mention of the Library reminded me of the items I found at Cowboy's. My mind drifted as I looked out the window and saw Maxine talking on her cell phone. I needed to get her attention so we could get moving if I was going to return the letters and make contact with Dr. Gifford by this afternoon.

"I plan to begin my post-graduate studies in the fall," I said returning my full focus to Miss Evelyn. "That's why I love these trips to Canton's First Monday Trade Days. It's an escape from the day to day and a little like going on a treasure hunt since we never know what we're going to find."

Miss Evelyn winked at me. "I believe it's called retail therapy or in your case 'junking' therapy. Shopping can help mend a broken heart or two. I know for a fact, darlin'," she said.

Unable to meet her eyes for a moment, I looked down at half of a squished cinnamon roll still on my plate. In the short pause, I took the opportunity to change the subject. "So, Miss Evelyn, how have you been? Are you still volunteering everywhere?"

"Well, honey, not as much as I was. Maria's still with me, but she's had some health problems recently too. I've got a young woman who comes twice a week to help out doing odd jobs or whatever needs to be done. It's been good to have her since Maria had shoulder surgery a while ago and she's not able to dust up high or lift anything very heavy. Although, I hate to say it—oh, never-mind."

"What Miss Evelyn?"

"It just seems ever since this young woman's been coming round things have gone missing. She tells me it's my imagination, but I was just telling your Grandmother Star and Aunt Edna about it the other day. In fact, Edna Jean told me she and Maxine also had some items missing from the Lee County Living History Museum. It's all very odd." She picked up her café cup for a sip of coffee.

Daryl Ann returned to the table and took a last swig of her coffee. "Okay, Miss Evelyn, shall we head on up to Canton then? It's already ten o'clock."

"Yes. We should probably go on. Come on, Jimmie Rae, let's get Maxine off her cell phone and get on the road," Evelyn Sue said with the perfect combination of authority and enthusiasm the years of herding third graders provides.

"I wonder who she's talking to," I said grabbing both our bags, and leaving a couple of dollars on the Formica tabletop. "Thanks!" I waved to our waitress as we headed out the door.

"I believe Miss Maxine Bea Huntington has a beau," Evelyn Sue said with a wink as we walked outside.

"No! Well, some friend she is. She's never mentioned him to me."

Maxine was pushing her purple cell phone into the side pocket of her cargos. "Hey, girl," she said walking over to where we were standing. "Star is looking for you. She kept texting me while I was on the line. Is your phone on?"

"Sure," I said as I pulled it out to check. This carrier just has lousy reception out here. I'll call and check in with her once we're on the road. See you both later," I said to Daryl Ann and Evelyn Sue as they got into Daryl Ann's Lexus GX.

"Be safe, girls," Evelyn Sue said to us as she shut her car door.

We watched Daryl Ann pull her car onto State Highway 19 and head north.

"So, tell me all about this new guy you've been keeping from me," I said to Max as we headed over to Old Blue.

"You'd better call Star first."

"You're stalling."

"Yeah, call Star."

"Wait till you see what I found at Cowboy's."

"What is it already?"

"These," I said opening the truck door and reaching across the seat to retrieve the fragile yellowed letters.

"Jimmie Rae, what in the world are you doing with those out here?"

"That's what I've been trying to tell you. I found them along with what I think are several other stolen items from the Armstrong Browning in the ladies room of this decrepit gas station back that way. "

"I don't get it, Jimmie. Why would anything from the Browning Library be out there?"

"I don't know. I left a message for Dr. Gifford. If she doesn't call me back soon, I'll call her again. We may cut our shopping short and head back to Waco to get this figured out. Do you have any folders or anything I could keep these safe in?" I knew Max, a third year law student at Baylor, was incapable of traveling without at least one manila folder. She reached into her bag and handed me one. I placed the letters inside and put the folder in a cloth grocery tote I pulled out from behind the seat. Finally, we got into Old Blue and pulled onto the road a few miles behind Daryl Ann and Evelyn Sue.

I put on my headset and pushed the first number on my phone for Star. One ring later she answered. "Thank goodness you called Jimmie Rae."

"What's wrong?"

"Edna Jean was in a car accident last night. She's over in College Station. They may have to Care Flite her down to Houston."

"Oh my gosh. What happened?"

"When I last saw her, all she said was Maxine ran her off the road."

Chapter Three

"Memorial Day Sale! Shop The Page Turner now for your summer reads. We have a wonderful collection of books. Come find an armful of favorites!"

"You know Max would never hurt Aunt Edna. In fact, Maxine's car was stolen a couple of days ago. She doesn't even have a car right now," I added to further prove her innocence.

"Jimmie Rae, I can't make out what you're saying." Star's voice wavered as the road dipped out of range for my cell phone service.

Maxine looked at me and mouthed, "What's going on?"

I waved her away. Multitasking was never one of my strong points and trying to hold two conversations and keep Old Blue on the road was like juggling lead balls in the dark.

"I'll fill you in tonight," I said to Star.

Her reply was fragmented but I made out, "Love ya and on my way to the hospital" before the call completely dropped into oblivion.

I snapped my cell phone shut.

Max looked at me with her large empathetic blue eyes asking the questions she hadn't said yet. The idea Max would ever do anything to hurt Aunt Edna was preposterous. The memory of Cowboy, Lonnie, and an old pink Cadillac back at the Antiques and Gas Emporium nagged at me. What if someone else driving Maxine's car ran Edna off the road?

"Girl, I don't know what is going on," I said turning the old steering wheel to follow the curves in the road. "Maybe, that *was* your car back at Cowboy's. Maybe whoever stole it caused Edna to have a car accident late last night, but she thinks it was you."

Max dropped the sequined coin purse she'd been fidgeting with on the floorboard, and cast her full attention to me. "What? Me? Tell me exactly what Star said."

I relayed the story to her. Although I had to watch the road, I knew her well enough to read her non-verbals loud and clear. The way she tugged at her left earring and swept her long bangs away from her face told me she was at a loss for what to do about Edna.

She looked out the passenger's window and tapped the door handle. She turned toward me and touched my arm. "Jimmie Rae, this is getting weird. Let's go back. I want to tell Edna I had nothing to do with her accident. I can't believe she'd ever think I could do such a thing. She's like my second mom. You know that."

I sneaked a peek at Maxine seeing the earnest concern in her face. "Of course, I don't believe you had anything to do with Edna's accident. Honestly, I doubt anyone else does either, but the fact is someone caused Edna to have a car wreck and she thinks it was you." I shook my head trying to clear the conflicting thoughts. "Look, we're here already. Let's just shop fast and head to the hospital as quick as possible. Okay?"

Max nodded her head in agreement. "I'm thinking the same thing. We need to figure out what the heck's going on. Last week I contacted the police about my car and even if it was my car at Cowboy's, Edna Jean's accident trumps that."

"Agreed," I said looking at her briefly and then back to the road. "Besides, I really need to get some more quilts from that Missouri couple and see if the guy with the large glass cloches is there. I don't know anywhere else to buy that kind of stuff so cheap and I need the extra cash from my mall sales now that Joe is being such a jerk. I'm still paying the mortgage and utilities while he supposedly gets his law practice going. That wouldn't be so bad if Clara over at Baylor Accounting hadn't seen his car parked at the pool hall dive outside of town early Tuesday morning."

Max shook her head in disgust and reached down to retrieve her coin purse. "Yeah, I understand. I need to generate a few more dollars too, especially now that my car is missing. That combined with the living expenses my scholarship doesn't cover means I need some big sales for Memorial Day weekend. I just pray Edna will be okay. I can tell you it wasn't me. I was with Steve late last night."

The roadside vendor stands became more numerous as the two-lane highway swelled into four lanes and we entered the city of Canton, Texas. What was otherwise a quiet, rural town in north-central Texas morphed into a combined festival, carnival, and shopping Mecca one long weekend each month year-round regardless of the weather, politics, or anything else going on in the rest of the world.

Although Canton's Trade Days was called First Monday, it was really the preceding Wednesday and Thursday for serious buyers who were mostly collectors and antique dealers. Oddly enough, by Monday everyone would be packed up and moved on to the Second Monday Flea Markets around the great state of Texas. This one was the mother of all monthly Texas flea markets though.

Far from the days of its humble beginnings as a "trade day," when people would meet under the large shade trees to barter for food, household goods, or weapons, now First Monday meant multiple flea market venues spread out over acres and acres of the land around the downtown square offering every kind of household item, decorative item, military paraphernalia, animals and fowl, antiques, collectibles, and every type of "fair" food imaginable. As we entered the city limits a familiar sense of excitement eclipsed our worries about the Browning items, pink Cadillac, and Edna. Sunshine shone through the colorful banners lining the main drag at the first four-way stop in town. By the time we'd reached the main intersection, whirly-gigs danced and bright quilts waved in the light breeze. Happy shoppers trailing treasure-laden utility carts behind them passed in front of us.

"I want to hear more about Steve, but first let's get what we came for, look around for anything else, and beat feet back to check on Edna. Sound okay?"

"Sounds great, but what about those letters you found?" Maxine asked pointing to the seat back where I'd stashed the cloth grocery bag that contained them.

"I almost forgot about them. Crap! Okay, same plan, but tomorrow I take these letters back to the Library and if they're the real ones, I'll personally lead the police back to Cowboy's Antiques and Gas Emporium to retrieve the rest of the stuff."

I turned into our usual parking lot on the north side and found a spot for Old Blue. I stole a quick glance at Maxine. "By the way, remember you're not getting back into my truck without promising me you'll tell me everything about this Steve guy on the way to the hospital. I can't believe you kept this big news from me."

Max smiled in reply as she retrieved our utility carts from the back of my truck. "Girl, believe me it'll be worth the wait. He may just be the one," was all she said as she winked and headed toward one of the Trade Centers south of the parking lot, pulling her empty metal basket behind her. She stopped and turned around. "Happy shopping, Jimmie! I'll catch up with you in an hour near the bathtub guy. I've got to pick up a leather purse I had made for my mom's birthday. We'll talk then, okay? I promise."

I threw the strap of my bag over my head, settling it across my body so I could pull my cart with greater ease. Minutes later, I was deep in the heart of the "old" side of the flea market moving quickly toward the back row where the glass cloche guy usually set up. Distractions were everywhere. The savory smell of smoked BBQ tantalized my senses as Blues singer Susan Tedeschi's sultry voice resonated from an iPod speaker near a used lawn mower vendor. I could stand it no longer and stopped at a vintage jewelry booth to check what the dealer had in her long line of glass cases.

Texas sun reflected off the knife like light off a mirror. It lay in blood red satin. I squinted and shifted, trying to see what other delights might be in the glass case beside it. Early afternoon beads of sweat were already forming beneath my long, brown curly hair. I pulled a clean bandana from my messenger bag, and with a few quick folds, the bandana now held my hair off my face like a headband. I was ready for action. Now I saw what I missed before, an unusual early-twentieth century oval Italian mosaic pin above the knife. I hadn't seen it before due to the sun's glare.

"Excuse me, how much is that pin?" I asked the woman wearing the carpenter's apron over her blue cotton dress.

"Which one, hon?"

"That one," I said pointing to it. "Above the knife."

"Oh, that one is quite old." Her pursed lips and concentrated look upon the pin told me she was trying to decide how much I would pay. She sighed deeply. "How about eighteen bucks?"

"Fifteen?"

"Done."

I tucked it into my bag and moved on fighting the urge to pull the antique pin out and admire it again. I had to keep moving if Maxine and I were going to head back soon to see Aunt Edna. It would help if Dr. Gifford would call back too, but I knew she was probably busy with meetings since she was scheduled to go to Italy in a couple of days. However, if the letters in the manila folder were genuine, those jerks at Cowboy's would be in more trouble than Lady Gaga at a Tea Party political convention.

I found the glass cloche guy, and bought four from him. I loved using glass domes to highlight small vignettes of Victorian postcards, bits of aged tatting, and other vintage smalls. I stopped by several more vendors and made small purchases to resell in my booth.

As I waited my turn to cross the small raised pedestrian bridge over the stream meandering through the market grounds, I caught a glimpse that caused me to bump into the person in front of me.

"Sorry," I said quickly as the woman turned to give me a dirty look. My hands began to sweat against the metal cart handle. I turned my head again and sure enough, there was a big man with a pathetic red ponytail that looked just like Lonnie, one of the big jerks I'd just left down the blacktop and hoped to never see again.

What in the world is that creep doing at First Monday for crying out loud? I looked again across to the spot where I thought I'd seen Lonnie, but he was gone. *What if the bubba brothers were looking for me because I took the Browning letters?* I had to find Max and get out of there. My pulse began the same frantic pace I'd felt a few hours ago. *Forget the quilts, corny-dog, and fresh squeezed lemonade—I had to get out of here fast.*

Since my utility cart was full of large glass cloches, it was difficult to quickly navigate over the non-paved terrain of the flea market's back row. I was supposed to meet Max at the bathtub guy's space, but it was on the other side of the market. I tried phoning her, but only got her voice mail. Keeping an eye out for the jerks, I headed for the open sheds a few rows over. It seemed unreasonable those nuts would follow me to Canton for some old letters. More likely, they were after me to shut me up about what else I'd found at their little shop of horrors. I pondered this as I dodged other shoppers, stopping only to wipe my forehead and re-adjust my purchases. Realistically, those morons wouldn't think to check their inventory. They had no real reason to think I'd taken anything or knew anything.

Jimmie, you're getting paranoid. Relax, shop, and don't worry about those jerks. The police will take care of them if they really have stolen Browning items. Calmer now, I stopped to sit on a bench for a water break.

I checked the time on my cell phone. Break time was over. Time to shop fast. I dragged my small cart around faded metal signs, rusty garden gates, weather worn wooden doors, and every kind of aged metal anything. An older couple sat on green webbed lawn chairs tucked in between the collection. An intricate quilt made up of tiny triangles caught my attention. By the looks of the fabric, the quilt was late nineteenth or early twentieth-century.

"How much for the quilt?" I asked, pointing to it. I'd learned quilts were like a barometer, depending on how much they went for would determine how much everything else was and I had seen plenty I was interested in.

"It's forty dollars, miss."

"I'll take it."

"I'll give you fifty," said a voice behind me.

I turned around to stare down Daryl Ann Sumner. She was known around our antique mall for playing dirty: swooping in on other dealers and offering more cash for merchandise or luring customers to her booth and away from other dealers' booths. Her dealer ethics were questionable at best. Since she usually had more money than common sense, I doubted the quilt would end up in my cart. The next words from her mouth confirmed it.

"In fact, I'll give you one hundred dollars for the quilt and that little blue cabinet over there."

The man and woman looked at each other. The woman shrugged her shoulders. The man looked to Daryl Ann, then to me. "Done. Sorry, miss. We need to pay for my wife's medicine next week," he said. "Medicare never covers the entire cost."

I gave him an understanding smile and Daryl Ann my sweetest smile.

"Sorry, Jimmie, darlin'—don't be mad, okay?" Daryl Ann said as she handed the man a crisp one hundred dollar bill. "I need more display pieces and I just bought a primitive pie safe last weekend over in Alexandra it will be adorable with that little cabinet and quilt."

"I'm not mad, Daryl Ann," I said.

"Well good. Hey, have you seen Evelyn Sue? She was supposed to meet me over at Tator's Canteen fifteen minutes ago," she said.

"No," I said eager to move on. "I haven't seen her. I'd better be going. Happy shopping, Daryl Ann."

"Better luck next time, Jimmie Rae," she replied.

I believed in karma and knew she would get hers. Two aisles over, good fortune rolled my way. I found worn woven baskets full of bright quilts; their intricate pieces hand-sewn from softly faded Depression-era sackcloth and organized in patterns from bow tie to flying geese. There were also bookcases full of old books. A hand-written sign declared the books were five dollars each. I thought of Star's bookstore, The Page Turner, and speed dialed. She picked up on the third ring. "Hey, Star, how's Edna doing?"

"She's in surgery right now. She has internal injuries."

"Do you have anyone with you?"

"Good Lord, yes. Jack, Janet, Joey, Melinda and their kids are all here. Stacy and Henry are on their way. Honestly, I wished I'd just waited to call anyone. I'd rather be alone now," she said.

"Fat chance of that. You know we'll be there tonight. I can't believe Aunt Edna would ever think Max would hurt her. Maxine thinks of her like a second mom."

"That's what I want to think too, but Edna is quite convinced Maxine tried to kill her. When are you going to get here?"

"We're at Canton. We each had a specific list and then we're out of here and straight to the hospital. Hey, they've got old books here for five dollars each. Do you want me to pick up some for the store?"

"Yeah, sure. Whatever you think. I'd better get back before the brood comes looking for me. Love ya, darlin'. Be safe. See ya later."

"Love you too, Star. Don't worry. It'll all be okay."

Edna Jean was Star's baby sister and also happened to be one of my favorite people. Ever since my folks came up missing when I was seven, Star and Aunt Edna had been my surrogate moms. The memory of the July morning when the avocado wall phone rang with the news from the Peace Corps headquarters that my mom and dad, Nora and Phillip, had not returned from a remote village in the Chilean mountains and were assumed dead caused me to shiver even on a hot day at a Texas flea market more than thirty years later.

Distracted, I picked up a book. As the pages opened, I realized it was an 1875 English engraved botanical guide in perfect condition. The hand-colored details of each flower and plant were incredible. One page alone would sale for up to fifty dollars. I placed it under my arm and moved on to the baskets of quilts. The sign read: "Quilts, your choice, $25 each." I handed the dealer five twenties and one five dollar bill. Daryl Ann approached as I tried to figure out how to stuff four quilts into my already full cart. I waited until she was closer to open the botanical guide again.

"Looks like you found something after all," Daryl Ann said.

"Yeah, just some old quilts and an old book."

"Let me see that book. Do you know what it is?"

"You mean this nineteenth-century mint condition English botanical guide?"

"How much was it?"

"Five dollars."

"Oh. And I suppose the quilts were twenty a piece."

"Actually, they were twenty-five each."

She rolled her blue eyes and shook her sleek blond hair. "Better luck next time," I said.

As I wound back through the maze of antiques and junk toward the parking lot and Old Blue, my always-on-the-prowl-eyes caught sight of small sequined feet from behind a rusty metal shed. They weren't standing.

Once again, unease slipped around me. I knew those tiny feet. Just a few hours ago I had considered the questionable practicality of Miss Evelyn wearing such dainty sandals to First Monday. As I approached, I recalled how she was an icon of all that was wonderful about my hometown in central Texas. Niceton was an all-American place. Miss Evelyn Sue, with her vintage beehive hairdo was its matriarch. Most everyone in town had had her as their third grade teacher, with the exception of the crazy year in 1966 when she was asked to teach fifth grade. It was the first and last time.

I knew my brain was rolling through these thoughts stalling for time – hoping the delicate sandals would hop up and make everything okay, but that wasn't happening. I dropped the handle of my cart letting my new purchases roll on the ground and moved quickly toward the small feet sticking out from behind the building. As I feared, they were attached to Miss Evelyn Sue Dinsmore. Although her vintage beehive hairdo had survived years of childish pranks, from its crown to her torso now lay in a pool of blood. Miss Evelyn Sue Dinsmore had been shot.

Chapter Four

"Yard Sale: Too much stuff! Workout equipment, stereo w/speakers, mountain bike, typewriter, books, misc. household. Friday only, 8 a.m.–4 p.m. 290 W. Magnolia."

Miss Evelyn was a fine-boned, petite woman and it looked like the bullet had made a real mess of her mid-section. Trying to control my gag reflex, I focused on her sweet pale face and tall hairdo. Who would do this to her?

I needed help. I used my left index and middle fingers to find a weak pulse at her throat. It seemed Evelyn Sue was still alive. I pulled off the navy bandana I'd been wearing to keep my hair out of my face and tried stuffing it into the bullet wound to stop the blood flow oozing from her chest. It was useless and messy. I was afraid to move my blood-covered right hand from her chest wound. I tried applying more pressure and pressed slightly harder. I needed help fast and leaned back to look around the building. I was actually relieved to see Daryl Ann Sumners.

"Hey, Daryl Ann! Get over here fast!"

"Jimmie Rae? What are you doing down there? I want you to see these darling crib quilts I got for fifteen dollars a piece," she said in a sickening sweet voice. "Jimmie Rae, honey, what's wrong?"

"Not now, Daryl! Call 9-1-1!" I shouted.

She came closer. "Oh, my Lord! Oh, my Lord! Please tell me Miss Evelyn Sue is passed out drunk and that's not blood! Oh, my Lord!" Daryl Ann repeated putting a perfectly manicured hand to her temple as if to message away what lay before us, and dropping her cell phone near Evelyn Sue's feet.

"Daryl Ann, take a deep breath, pick up your phone, and call 9-1-1 now! We need an ambulance down here fast!"

She needed no enticement. She moved faster than I'd ever seen her move before toward the large metal building closest to us. I just hoped she was getting help and not puking somewhere. I looked down at my sweet friend again. This was too much. I'd never felt so useless and alone. Sweat and tears mixed into a salty mess and trailed down my face. My hands shook as my heart pounded a calypso melody. *Please send help. Someone. Anyone.*

I leaned back again to see if Daryl Ann was headed this way. No Daryl Ann, but Maxine was slowly coming my way pulling her cart behind her and carrying a plastic bag. I closed my eyes and took a deep comforting breath. Max would know what else we could do to help Evelyn Sue. As I watched her slow progress, I realized she had no idea what had just happened and was merely arriving at our agreed upon meeting spot. "Maxie, get over here now!" I shouted.

"Hey, Jimmie, good grief! I've been looking everywhere for you. Where the heck have you been? We were supposed to meet at the bathtub guy and here you are messing around behind the buildings. Say, have you got any idea why Daryl Ann would have this gun with her or why it fell out of her cart back there?"

Could Daryl Ann have had time to shoot her and return to an afternoon of shopping at the flea market? I looked down at Evelyn Sue's bleached out face. Now, I felt anger churning with gut-wrenching sadness. Daryl Ann was a lot of things, but a murderer seemed unlikely. Still, where was she now when one of her closest friends was on the death's front porch?

"Did you hear me, Jimmie Rae? I've got a gun." Max strode around the building's corner.

"What the…? Oh my gosh, what happened Jimmie?" Max dropped her cart and the plastic bag she'd been carrying and hurried to my side. I looked up at Max with tears in my eyes. She knelt beside me and took Miss Dinsmore's hand. Perhaps it was Max's touch, but Evelyn Sue opened her hazel eyes and said one word to us. "William." She tried to squeeze Max's hand, and then it relaxed. She was gone— dead. Oversized tears streamed down my face, but I didn't care. Against the party atmosphere of the flea market, Max and I sobbed like we'd just lost a parent. And in many ways we had.

I moved my bloody hands from the soaked bandana in her chest. Max took the kiwi green silk headscarf tied on Evelyn Sue's canvas tote strap, removed it, and covered her face with it. The stress of the day, indeed of the past six months, gripped me and I began to shake and sob deeply.

A man's voice interrupted the moment. "Nobody move. What's happened here?"

"I was trying to find her," I said pointing a bloody finger toward Max "and found her instead." An extra sob escaped my throat. Apparently my brain hadn't received the memo that the police were on the scene. I tried to pull myself together.

"Who are you?"

I looked up at him and realized how things must look. In an attempt to be in a less venerable position, I stood up and wiped my face on my forearm. “Jimmie Rae Murphy, officer.”

“And, Ms. Murphy, what happened? Is she dead?” He face squished and he swallowed hard avoiding looking at my bloody hands or at Evelyn Sue.

“There’s no pulse. Are there EMTs coming?”

“Yes. They’re on their way. Did you kill the deceased?”

“No! Of course not! I was trying to save Evelyn Sue.”

“So you knew the deceased?”

“Her name was Evelyn Sue Dinsmore, officer.”

“Are you implying my friend is a murderer? Are you arresting her?” Maxine asked, standing up with her hands on her hips defiant and ready to test her fresh attorney skills.

“I didn’t say you could move. Who are you?” he said sternly, his hands resting on his hips conveniently close to full leather holsters.

“Maxine Humphries, attorney at law, sir. My friend doesn’t have to answer any more of your questions, officer.”

Sirens screamed in the distance and as if calling everyone over, a crowd began to surround us. “Back up folks. Catch it on the evening news. You two, over here now! It’ll be a few minutes before the EMS boys can work through the traffic and get over here.

I tried to stand confidently, but my legs were shaking. I looked down at my hands and tried wiping them on my denim skirt, making now both my skirt and hands a bloody mess. My clothes were as ruined as the day. I’d gone from happy go lucky flea market addict to first on the scene of a murder of someone I’d known all my life to murder suspect in less than thirty minutes. I couldn’t believe any of this was really happening.

The officer looked perturbed. With squinted eyes he grimaced causing his large nose to point upward. I could tell the hot afternoon sun, lack of breeze, and increasing crowd wasn't helping his mood any.

I joined Max and the police officer off to the side of Evelyn Sue.

"Sorry officer. Forgive my friend. I'm happy to answer—sorry what is your name?"

"Rubbins"

"Officer Rubbins' questions, Maxine." I said giving Max a hard look. Lord knows I didn't need any more trouble today.

"Ms. Murphy, what happened?"

Max cleared her throat loudly and raised her eyebrows at me warning me to be careful with what I said next.

Officer Rubbins looked at Max and back at me. "Well, I'm not gonna wait all day. Want me to just haul you in now? What's in that bag?" he said pointing to the plastic grocery bag Max had been carrying before she saw Evelyn Sue.

"Excuse me officer, but you're overstepping your boundaries here," Max replied.

"Max, it's okay," I said cutting her off, "Hand the good officer the plastic bag you found while I tell him what happened. It's simple really. I was looking for her and found her," I said lacking words and pointing my finger instead at Max and back toward Evelyn Sue.

The deafening sound of the ambulance and another Sheriff's car arriving interrupted the interview. "Wait right here, you two, do not move. I have to take you to the station for questioning."

Three paramedics arrived, removed the scarf and began to work on Evelyn Sue.

I watched as they tried to resuscitate her, but it didn't appear they were having any luck. I stood with her blood drying on my hands and clothes in the afternoon heat, sweat trailing where tears already stained my face.

"We're going to the station where you'll both need to give a report, but first you're going to tell me what's in that bag," he said again.

"It's a gun, I believe," Max answered.

"Who does it belong to Ms. Humphries?"

"I wouldn't know Officer Rubbons," Max said echoing the police officer's condescending tone and whether she meant to or not, mispronouncing his last name.

"Is this the murder weapon?"

"How would I know?" Max said. "It fell out of my friend's shopping cart a couple of aisles back. I followed her back up here."

"Is this your friend?" he said looking at me.

My blood covered hands and arms and blood soaked clothing was marking me as the murderer instead of the Good Samaritan.

"Yes," Max said.

"Maxxx!"

"No! I mean, yes. Jimmie Rae is my very best friend, but she didn't kill Evelyn Sue Dinsmore," Max said looking at me in an apologetic way. "That gun didn't fall out of Jimmie's cart."

"Are you sure about that?"

I didn't like the way Max looked at me as if contemplating my innocence.

"Max!" I interrupted before Max could offer one of her long-winded evaluations of the situation. Law School was having that effect on her. I continued, "Look Officer Rubbins, I know you have to question us, even print us, but I didn't kill Evelyn Sue Dinsmore. She was our friend. We're all in an antique mall together and came here today to buy items for our booths. One of us getting murdered was not on our list of things to do. I'm sure our friend, Daryl Ann Sumners, will vouch for us. She brought Evelyn Sue here today in her Lexus. Now, I've got to get cleaned up and get back to Niceton where we've had a family emergency."

"I'll bet you do, Miss," Officer Rubbins said. "Wait right here—I think Detective Mitchell will want to visit with you before you even think of leaving our sweet town."

"Crap, Maxie! What now?"

"I tried to tell you to shut up, Jimmie! You gotta trust me for once, okay? Now we're in a bit of a stink. Answer their questions. You're innocent, so give them the plain, simple facts. Don't go off on one of your big tangents, okay? This was probably just a random act of violence," Max said offering me some wet wipes from her burlap flea market bag.

I took one and began wiping my hands. "Yeah, maybe. But it seems like if that were the motive they would have taken her purse too," I said pointing to her large tote bag.

"Good point," Max said. "Maybe Evelyn Sue refused to let go of her tote. She was one tough broad."

"Not tough enough against a bullet," I said shaking my head glumly.

Officer Rubbins allowed us to take our carts to Old Blue and lock our stuff up before we headed to the police department to be interviewed by Detective Mitchell. As I bent over to retrieve the Victorian botanical book that had fallen out of my utility cart, I noticed a cigarette butt with pink lipstick. Real Pink Rose lipstick from the looks of it. The same color Evelyn Sue applied at the café a few hours earlier. "Max, look," I called and pointed.

"What?"

"It's a cigarette butt with pink lipstick. Could be evidence."

"That's doubtful, Jimmie. It's outside the crime scene. More likely it was already there. Unless you're saying Evelyn Sue was back here smoking. Is that what you're thinking? I don't think she smoked, Jimmie. Anyway, come on, I want to get this over with and get out of here. We don't want to piss off the local police anymore than we already have."

We loaded our flea market purchases as best as we could in Old Blue's cab and I locked the door. Officer Rubbins was waiting to take us to the Canton Police Station.

Chapter Five

"Empty Nester's Garage Sale: 916 Elm--Saturday only from 8:30 – 3:30. (Early birds will be shot!) Bunk beds, clarinet (like new,) clothes, toys, and lots of other great stuff."

I sat in a narrow corner office painted battleship gray, growing more impatient with each passing second. It was already 4:30 p.m. My reflection in the oak framed mirror on the wall near where I sat looked more normal than it had in the restroom a few minutes ago. I was forced to part with my stained clothing as they were beyond ever being clean again. Fortunately, I had extras in my bag. I changed into a fresh camisole, T-shirt, and denim shorts. My face was slightly sunburned and my curly, dark hair refused to lie down and relax. Too much humidity and sweat had erased any attempt of taming it. I tied it back off my face with a white bandana from the bottom of my bag. It had taken some time to wash the blood off my hands and arms. The memory caused an involuntary twitch.

Beyond the door, I could hear radios and telephones. A couple of fellows had been on break for the last hour, discussing everything from tractor pulls to the newly acquired Dallas Cowboys' quarterback.

A man of average height walked in and took his place behind the desk labeled DETECTIVE R.C. MITCHELL on the brass nameplate. He was reading a file and settled himself in the burgundy leather chair without looking up at me or acknowledging I was there.

He appeared to be in his early sixties. His face was tan as his arms. He wore a polished cotton blue short-sleeved western shirt tucked into classic khaki slacks. A silver bolo tie added a bit of flair. His black Roper cowboy boots were highly polished. On his wrist he wore a heavy silver and turquoise banded watch.

Detective Mitchell reached into the small top drawer of his desk, withdrew a cigarette, and placed it between his dry lips. It was obvious he wanted to light it. Instead, he lay it back down on his desk, opened his drawer again, and pulled out a toothpick. He looked across the desk at me.

"Miss Murphy this report stinks to high heaven. You mean to tell me you two ladies just so happened to find a murdered woman--someone you both knew--and just so happened to have a gun which has recently been fired and neither of you knows who killed the woman or if this is the murder weapon?"

"Yes, sir. That's true. I'm sure if you could talk to Daryl Ann Sumner she could clear this whole thing up."

"And who might she be?" Detective Mitchell asked chewing on his toothpick.

"She's someone my friend, Max, and I know from our hometown. She owns an antique shop there and has a booth in the same mall as Maxine and me. She brought Miss Evelyn Sue to Canton today. She drives a Lexus."

"Happen to know the license plate numbers?"

"No."

"Well, this Ms. Sumner is not in the report. She isn't sitting in my office with a recently fired murder weapon and blood on her clothes, now is she?" he said.

"No," I admitted again. "Sir, I understand how this may look, but Maxine Bea Huntington and I didn't have a thing to do with Miss Dinsmore's terrible murder. We both loved her. She was our teacher and has become our friend since we all have booths together at the same antique mall," I said looking him in the eyes.

"You've got our fingerprints and I know you have to get our statements, but we need to get on the road. My great aunt was in a car accident earlier this morning and she's in the ICU at College Station Medical Center. With all due respect sir, my friend is a law student and she said you couldn't keep us without sufficient evidence. Do you have sufficient evidence?"

It was his turn to admit he did not. "I suppose you're one of those women libbers. I should have known. Wait right here."

He got up, took the file and cigarette, and left the room. Ten minutes later he returned smelling like fresh cigarette smoke. He cleared his throat. "Okay, Miss Murphy, we are playing this by my rules. You two are going to Niceton tonight, is that correct?"

"Yes, sir."

"When you arrive after-while, you call this number and report to my nephew. He's the supervising police detective down there. I'm e-mailing your file and you are to stay in touch with him. Do not leave the Niceton city limits without notifying him first. Do you understand?"

"Yes. May I ask who your nephew is?"

"Billy Jack Mitchell. Finest cop in the great state of Texas," he said with pride.

"Oh, great."

"So, you know him then."

"Oh, I know him." Billy Jack Mitchell was my high school sweetheart twenty years ago. I hadn't seen him for ages. He left Niceton High to follow the rodeo circuit our senior year. He'd done fairly well and even competed in the National Finals until he injured his hip and tailbone in Utah. I'd lost touch with him over the years, although Max heard on the grapevine that he had gotten himself together and become a top-notch police detective down in Brownsville. Now, apparently, he was back in Niceton, working at the Police Department.

"Well, if you don't, you soon will. He'll be stuck to you like a fly in my momma's buttermilk chess pie. Don't worry none though, he's real smart and good-looking like his uncle," Detective Mitchell said with a smile and a wink. "Now, Miss Murphy, I need to get some real work done. It's been nice. Go sign the papers Officer Rodriquez has and stay away from dead bodies. Go straight to Niceton and call Billy Jack. He's expecting you. If he doesn't hear from you, you'll be hunted down. Do you understand, Miss Murphy?"

"Yes, but I do have a couple of stops to make on the way…"

"Miss Murphy, I'm not your keeper. Just do as you've been asked and you'll stay out of trouble. I'm giving Billy Jack a call right now; so don't disappoint me, okay Miss Murphy? Good evening," he said opening his door.

Max was waiting outside. I met her eyes and motioned one minute. An officer handed me some papers to sign and a letter with Billy Jack's contact information. "You understand you may be asked to return to Canton to appear in court?"

"Yes."

"Okay, sign here."

I looked over at Max. She nodded her head and I signed. "Officer Duncan will be taking you back to your vehicle at the Trade Days."

Outside the sun was closer to kissing the western horizon and it was as muggy as a lone August rainstorm. Old Blue was a welcome sight as I unlocked the doors and transferred our day's shopping to covered totes in Old Blue's bed. Max and I jumped into the narrow front seat. I turned the engine and waved good-bye to Officer Duncan.

"I can't believe Evelyn Sue is dead," I said.

"Me either. But I'll bet my custom tooled red cowboy boots Daryl Ann had something to do with this. Why would she disappear unless she was hiding something?" Max asked.

"Yes, but if she is the murderer why would she head back to the scene?"

"Because she is either that dense or she thought it would throw everyone off her trail. She's probably halfway to Mexico by now," Max said as she applied a fresh coat of lip balm. "I tried to tell those idiots they should be looking for Daryl Ann or at least looking for her vehicle."

"I tried to tell Detective Mitchell the same thing. I didn't know her plates," I said shifting into fourth gear as we gained speed on the open road.

"It's GDDL4U. Remember, when she got that new car last fall, she ordered vanity plates?"

"I was in Waco, remember? The detail of Daryl Ann's new car and vanity plates were never part of our conversations," I reminded Max.

"Okay, probably not. Anyway, she made a big deal about it last year. Evelyn Sue thought they were so clever. She even considered trading in her old boat for a Lexus with vanity plates. I wonder what will happen to all her booty now?

"Maxine Bea! The woman is barely dead four hours and you're already smacking your lips over her estate? You should be ashamed."

"Oh give me a break, Miss High and Mighty! You know you've thought about it too. I mean, yeah it's pitiful someone blew her away, but there's an estate with literally generations of original Texas antiques worth millions and no heirs. From a professional standpoint, the Lee County Living History Museum could really use a boost of new acquisitions. We've had so much go out the door lately."

"What do you mean?"

"Remember, I told you Edna, Evelyn Sue, and I were just discussing this over lunch at the Lone Star Café last week."

"Oh yeah, right."

Max continued, "I first noticed small things, like Victorian baby shoes and a few silver pieces, missing from our home exhibit. Then, more recently, we came in one day and a silver punch bowl and Mrs. Earle's nineteenth-century Staffordshire collection were gone. That's when I began checking Niceton's Third Monday Flea Market and getting eBay savvy."

I processed this new information for a moment. "Max, you do understand what has happened today?"

She looked across at me with a new realization. "Yes, of the three of us who discussed the possibility of a theft ring, I'm the only one not dead or in the hospital. Let's call Billy Jack and tell him we are making a beeline to see Edna in College Station tonight. We have to find out what happened to her. He'll understand."

I hoped she was right, but remembered all too vividly my last conversation with Billy Jack Mitchell. It was less than a lesson in good verbal relationship communication. He was broken-hearted and ran away to join the rodeo that night. I hoped the last twenty years had mended more than his hip.

Chapter Six

"Garage Sale: Tupperware, some furniture, dishes, linens, books, clothes, lamps. Friday-Saturday, 348 E. Oak. NO early birds."

Max handed me her cell phone. "Mitchell here."

For a woman who taught freshmen students at Baylor, I was suddenly at a complete loss for words. "Um, Billy Ja, I mean, Detective Mitchell, Hey! This is Jimmie Rae."

"Oh. Yeah, R.C. said you'd be calling. You murdered someone or something like that? First you break my tender little teenage heart then you become a murderer. Talk about karma."

He was enjoying this too much. "Look, Billy Jack. Let's try to be grown-ups about this. What happened between us is past. What happened today was just plain bizarre. Maxine and I are calling, like your uncle told us to. We're on our way back to Niceton, but we're going to College Station first to check on my Aunt Edna."

"Oh, really. That wasn't the plan he told me. My instructions were to stick to you like a fly in my grandma's buttermilk chess pie. If you're over in College Station, that will be a little tough. Why don't you be a good girl and follow the plan? Otherwise you'll force me to call my guys, find you, and keep you as our overnight guest. Detective Mitchell was doing you a huge favor, so don't screw it up."

"Look, Billy Jack, it's not that easy. Maxine and I may be in a lot of danger. We'll be in your office first thing in the morning."

"Jimmie Rae, the only danger you're in is what will happen if you don't follow the plan."

"Yes, I understand, but I really need this one favor. Please, Billy Jack?"

"Sorry, Jimmie, no-can-do. Unless..."

"Unless what, Billy Jack?"

"Does Star still bake that incredible Texas Sheet Cake?"

I rolled my eyes. *Good grief*!

"Jimmie? You still there?"

"Billy Jack," I began. He cut me off before I could finish.

"Never-mind, Jimmie. Just stick with the plan or my boys will find you two, okay?"

I raised my eyebrows and looked over at Maxine. "What?" she mouthed. I rolled my eyes again. Maxine grabbed her phone from my hand and covered the speaker. "Just do whatever he wants, Jimmie. Goodness!"

"Billy Jack? Sorry about that. Say, I remember how you always loved Star's Texas Sheet Cake. How about I bring you one in a couple of days."

"I'm available for dinner if that would be more convenient for her," he offered.

"Sure, Billy Jack. You can come over for dinner."

"Oh, okay. You could always sweet-talk me, Jimmie. Remember that time after our junior prom?"

"Billy Jack, let's just stick to the present and let the rest go. Okay?"

"You owe me, Jimmie Rae. If your sweet ass isn't in my office by 7 a.m. you'll regret ever knowing me. Your life will be a living hell."

"Understood. So nice to talk to you too, Billy Jack."

A stop at the Dairy Queen in Athens and two Lucinda Williams CDs later, Max and I parked Old Blue in the visitors' parking at College Station Medical Center. Visiting hours were almost over, but we were determined to see Edna.

Star saw us before we saw her. As we got off the elevator she rose to meet us. Enough of my kin were sitting in the burgundy and chrome seats to warrant a family reunion. Only in place of tables laden with food and surrounded with the sounds of a ballgame and laughter were crumpled vending machine wrappers, long faces, and low murmurings.

She wore a beige linen blouse and matching skirt with her favorite brown leather Birkenstock slides. A turquoise cross matching her earrings hung on a silver chain around her neck. She wore her long silver hair in a single braid.

"Jimmie, Maxine, I was getting worried about you girls." Star hugged us both, her scent of lavender and mint enveloping us. I searched her face for some hint of how she was doing, how Edna was doing, or if everyone was driving her nuts. Star was too good an actress to give away anything though. All things considered she seemed to be holding up strong as always.

"Come on over and give everyone a hug," Star said.

In the ICU waiting area, a flat screen television hummed in the corner, the detective show ignored for the real-life dramas unfolding around the room. Uncle Keith and his wife, Janet, sat on either side of Star. Their eldest son, my cousin, Johnny, sat talking to my Aunt Stacy's son, Reed, about the great season the Houston Astros were having. Johnny's wife, Melinda was knitting and talking to Janet. Johnny and Melinda were expecting not only their first child, but Star's first great-grandbaby. Since Aunt Edna was a widow and had only one daughter, Mayleen, who lived in Alaska and seldom made her way back to Texas, we were her closest family.

"Hey, everyone," I said quietly. "So how's it going?" We made our way around the small space hugging and making small talk with the others.

Star answered as she sat back down in her spot between Keith and Janet. "Oh, she's doing okay. They want her to stay in ICU overnight and plan to move her down to the main floor tomorrow if everything goes well tonight. What kept you two so long anyway? I was getting worried."

Maxine and I exchanged looks. "What happened?" Star said.

"The short version is Evelyn Sue Dinsmore is dead."

"What? Here, you two sit right down and tell us what happened." Star said patting Keith's chair with a gentle nudge for him to relinquish his chair for me. I took Keith's seat while Maxine settled herself in the empty chair beside me.

For the next few minutes we relived the terrible events of the afternoon at the flea market, including the interview with Detective Mitchell and having to meet with Billy Jack Mitchell the next morning.

"Jimmie, girl, are you sure you're okay?" Keith asked patting my shoulder. "I can't believe anyone would kill such a sweet old lady. Well, come to think of it, she wasn't so sweet when I was in third grade," he said with a mischievous smile.

"Well, that was because you, my son, were what we kindly refer to as 'a hand full.' You can believe Evelyn Sue Dinsmore came to your defense more than once when Principal Rooney thought a good paddling would work better than missing recess," Star said resting her hand on Keith's arm.

I just can't believe she's really gone. It had to be a random act, right?" Star said.

I looked at Maxine, hoping she'd answer since I didn't think I could say anything without accusing Daryl Ann of a murder without any proof at all. Only that she had mysteriously left her dear friend to die and had never shown up again to the scene of the crime.

"It was hard to tell," Maxie said in her best attorney voice. "Interestingly, Daryl Ann seems to be missing. They hadn't had a falling out, had they?" Maxine's tone was causal and professional when she asked about Daryl Ann. Her objectivity about it all would serve her well when she finished law school.

"No, not that I know of. However, Stella Pierce and Evelyn Sue had a running feud over property lines and anything else Stella could come up with. I heard they had a pretty loud spat over at the city offices a few days ago. Ever since she got elected to the city council Stella has made Evelyn Sue's life awful."

"What was the original fuss about?" I asked.

"I don't know, but I remember overhearing my mom and dad talking about how vile Mrs. Stella Pierce was to spread the story that Evelyn Sue had a baby out of wedlock."

I looked up at Keith and caught him exchanging looks with Janet and Star. Star cleared her throat. I ignored her. "What? I never heard that. You never told me that, Max," I said.

"Of course, not, silly. It was gossip," she said springing up. "I'm parched. Anyone want a soda? I'm loaded with change. I cleaned out my change jar and couldn't believe how much was in there."

"No, thanks," my family chorused back. Max shrugged her shoulders, grabbed her bag, and walked toward the vending machines at the back of the room.

Star pulled at her braid, a sign I'd learned meant she was uncomfortable with the subject matter. She cleared her throat again. "Maxine's right, it's only silly gossip." I noticed Star did not add anything else about the subject of a possible Dinsmore heir running around. Star continued, "I just can't believe she's gone. I'd really grown quite close to the old girl. She used to be so cold and hard to get to know, but after she retired, she seemed more mellow and friendly. Shoot, she volunteered for anything and everything."

Star picked up her braid again, absently removed the band, re-braided it, and secured it again. She smoothed her linen skirt. Fidgeting was not one of her habits, so I could tell all this bad news was getting to her. I touched her arm. When she looked over at me, I saw tears in her eyes. My heart went out to my grandmother. First her sister was injured in a near fatal car accident, then one of her dear friends was murdered. What a day she'd had. I got up and reached down to hug her. "I know," I said taking her strong hands in mine. "We'd just talked about how busy she's been this morning over coffee before we hit the road for First Monday."

"It was so awful, Star," Maxie said walking back over to where we were sitting. She popped the ring on top of her soda can. "Jimmie really kept her wits and tried to save Evelyn Sue. You should be proud of how she handled it."

"Well, of course. I'm just so shocked. Evelyn Sue, Edna, and I were just having lunch down at the Lone Star Café the other day," Star's voice trailed as she wiped a tear from her eye. "I guess I'll call down to White's Funeral Home tomorrow morning and see what arrangements have been made. Of course her housekeeper, Maria, will probably need some help with everything. Then again, there's been a young woman helping her out too. But then, I don't think Evelyn Sue trusted that girl much. Anyway, why don't you two go on in to see Edna. I'm sure it would be okay for a few minutes," Star said. "And Jimmie, I want to talk to you before you leave, okay?"

"Sure, Star."

The room was quiet as we entered. The blinds had been drawn against the setting sun. Aunt Edna lay resting against a couple of uncomfortable foam pillows with an

I.V. slowly dripping from above into the needle in her vein. Short spiky white hair framed her determined facial features. The steady beat of a heart monitor droned in the background. I placed her free hand in mine.

"Aunt Edna, it's Jimmie Rae and Maxine. Can you hear me?"

I watched as she struggled against the medication to wake up. She opened her eyes and looked frightened.

"Edna, what's wrong?"

"You tried to kill me," she said to Max.

"Of course, I didn't try to kill you, Edna! You know better than that. I've always thought of you like a second mom. Now, take a deep breath and tell us what happened. We want to go after the creep who did this to you."

We had her attention now. I released her hand and she reached out to Maxine who took it gently. "That's better. Try and tell us what happened," Max said.

"I'm sorry, Maxine Bea. Of course, I know it wasn't you, but it sure looked like your old Cadillac. Now, why don't you two run and play and let this old woman get some sleep?" Her voice was barely a whisper.

"I'm sorry. Star called and of course, we had to see you," I said moving closer to her and Max. "I'm not even going to be silly enough to ask how you feel. Can you try and tell us what on earth happened?"

"I'll try, but I'm so tired." Edna pointed to her cup full of ice chips and I used the plastic spoon to fish one out for her. "Thanks, hon," she murmured. "I was out at the Living History office late," she began. "I was trying to get the rest of the volunteers organized for the Homecoming Celebration next month. It was getting dark and I was on the road alone until bright lights came up behind me from nowhere. I tried out running them, but they kept accelerating then falling back very erratically, you know. I thought it was a drunk or someone in trouble. Finally, they came up fast behind me their bright lights blinding me and

I lost control of my car. I couldn't make out the driver, but there was no mistaking whose car it was."

Even though I had a good idea what her next words would be, we needed to hear her say them.

"It was Max's."

She looked up at us—her brown eyes large and serious. I lay my hand on her arm and said, "Edna, you know Maxine Bea Huntington would never do anything to harm you."

"No, Edna It wasn't me. Remember someone stole my car about a week ago? Are you sure it was my old Cadillac?"

"Well, it had the same stickers in the rear window. You're the only one I know with a Baylor Law School, Luckenbach, Texas, and Hard Rock Café sticker in the back window of a 1975 Mary Kay pink Cadillac.

"I met with Mary Jayne Brown yesterday," Edna continued. "We were talking about the upcoming Homecoming Celebration when she told me the most extraordinary thing about Evelyn Sue."

"Mrs. Veigel, how are you doing this evening? Oh, it looks like you have guests. Who are these pretty little things?" said a large lady with skin the color of cocoa as she entered rolling an electronic blood pressure and thermometer machine. Her picture identification card read: Sheree Smith, R.N.

She placed a syringe of fluid into Edna's IV tubing and said, "Okay ladies, sorry the party's over. Mrs. Veigel needs her beauty sleep. Today she's been working hard on healing her insides. You all can come back tomorrow if you want." She winked at us and rolled the machine back out of the room softly humming.

"Edna, I know you need to rest, but first can you tell us what Mrs. Brown told you."

Her eyes closed.

"Aunt Edna? Can you hear me?"

It was no use. She was in a deep sleep.

I squeezed her hand. "Tell you what, you get better and Max and I will get down to the bottom of this.

Max and I walked back out to the ICU waiting area. Everyone had gone home except Aunt Stacy. "Star would you like me to stay with you tonight too?" I offered.

"Oh, no thanks, Jimmie. Stacy insists on staying up here with me. No need for you to stay. You've had a tough day too. We'll be fine. I do have another favor to ask though."

"Anything."

"I need you to pick up an old radio out at the Flying W Ranch. I found a fella out there who fixes them up like brand new just like his daddy used to. Anyway, while I'm tied up here, I'd appreciate it if you could run out there tomorrow and pick it up. I got it fixed up for Keith's birthday next week. Here's his business card with a map on the back. Think you could do that for me sometime tomorrow?"

"Sure, Star. Anything else?"

"Yes—you girls get on home safely and don't find anymore dead bodies. Deal?"

"Sure, Star," I said and kissed her cheek. "The last thing we want is more trouble."

Chapter Seven

"Saturday only—Truth Estates, Lot 43B. Cash Only."

Somewhere between the full moon, cold sweat, and crazy dreams I couldn't sleep. At 3:19 a.m. I awoke from a bizarre dream and realized I hadn't made contact with Dr. Gifford to tell her about the letters and other items at the bubba brothers' junk shop. With all the mess that followed finding Evelyn Sue dead, the creeps at Cowboy's had literally become the last thing on my mind.

At 4:30 a.m. I gave up and decided I would just go to the Armstrong Browning Library early and check the archives myself. It was about an hour's drive to Waco and depending on what I found, or didn't find, I would figure out what to do next.

A half hour later, I shifted Old Blue into third as we eased onto the highway toward Waco. The late spring sun hadn't risen yet but the eastern horizon was pale lavender and pink. The humid air coming through the old windows hinted at the salty Gulf to the south. Stevie Ray Vaughn's soulful voice sang out in his rich Texas blues style as I dropped the gearshift into fourth. I took a careful sip of hot coffee thankful I had given Star an espresso maker for Mother's Day a few weeks ago. She would find my note when she got home from the hospital and went for her morning fix.

I hated driving around with Old Blue so loaded, but there seemed no other way. I planned to get to Waco by 6 a.m. and check the archives. By seven o'clock I figured I would have sufficient information to pass on to the police and that would justify not being at Billy Jack's office at the scheduled time. I reasoned that if I waited for everyone to wake up, I would be tethered to the demands of the day and not able to follow my hunches about the Browning letters and the other Browning items at Cowboy's.

As I approached Rosebud, Texas city limits my cell phone screamed like a sorority girl on a bad hair day. It was Max. "What are you doing up at this hour?" I said.

"Let's meet at the Lone Star Café in fifteen. I thought of some things that may be important to finding Evelyn Sue's killer. Maybe we should find out where Stella Pierce was yesterday. Also, I've thought all night about what happened to Edna. Who do you suppose ran her off the road? I don't think it was a coincidence. I'm just itching to find out what Mary Jayne told Edna that she wanted to tell us. I'm beginning to think there's something very connected and strange going on, and don't you wonder if those letters and things you found yesterday are real? Anyway, beat feet over to the Lone Star in a few. We can talk before we have to be in Billy Jack's office at seven."

"Hmmm, yeah, about that, I won't be making it."

"Of course you will," Max said in a reprimanding way.

"No, I won't. I'm half an hour away from Waco."

"What? Jimmie Rae have you lost your ever-loving mind? You're going to get us both in trouble! May I remind you, it doesn't bode well for Baylor law students to be locked up?"

"I'm sorry, Max. I couldn't sleep. My mind was going ninety to nothing too. Instead of lying there and thinking about everything, I decided to check and see if the Browning letters I found are the real ones or fakes. I'll be back to Niceton by mid-morning."

"Okay," Max said. "Here's our new game plan. I'll go to Billy Jack's office alone, but you have to promise me you'll call him before seven. I'll stall him as long as I can. I'll see if I can catch up with Stella Pierce and Mary Jayne. My buddy, Thomas Williams, may also be able to fill in some of the blanks about Evelyn Sue's murder."

"Who?"

"Never mind, kiddo. You do what you need to do in Waco and I'll meet you at Blessings around noon so we can unload your truck. Hey, by the way, Jimmie Rae?"

"Yes?"

"Since you're already there, could you please go by my apartment and pick up a box I left near the kitchen counter? It's marked, "BAM." It is my tiara collection—I thought it would be cool in front of the vintage Texas Chainsaw Massacre poster."

"Oh, girl, you are warped!"

"Gee, thanks, Jimmie."

"See you later, Maxie," I said.

"You be careful, Jimmie Rae and don't forget to call Billy Jack. I have the feeling it's going to cost you," she said.

I laughed. "Don't worry, sister. It's all good! By noon we'll have this thing figured out so we can get on with our lives. Besides you still owe me an explanation about Steve. I want to know everything. See you later!"

I still wished I was as confident as I sounded. The sun was reaching over the eastern horizon as I came up Highway 77 and passed the infamous Waco restaurant landmarks, Healthcamp Burgers and the Elite Café on the circle, and made a sharp right onto the access road. Traffic from Interstate 35 buzzed next to me. I turned right onto Eighth Street.

The Armstrong Browning Library was nestled in the southeast end of Baylor University. Its magnificent Italianate architecture was shaded by century old pecan trees and gnarled live oaks. The sheer sense of delight I felt the first time I visited as a teenager was still alive.

A statue of Pippa, the little girl from Robert Browning's poem, "Pippa Passes," welcomed me back with the quote, "God's in his heaven – all's right with the world!" *If only.*

No one else was around at this hour. It reminded me of when I was so obsessed with finishing my thesis and Dr. Gifford had allowed me to work at the Library anytime I wanted. I had grown comfortable with the old building's sounds when the campus was quiet early in the morning like this.

I parked Old Blue and approached the back door "Employees Only" entrance that required punching an access code on the keypad and scanning my "staff" ID card. I pushed the door open. Emergency exit lights gave the narrow hallway an eerie glow. I passed my card again and entered the Library's Administration Office to pick up my paycheck. The mailroom was two doors down from the receptionist's desk.

An electronic beep stopped me dead in my tracks. The sound indicated someone was trying to gain access to a room they were not permitted in. A chill ran through me. I was not alone. Next, I heard light footsteps treading on the tile floor back toward the office. I crouched into a defensive position and waited.

"Oh, Jimmie Rae, thank heavens! I'm so glad you're here. I need to borrow your I.D. card for a second."

Kate Wilson, the Armstrong Browning Library's part-time receptionist, stood there as if nothing were unusual at all. I had no idea why she would be at the Library at this hour. Dr. Gifford had not granted her permission to come in early to the best of my knowledge. Kate was from

Niceton too, although I didn't know her well since she was about ten years younger than me. Her skin looked like the alabaster from a couple of the Library's statues except for the dark shadows beneath her eyes.

"Kate, what are you doing here? You scared me to death! I thought you'd gone back to Niceton for the weekend. Is everything okay? You look exhausted."

"Everything's just fine. I came by to do a little filing. I'm getting ready for our trip to Italy," she said. Her large blue eyes didn't match her small face. Her Baylor football jersey and loose blue jeans only emphasized her tiny body.

"That's right," I said relieved. "You're going with Dr. Gifford to receive the new acquisition from the Bartelli family in Florence. Francine was telling me all about it. When do you leave?"

"We're driving to Dallas Sunday morning to catch our afternoon flight. So, how about it? Can I use your pass card real quick?"

The teacher in me wanted to correct her grammar, but I let it go. "I thought you had the same access as I do. Why would you need my pass?"

"Well, it's just a formality really. Dr. Gifford is working on why my pass doesn't open the archives room. I'll only be a moment. I just need to check something."

My cell phone screamed out again for the second time in an hour. I needed to remember to change the tone to something more soothing. "I'm sorry Kate, I've got to go. Maybe you should call Dr. Gifford and check with her," I said over my shoulder.

My curiosity was peaked. Why in the world would Kate be at the Library "filing" so early on a Friday morning and why would she need access to the archives? As a part-time receptionist, she didn't have any reason to be in the archives room. I suspected she had lied about Dr. Gifford too.

It didn't make sense, yet there wasn't time to ask questions. My grandmother was calling. "Hey, Star. What's going on?" I said as I unlocked the door with my free hand and entered the small office, tossing my leather messenger bag onto my office chair.

"Where are you, young lady?"

Star was not in a good mood. "Good Morning, Star. Didn't you get my note? I'm at the Armstrong Browning doing some early morning research."

"Why did I think you were supposed to be sleeping here last night or be at the police station in forty-five minutes? Could it be because Detective Mitchell has already called here reminding you of your 7 a.m. appointment?"

The tone of Star's reprimanding voice told me she had not had her morning java yet.

"Lands, child, don't I have enough to worry about with Edna without you running all over the creation finding dead bodies and such," Star said.

"Star, hey, slow down and take of sip of coffee. Come on, you know you'll feel better." I could hear her take my advice.

"Good, now don't you feel a little better? Okay, I'm sorry I took off early, but there's something here at the Library I have to check before I meet with Billy Jack. I didn't get a chance to tell you about it because of everything else that happened yesterday. You'll have to trust me, Star. You've taught me well and I'm a big girl now." I heard her take a long sip of coffee and could tell she was calming down.

"Sorry, hon, it's just that with everything that's happened I'm afraid for you and Maxine. Wait, Jimmie Rae, the hospital is on the land line."

Another caffeine fix would be good for me as well. As I held the phone between my shoulder and ear, my hands went to work automatically filling our Italian–-or rather, now *my* tomato red Italian espresso machine. Star came back on the line as the grinding cycle finished and the brewing had begun.

"They think Edna may have some additional internal bleeding. They may have to take her back to surgery. I've got to go, girl. Do what you have to, but please be careful and get back here as soon as possible."

"Of course," I said. "Give Edna a hug for me. I'll say prayers for her. I love you, Star. See you soon."

"I love you too, hon, be careful. Bye-Bye."

I grabbed my favorite Italian demitasse for a much needed espresso shot. There was snail mail in my in-box tray. I fanned through it. There was an envelope from my attorney's office. I placed it on the bottom of the stack. I didn't have the heart to open it. Instead, I foamed some milk from my mini-fridge and topped off my cup. Café crema was just what I needed. At least our Italian honeymoon hadn't been a total waste.

Chapter Eight

"Divorce Sale: Sat. only, 8 a.m.–4 p.m. Wedding Ring Set -CHEAP! Entertainment center complete with big screen TV, CDs, textbooks, misc. household items, and many other items too numerous to list."

For the past couple of years, this small office had become more of a home to me than the house I had shared with Joe. Placed in front of a large window, my oak desk overlooked the garden area in front of the Library. Almost all my office furniture and accessories had come from forages to antique malls, estate sales, and flea markets from San Antonio to Dallas to Houston, and even over in Lafayette, Louisiana. A few publicity posters from the Library hung between vintage floral prints and black-framed Victorian lithographs.

Although, our separation was amicable, admitting it had to come to a legal divorce was difficult. Initially, I had written off our disagreements as him being stressed out his first year as a professional attorney. When he asked for more "space," I suggested we go away together. His expression told me there would be no reconciliation. I reluctantly agreed to let him move out. That was six months ago. In the light of day, the memory stung unexpectedly like a fire ant bite.

I tossed the unopened mail on my desk. The ticking of the mantel clock reminded me of the time. I finished my latte, wiped out the cup, and refocused my attention to the mission at hand.

Locking my office door, I looked up and down the staff hallway and noticed Kate was nowhere to be found. I headed down the hallway to the basement stairs to check the east archival room for the letters.

For the past seven years my time had been split between teaching freshman composition and working at the Library. I began as a research specialist while still a grad student then progressed to an assistant archival curator after I received my master's degree.

I still thought it was incredible this massive building dedicated to a couple of Victorian English poets was in Waco, Texas of all places. The Armstrong Browning Library began and continued as a true labor of love.

In 1918 as a young English professor, Dr. A.J. Armstrong presented Baylor University with his incredible collection of Robert and Elizabeth Barrett Browning's writings, personal possessions, and household items from the everyday silver teapot to the most extraordinary sixteenth-century Italian tapestry. For the next thirty years he diligently worked, raising funds to create a special place for the items to be displayed. Dr. Armstrong finally realized his dream in 1951 at the dedication of the Armstrong Browning Library. He died three years later, leaving a legacy of the world's largest collection of Barrett Browning items.

Custom crafted bronze doors depicting the Browning's poetic themes welcomed visitors into a quiet, peaceful sanctuary away from the chaos of modern life. From the beautiful polished granite floors and paneled mahogany walls to the fifty-three spectacular stained glass windows depicting different poetic themes, the Library building served as graceful architectural and literary reminder of another time and place.

I felt a kinship with both Dr. Armstrong and the Brownings as a fellow poet and person who appreciated items from the past. I envisioned the Brownings as eloquent fellow junkers. After all, Elizabeth and Robert had furnished their small rented Florentine villa, Casa Guidi, with finds, many which were fifteenth and sixteenth century pieces, from the local Tuscan flea markets held daily throughout Florence.

Once down two flights of stairs to the basement I was at the door of the Archives room. Checking the hallway once again I saw nothing. Where had Kate gone? Only the sound of the industrial air conditioner droned. I swept my identification card through the electronic track. A green light flashed accepting me inside the room.

With the metal door firmly shut, and white cotton gloves stretched over my fingers, I began to search for the letters. As I suspected the file had been tampered with. Usually, a paper marker is used to indicate if someone is working with an archival item. The marker would be placed in the exact location of the removed item so once the research was complete, the document could be returned to its proper location.

Elizabeth and Robert had posted letters to one another following their secret marriage before they left for their new lives together in Italy. There was an empty space where these letters should have been filed. Removing the delicate letters from the Max's manila folder, I placed them in the file where they belonged. I realized this file of precious letters should be fuller. Other letters were missing too. Bet I knew what teal and black tiled restroom held the other missing two hundred-year-old love letters.

I checked my cell phone for the time--6:58 a.m.— it seemed still too early to call Dr. Gifford who was not known to be a "morning" person. I decided to retrieve

Max's box first then call Dr. Gifford. Right now I couldn't explain how the Browning letters had ended up in a ladies room so many miles from Waco. Lonnie and Cowboy really didn't seem the poetic types. Even worse, I feared I had stumbled into a larger problem--what if those two knuckleheads were part of an elaborate black market ring?

And didn't Max just tell me yesterday there were also missing items from the Lee County Living History Museum? It was beginning to come together and make sense. It seemed a stretch to think everything that happened might be connected yet my intuition told me it was true-- especially with Edna in the hospital and Evelyn Sue dead. Who was next, Max? Star? And how in the world did Daryl Ann fit into all this? Did Stella Pierce know anything about it? Could she be the murderer? The thought hurried me through the task of locking up the Armstrong Browning Library and getting back to my truck. The last fifteen-minutes posed more questions than it answered and gave me a serious case of the hebbie-jebbies, but I now knew I had a lot to find out from a few of Niceton's citizens and city council members.

I was about to head back to Niceton when I remembered the box Max asked me to pick up at her apartment. When she was in Waco, which wasn't that often any more, she lived on the second story of a three-story 1920's boarding house with two other women. They each had a bedroom and shared a common living area, kitchen, and one bathroom. Since Max grew up in a large family the occasional inconveniences were well worth the small amount of rent she paid. Especially now, since she split her time between Waco and Niceton.

This would only take a second I thought as I pushed the silver column shift in park and killed the engine. I grabbed my leather messenger bag and Max's pink flamingo key chain in case no one was home. The house was unusually quiet for a weekday even if it was between semesters. I knocked lightly on the heavy green door. It opened the length of the door chain.

A young woman answered. "Yeah, what?" she asked wearily.

"I'm a friend of Max's. She asked me to get something for her."

"Who are you?" the woman asked.

"I was about to ask you the same thing. I'm Jimmie Rae, Max's best friend…" my voice trailed. Suddenly, the woman slammed the green door in my face.

Chapter Nine

"Estate Sale: 806 Oak St., 7 a.m.–4 p.m., Friday & Saturday—50 years of accumulation—Everything must go! Maple bedroom set; 100s of country & western albums; Tupperware; clothing; Frankhoma collection; café-ware; cowboy boots, lawn mowers, plus MORE."

I realized it wasn't a slam but rather an unlocking of the door in my face. "I should have realized, you're Jimmie Rae, of course. Come on in. I'm Max's cousin, Belinda, but everyone calls me 'Birdie.' Max told me you'd probably call or something." She walked over to the small 1950s style chrome and yellow Formica table stacked with textbooks and sat down. She looked nothing like Max. Her hair was short, blondish with black wisps peeking through, and her eyes were dark brown. She wore an oversized Will's Point, TX Bluebird Festival t-shirt which strained to cover her curves.

"When did you move in?" I asked as I moved toward the kitchen area to retrieve Max's box.

"Last week. I just graduated from East Texas Community College and start summer classes at Baylor next week. Momma and Daddy thought it would be okay if I roomed with Max this summer and got my first taste of real university life. Of course, they don't know I've jumped in up to my eyeballs—I really love being on my own."

I found the box marked "BAM" and headed toward the door. "Thanks. I'll be going now." I placed my free hand on the doorknob. "It was nice to meet you, and by the way, don't drag any boys home, they're only bad news." As I turned to let myself out, I realized my tip of the day was wasted.

"Say, Birdie, like where's the Coco Puffs?" A familiar male voice asked. My ex-husband appeared from the kitchen door wearing a Baylor ball cap worn backwards, cowboy print boxers, and a boyish grin. "Oh, I didn't know you had company," he said walking around the partition. He stopped dead in his tracks. "Well, this is awkward," Joe said turning his cap around like it would magically erase the moment. "So how ya been, Jimmie Rae?"

"You know her, Joe?" Birdie said.

"Never-mind Birdie!" I answered. "My advice is too late. You've just slept with my husband!"

"Ex-husband, Jimmie," Joe said.

I looked at him and felt the all too familiar bile boiling in my stomach. "You could have at least waited for the official divorce papers! But hey since you asked Joe, you want to know how I've been? Now, that it's over, I'm better than ever! You slithering, slug-eating, backstabbing, cradle-robbing, pathetic excuse for a human being! You think you're such hot stuff, huh? Here, maybe this will cool you off!" I set the box down, picked up the pitcher of orange juice on the Formica table, and threw it on him.

He was obviously stunned. He just stood looking down and watching the sticky juice run down his naked chest to the top of his boxers and drip on the floor. "Well, that was mature, Jimmie," he said grabbing the kitchen towel off the table and trying to sop up the mess.

I could care less. I straightened my pink rhinestone 'Texas' T-shirt, pushed the fallen curls from my eyes, picked up the box, and opened and slammed the green door so hard, small bits of plaster came down around my head as I took the steps two at a time.

Joe's voice followed me over the stair railing. "Hey, Jimmie, check your stinkin' mail! The divorce was finalized last Monday!"

I tossed the box of jeweled crowns on the front seat, jumped in Old Blue, and slammed the door. I sat in the mugginess staring ahead as tears slipped down my hot face. All those months of loneliness--the emptiness gathered at once and forced itself into convulsing sobs. I reached into the glovebox and grabbed a fistful of napkins. I dried my face, blew my nose, and regained my composure. The last thing I wanted was for those two to see me bawling like I cared.

Joseph Trent Murphy was hardly worth such a fuss. I reached for my leather bag – did I forget to throw the mail in while I was in my office? Was our divorce final? Regardless, it was finally obvious to me I was just the creep's financial aid source for law school. Crap! I slapped the dashboard at the realization ignoring the hot tears burning down my face. In my rearview mirror I saw Joe's truck parallel parked on the street. I'd somehow missed it before probably because this was the last place I expected to see it. I wiped my tears on my arm and Carrie Underwood-style I grabbed my keys, hopped back out of Old Blue, and left a lasting impression on Joe's precious red Silverado truck.

There! I hopped back into Old Blue and blew my nose. One thing about me though, I don't forget and I believed karma would pay good ole Joe a visit. With a fresh hit of patchouli oil behind my ears and swipe of lip balm, I popped a piece of sugarless gum in my mouth, and turned the key. I backed out of the driveway and away from my years of married life with Joe for once and all.

The fresh “Estate Sale” sign flashed at me at the corner of First and Oak like a beacon on a stormy sea. “Come On!” it tempted me. I flipped open my phone again to check the time— 8:24. “What the heck,” I thought. I needed to calm down and an estate sale would put me in more pleasant frame of mind to deal with Billy Jack later. Kind of like a Zen for junkers. I toyed with calling Max and ruled against it. She would probably be talking to Billy Jack and I certainly didn’t want to interrupt their discussion. A quick peek at the estate sale would indeed be valuable on many levels I reasoned.

Minutes later my hands were reaching for a dark green McCoy flowerpot when my cell-phone released its hair-raising soprano. Caller ID revealed it was Max before my index finger poked the “OK” button.

“Maxie, I’m on my way back,” I fibbed, not adding I was at an incredible estate sale. One run by a family instead of a professional dealer, meaning all the good stuff hadn’t been nabbed by the dealer running the sale and the prices were reasonable. As I tried to balance my phone against my shoulder, a dirty blonde forty-something woman in a ladybug sequined T-shirt reached across me and snagged the McCoy flowerpot.

“Ain’t this just the steal of the day,” she said holding her prize close to her ladybug. “And only three dollars.” We exchanged fake Cheshire-Cat grins and she left. I was alone in a stranger’s back bedroom in Waco, Texas with only black-velvet Elvis pictures and boxes of Conway Twitty memorabilia for company. I stood dumbly holding my intrusive cell-phone with Max, attached at the other end.

“Maxie, what’s up?”

“Where are you? You’re at a sale, aren’t you?” she said. She knew me too well.

"Yes, and I just missed out on a cool *three* dollar McCoy," I admitted.

"Woman, don't you realize how serious this is? Billy Jack isn't fooling around. You can't be screwing around at sales today," she said in her best attorney voice. "You need to get your butt back here now. Billy Jack is on the war-path."

"But Max, this is a really great family estate sale. Besides you didn't tell me my ex was sleeping over at your apartment."

"What?"

"Yeah, I went over there and your baby cousin, Birdy, was shacked up with Joe or vice versa. Anyway, I'm just doing a little Zen junking then I'm on my way. I promise I'll be in Billy Jack's office by ten."

"Well, girl, you'd better be. He was hotter than your cousin Mayleen without her estrogen patch. I tried covering for you but he wasn't buying any of it. He's not going to let you off or forget you stood him up. Also, my friend Thomas has been doing some checking and Daryl Ann is no where to be found."

"Maxie, come on, that's because she's in Mexico sipping a Bloody Mary and watching the sun mambo over the waves by now."

"I don't think so. Her car was found abandoned at the Hillsboro Outlet Mall parking lot late last night. No one has seen her since yesterday at Canton. The police are treating her disappearance as 'suspicious.'"

"Oh. That's no good. On that subject, there are a lot more letters missing from the Library too. Hey, let me get out of here and I'll see you later, girl."

"Promise me no more garage sales, yard sales, junk stores, antique malls, or estate sales, Jimmie Rae. Okay?"

"I promise, Max."

"And Jimmie, you may want to call Billy Jack. It may help justify your alibi."

"Bye-bye, Maxine!"

I snapped my Trekkie looking cell phone shut before she could say another word. I placed it back in my pocket, as I continued to scan the bedroom for treasures. The bedroom suite, a maple set, was already marked "SOLD."

Then I saw it. In the darkened room I had mistaken it for another velvet Elvis. I climbed over the Conway Twitty albums and across the full size bed to grab it off the wall. It was an amateur rendering of the Texas hill country in springtime. Painted bluebonnets dotted the rise and fall of the horizon offset by a sprawled out live oak in the foreground and a distant dirt road leading to an old barn. It was large-–every bit three feet by two-–a real gem, and only twenty-five dollars. I'd seen smaller ones at a recent Austin flea market starting at a hundred. I took my prize to the woman running the sale. The ladybug shirt woman was ahead of me.

She turned around as I approached. "Where'd you get that?"

"It was above the McCoy," I said. She knew she'd been beaten at her own game and I knew I'd better cough up the cash and load.

The sky was illuminated like candlelight as the sun tried to penetrate the thin Gulf clouds. Sweat beaded under my curly brown bangs, acknowledging another warm, humid late May day.

I set a brown paper bag of odd estate sale smalls on the floorboard, and placed my bluebonnet painting at an angle to rest against the worn brown pick-up seat, and Max's box of tiaras. I rolled the windows down half way to get some fresh air. Old Blue jumped to life.

The noise of her engine was loud, but once she started she purred like a fat barn cat. Although the ride was jerky and third gear was tricky, I loved Old Blue because she smelled of hard work, tobacco, and Wrigley's' spearmint chewing gum— a quiet tribute to my late granddaddy, John Eugene Spell.

I tried to focus on my happy thoughts as I drove back to Niceton. I looked around the full cab swelled with treasures and tried to focus on how they would look in our booth at Blessings Antique Mall. My mind refused to cooperate and immediately flashed to finding Evelyn Sue Dinsmore's sprawled out body and bloody face. Her beehive hairdo limp and her perfectly matched outfit stained in crimson. It was no consolation that her jeweled sandals were as immaculate as when she put them on her size five feet that morning.

Finding Daryl Ann and chatting with Stella Pierce and Mary Jayne Brown would be pivotal to getting Billy Jack off our backs and solving the murder. Where could Daryl Ann be? Why would she kill Evelyn Sue? Where were the other missing Browning letters and other possessions? It seemed too odd the two could be connected; yet I've always believed life is stranger than fiction. This line of thinking jarred my memory to call Dr. Gifford. I opened my cell phone, pressing speed dial number four when I saw the flashing lights in my rear-view. Billy Jack had found me first.

Chapter Ten

"Huge selection of vintage radios- 1920s to 1960s- Floor and table models. Also large variety of vintage radio tubes and parts. Vintage Soundwaves, Booth #333, located at Blessings From the Past Antique Mall, 213 East Main Street, Niceton."

"What the hell were you thinking, Jimmie Rae?"

Billy Jack Mitchell peered at me with the same lupine blue eyes that stole my heart some twenty years before. His face had aged and his brown hair, though still full, was buzzed in a crew cut. He was leaning against his desk. He wore a crisp, white western shirt with pearlized snap buttons and carefully creased indigo Wranglers. Polished black ostrich cowboy boots made him appear taller than his five-foot-eleven-inch height.

Like a reprimanded child I sat opposite him in a green and chrome office chair. "Look Billy Jack, I went to Waco this morning because a lot of unexplained things happened yesterday. Miss Dinsmore's untimely death was only one of them."

"Oh, really? Do tell, Jimmie."

"Okay. I have reason to believe Edna's car accident and Daryl Ann's disappearing act are all connected to Evelyn Sue's murder."

"Oh?"

"Hear me out. I stopped at a junk store yesterday on the way to the Trade Days and found either the most extraordinary fake Robert and Elizabeth Barrett Browning memorabilia or the actual rare items stolen from the Library where I work at Baylor." I paused and looked at him for effect. His expression did not change, but he did write for a few minutes on the legal pad in his hand. He looked up, so I continued.

"Browning?"

"Yes, as in the English poets, Elizabeth Barrett and Robert Browning. You know, 'how do I love thee'?"

"Why Jimmie Rae, I didn't know you still cared."

I chose to ignore his comment and continued, "This morning I was checking to see if we were missing any of our Browning letters, which we are, if you care. I was in the process of contacting my supervisor, Dr. Eva Gifford when your boys changed my plans a while ago." I continued, "You know me, Billy Jack. You can't possibly believe Max or I had anything to do with Evelyn Sue's death."

He looked at me a long time, carefully measuring the situation. Finally, he tossed his legal pad on the desk, picked up his coffee cup, refilled it, and sat in the leather chair behind the massive wooden desk. "Save the sentiment, Jimmie Rae. It's not going to work. I know people change. Why even my own dear grandmother is capable of murder in the right circumstances."

"How could you even think that about Miss Lou?" I asked. "You know what?" I looked down at my sandaled toes taking a moment before I blurted out my thoughts. Raising my head and looking him in the eyes, I decided to go for it, "You're the one who's changed Billy Jack."

He smiled and shook his head in affirmation. "Life does that to people, Jimmie. Now, why don't you give me your statement about Miss Dinsmore? Then, I'll take your statements on the other points you've made."

"I gave your uncle my statement yesterday."

"Well, hon, that was yesterday. I'd like to see what you remember today and how it matches up with the other witness statements and with your own statement. Of course you may choose to decline. However, that doesn't bode well for your case."

"I see. So do I need an attorney to be present?"

"That depends on you, sweetheart. It's a risk not to have one and a pain to find one. Hey, aren't you married to one?" he asked with a smile.

Years of riding in every rodeo west of the Mississippi and more recently, becoming a cop, had only added interest to his face. His smile, once so easy, now appeared smug. Even so, he still had the same deep, mischievous dimples he had as a kid.

I stared at him. Billy Jack was definitely in the mood to torment me. "As if you didn't know or even care, we've been separated for some time, and according to him, the divorce is final. Yay." I could no longer sit still and pretend everything was ducky. I stood up, placed my hands on my hips, and continued. "Furthermore, although I worked my butt off so he could get a law degree, I wouldn't call that sleazebag even if I got the death sentence."

"Hmm. Touched a nerve, I see," he said, picking up the legal pad and adding to his notes.

I was ready to get away from Billy Jack. "If I give you my statement, may I leave?" I said.

"Yeah, sure."

I sat back down and tried to gain some modest amount of composure. For the next fifteen minutes, which seemed more like an eternity, I told him how I stopped at Cowboy's to use the facilities, and instead found the Browning letters. He stopped me several times and asked detailed questions. Then, I told him about the moments prior to finding Evelyn Sue. He wanted a detailed description of how I found her.

Tears fell as I recounted the shock of finding my long time friend and teacher, a woman I truly admired, as she lay dying. I told him how I tried to stop the bleeding with my bandana only to realize it wasn't helping. My nose began to run as snot and tears combined for the umpteenth time in the past twenty-four hours. What a beauty I must look like.

Billy Jack shoved a tissue box toward me. I stopped to blow my nose.

"I know that was difficult, Jimmie, but maybe there's something you remember today that you didn't yesterday," he said quietly.

"That's all I really remember, Billy Jack. May I go now? I need to unload my truck."

"You've still got Old Blue? She's one of the sweetest old Effys I've ever seen," he said.

I wiped my eyes and tried to pull myself together. "She's even sweeter now--I had air-conditioning and a CD player installed. The guys I took her to did a great job and kept her as authentic as possible."

"Great," he said getting up and opening his office door. "Okay, I've got work to do. You still owe me a Shiner at Lucky's later. We'll catch up on the last twenty years. By the way, don't go getting into anymore trouble," he said, attempting a smile. "Let me see what I can find out from R.C. and the guys up near that junk store you found."

Minutes later I parked Old Blue at the back door of Blessings. My stomach growled, rebelling against my plan to unload the truck before I ate lunch.

"Hey, girl." Max appeared from the back door and greeted me with a hug. "Sorry about the McCoy. Gee you look awful."

"Thanks, girlfriend! It hasn't exactly been my day so far." I pulled my hair back into a ponytail and wiped my nose again. "Forget about the McCoy pot. I ended up with a great old bluebonnet painting and some other good stuff," I said changing the subject.

"Good. You *did* go talk to Billy Jack, didn't you?"

"Yes, mom. I just left his office. He's certainly lost his sense of humor and good nature somewhere along the way, hasn't he?" I walked around my truck, dropped the tailgate, and reached for the covered totes.

"Well, I think life has left a lot of marks on him. You know his wife overdosed on sleeping pills, right?" she continued, not waiting for my reply. "He's raising his little girl – I think she's two." Maxine reached out for the tote I handed her and headed up the back steps to the loading dock at the back of the Mall never once coming up for air. "Then, last week my brother-in-law Frank told me Billy Jack's partner was shot in front of him during a drug raid in February. The bullet went through the guy just missing Billy Jack." She dropped the tote on the dock and returned to Old Blue and reached in for her BAM box. "Oh, that is a cool painting!" she said as she moved it to get her box out.

"So he moved back here so his folks could help him with his daughter? Hard to believe Billy Jack has a little girl," I said taking a tote up the steep dock steps.

"Yeah, he wants to spend as much time as possible with her. I guess between his wife's death and his own near death experience, he figured a desk job would be a good idea. That's hard to do working drug raids in South Texas. Besides, now his mom and grandma can help him out with Caroline too. I saw her last week. What a doll," Maxine said opening the metal back door, resetting the lock, and kicking the brick down so it wouldn't close and lock us out.

I watched my best friend to be sure she was done with her oration on Billy Jack. Being on the long-winded side would certainly be in her favor when she finished her law degree. Like an early spring Texas twister, her opponents wouldn't know what hit them.

"Gee, I had no idea. I guess having a spouse die and putting your life on the line everyday would have that kind of impact. Kind of puts life into perspective too--like finding your ex shacked up with a girl seem as insignificant as it is," I said joining her on the loading dock.

"Hey, Jimmie, I had no idea that was going on. Uncle Dan and Aunt Pearl won't be too happy that Birdie has flown the coop," she said giving me a light punch on the arm and trying to make me smile. "Really, I had no idea Joe was there. I'm very sorry you had to deal with that this morning. So, is the divorce really final?"

"Honestly, I'm not sure. I was so focused on Star and the archives and Evelyn Sue's murder, I accidentally left the mail on my office desk. Guess I need to go back eventually and pick it up. Actually, there may have been something from Mick's office. Anyway, your kitchen floor may be a little sticky. I cooled Joe off with pitcher of O.J."

"That's my girl!" She hugged my shoulder. "Now, let's get back to work. Do that thing you do with our old stuff to make it sell like chocolate during Lent. Speaking of church, did I mention there's a new minister in town?"

"Maxine!" called Glenda Phelps, the mall's owner.

"Oops, gotta go, kid."

"Okay, go on. I'm going to get a bandana. It already feels like a steam bath out here," I said.

Honestly, I thought to myself, Max is so smart yet so totally Attention Deficit Dysfunctional. Yet, somehow she kept it all together. Maybe that was *how* she kept it all together.

I was as bad as she was. My mind was going in a million directions yet I had to focus on unloading my truck first. I promised my growling stomach a cheeseburger and a piece of fabulous chocolate pie down at the Lone Star

Café as soon as I finished. To heck with the carb count today.

Years ago, as urban sprawl crawled beyond the big cities and the locals left for bigger paychecks, fancy coffee, and the conformity of suburban life, Niceton, Texas was on the verge of dying. But, leave it to the good ole Baptists to save the day. Everything began improving when they built a new, bigger, and better worship center out on Highway 77, and Judge Theodore Phelps, and his wife, Glenda, purchased the old nineteenth-century limestone and brick sanctuary in downtown Niceton. Since then, things had begun to look up in our small town. What was once a dying, dried up town had become a tourist destination.

With the successful opening of Blessings From the Past Antique Mall in the old First Baptist Church building on the town square, four other antique malls had followed suit. Soon, a bakery, two tearooms and a bevy of boutiques had jump-started Niceton's economy.

Even Star had a piece of the action. The Page Turner, a couple of doors down from Blessings, was a great independent bookstore—a rarity these days. My younger cousins helped her run it and she helped them pay for college textbooks. Ironically, the suburbanites who craved this type of slow-sit-a-spell mentality were some of the very ones who left years ago for the frantic paced urban life.

I still remembered the First Baptist building from my days of attending Vacation Bible School with Maxine. The Fellowship Hall with its pale pink and blue checked tiled floor, had welcomed me with the lingering aromas of homemade yeast rolls, fried chicken, and unknown gallons of sweet ice tea.

The original building had been built in a gothic architectural tradition. Strong, exposed interior beams like ribs held the framing together while long, narrow, arched lead-glass windows ran the length of each side of the locally quarried limestone building. A pair of massive blue and green stained glass windows flanked the sanctuary's focal point high above the baptismal. The center stained glass window revealed a nineteenth-century pastoral Christ figure leading white and gray sheep.

The first time I saw the converted space I knew the antique mall would be a huge success. Once used to submerge new believers, the baptismal tub had been removed and the area was now used to display items for sale. The impact of the open, yet cozy space invited customers to spend hours, if not the day, searching each booth for treasures.

Booth spaces flanked the entrance, both sides, and the back of the building. The Junk Chic booth Max and I shared was in the old choir loft to the left of the pulpit area. An added bonus was its convenience to the back door that made loading and unloading a lot easier. We felt fortunate to have such a premium spot and had spent many years figuring out new uses for the old space. We used the old oak hymn board, still intact on the limestone walls, for displaying vintage postcards and the old tiered oak floors now made for great staggered display spaces.

The mid-day sun was already causing moisture to drip off my forehead. I pressed my shoulder up to sop up some of the sweat. Although it was only late May, the temperatures combined with the humidity hinted at the agonizing summer heat to come.

Max had propped the back door open for me. Our booth was through the old choir room and out to the choir loft. I grabbed two boxes and proceeded through the metal backdoor. With my arms full, I didn't see the brick holding the door. My foot accidentally kicked it and the door replied by slamming shut, leaving me in the dark choir room with only the exit light for illumination. I set the boxes down and tried opening the interior door leading to the main sanctuary. Of course, the door was locked, leaving me alone in the darkened room.

All at once, the door leading up to the old baptismal squeaked open. The silhouette of a tall man backing into the choir room appeared in the dim light from the baptismal stairway. He was carrying a chair down the stairs.

"Max, give me a hand for crying out loud!" his voice boomed through the darkness. "Cripes! What did you do to the light? Come on now! Hold the dang door!"

Stunned into silence, I held the door open as wide as it would go. He pulled the 1930s Deco green velvet upholstered chair through with a few more choice words. He abruptly dropped the chair and swung around to face me. In one motion he pushed me against the wall. My cheek felt the cold, rough limestone wall while my arms ached as he held them tightly. I was pinned against the wall, his weight pressing against my back.

"I don't know who the hell you are, but one false move and you're history," his warm breath whispered in my ear.

Chapter Eleven

"Dealers Wanted: Come join the fun in Niceton's first antique mall, "Blessings From the Past," located at 213 East Main Street. First month, free booth space rental upon signing 12-month lease agreement. Great location, regional advertising. Don't miss this great opportunity! Call or stop by."

"I suggest if you'd like a proper introduction you'll get off me, bud!" my voice sounded hoarse as his weight bore me into the wall, making it hard to breathe.

"Not until you tell me who you are, sister." His breath stirred the wisps of hair around my ear.

My pulse was racing and my temper flared. I let my left leg bear both our weights and wrapped my right leg around his, and pivoted, crashing us both to the floor. I landed on top of him. In the red light from the "Exit" sign I glared at him and he glared back.

My attacker was about six-foot-three-inches and slim. He appeared to be in his late thirties or early forties. His face was smooth and his collar length dark hair was full but tinged with gray. A simple silver cross on black cord was hung around his neck and the word TEXAS was tattooed on his muscular forearm.

As I sat on top of his abdomen glaring at him, he laughed. Embarrassed and angry I jumped up leaving him lying in the floor now in full-blown uncontrollable laughter. I wanted to kick him, but instead I crossed my arms. "Ha-ha! What are you, some kind of perv? Don't answer that or I may be forced to bring you to tears, buster. If you can manage to pull yourself together I need to get this door unlocked so I can unload my truck."

The Mall door suddenly opened and the overhead light came on as if just needing an invitation to do so. Max peeked in. "Jimmie Rae, come on girl!" She saw me standing over the stranger as he continued to laugh. "Oh," she said winking at me. "Sorry to interrupt. Guess you two have already met."

"Actually, no, we haven't. This guerilla just accosted me in the dark," I told her. I followed her eyes and saw my attacker wore a pair of worn black cowboy boots, faded Levis, and an untucked worn chambray western shirt with the collar open and the sleeves rolled up.

"You lucky girl," Max said.

"You must be the notorious Jimmie Rae Murphy. Sorry about that. It was simply a case of mistaken identity," the man said as he got up brushing off his jeans. "Although I must say that is the most fun I've had in a while and I didn't hear any complaints from you."

Maxie raised her eyebrows. "I feel like I've interrupted a *moment*," she said emphasizing her last word. Max looked at me and I gave her my best "I'm not amused look."

I brushed at my denim shorts, tugged the hem of my pink t-shirt, and straightened the red bandana holding the curls off my face.

"Jimmie, this is Thomas Williams," she said, ignoring my obvious lack of interest. "Thomas, this is my best friend, Jimmie Rae, but you may know her better than me at this point," she said giving him a wink and punch on his arm.

"Good to finally meet you. I've heard a lot about you from this one," he said reaching his right hand out.

I forced interest and he shook my left hand in a firm handshake. In the light, I couldn't help but notice his clear brown eyes, a sizeable, deep scar on his left cheek, and a small dimple in his right cheek near his smiling mouth. Grey tinges at his temples only added mystique to his handsome presence. I also noticed he had worked up a sweat and smelled like sandalwood. I tried to ignore his sensuality and the feelings it stirred within me. Flashes of Joe and Birdy together, reminded me all men were pigs. Meanwhile, Max was pouring on the flirtations as liberally as Star used Tabasco in her shrimp gumbo.

"The name is Maxine Bea Huntington. Don't make me remind you again," she said coyly, tossing her long red hair off her shoulders.

I looked hard at Max, as if to say, "Who is this guy?" She gave me the "fill you in later" look back.

"Thomas, could you give us a hand over here?" Glenda called out.

"Sure, be right there." Thomas looked back to Max and I. "Jimmie Rae, once again I'm sincerely sorry. I hope you'll give me a chance to show you what a gentleman I can be. Besides, I expect you to fill me in on your version of Max's stories later," he said extending his hand again. "It's my distinct pleasure to meet you, Jimmie Rae Murphy."

Still perturbed, I feigned a pathetic handshake and wave as he pulled open the heavy oak door, leaving us alone with the green velvet 1930s Deco chair. Max and I watched as he strode out the door to help move a huge, ornate nineteenth-century German armoire.

"Max, we need to talk."

She replied with a low sexy whistle. “I know. Isn’t he the juiciest looking thing since the last year’s peach crop?” She grabbed my arm, “Tell me exactly what happened. Don’t skip any details. Just what were you two doing in a dark room in the middle of the afternoon? You sneaky little thing, you.”

“Max! Your hormones are in overdrive! It wasn’t like that at all. Look, not that it matters, but I accidentally kicked the brick from the door and then realized the door was locked. He was dragging that chair down the stairs, yelling for you. Next thing I knew he had me pinned against the wall.”

“Now, we’re getting somewhere,” Max said with renewed interest.

“Well, I pulled a move and managed to trip us both so he would let me go. Then I ended up sitting on his stomach,” I said unable to keep my eyes from rolling.

“No wonder he was laughing. You certainly know how to make a first impression,” she said.

“On whom?”

“Thomas.”

“Oh, yeah, I guess. Look, after the day I’ve had, the last thing I need is to be interested in some old guy.”

Max rolled her eyes. “Jimmie Rae, child, Thomas happens to be intelligent, charming, worldly, interesting, extremely handsome, and most importantly, single. Besides, he’s only forty-three which may I remind you, is only a few years older than us.”

“Six to be exact. He’s way too old to be single. There’s got to be some reason why and it can’t be anything good. Look, I really could care less, I need to talk to you,” I said.

“Let’s unload first, and then we’ll talk over cheeseburgers at the Lone Star.”

“Max, you’re a vegetarian.”

"Linda Jean now makes veggie burgers too. It's part of the customer service philosophy going on around here. If you build it they will come."

"Okay. Anyway, we're going to need our strength for our field trip tonight," I told Max.

"And just where might that be?"

"Back to Cowboy's Antiques and Gas Emporium."

Chapter Twelve

"Garage Sale, Saturday only, 7-noon, kids clothes, toys, bikes. Everything has to go! Will consider all offers."

About an hour and a half later, Max and I were sipping iced tea and finishing our chocolate pie at the Lone Star Café. Over lunch, we compared the accounts we had each given Billy Jack. She also recounted some of the conversation she, Star, Edna, and Evelyn Sue had last week as they finished their plans for the upcoming Homecoming Festival.

"Did you ever catch up with Stella Pierce?" I asked.

"No, but I saw your cousin, Jen, at the post office and she told me Stella had paid her a visit the day before yesterday threatening to shut down The Page Turner because Star has added those two black metal bistro tables and chairs to the entrance. She said it was a safety hazard and a violation of city code."

"Oh, really. She must have absolutely nothing else to do," I said. "Guess I should check in with Jen to see if she needs someone to run interference while Star's tied up with Edna. So did you actually catch up with Stella?"

"No, I tried calling her office and even went to her house, but she didn't answer at either location. She shouldn't be too hard to catch up with though. Just look for the shaking heads or really pissed-off people and chances are you'll be hot on her trail," Max said.

I laughed.

"Seriously, though I know she had Evelyn Sue's full attention. I heard Stella was threatening to take Evelyn Sue to court over that new fountain she kindly donated to the Niceton Public Library."

"Like she needed anything else to worry about," I said.

"What do you mean?"

"Oh, just that Evelyn Sue told me yesterday that she was afraid she might be losing her mind because so many of her family's heirlooms were missing from her house."

"Yeah, she told us that too," Max said. She took another sip of iced tea, "You don't suppose Maria could be doing more swiping than wiping."

"Well, that's highly unlikely. Maria has lived with Evelyn Sue for at least the past twenty years. They taught ESL classes together at the Niceton Public Library every Thursday evening. I just can't imagine she'd do anything against Evelyn Sue. They've always seemed to have a close friendship. Evelyn Sue even let Maria's kids and grandkids use her place for their family fiestas."

"True," Max agreed. "Still I told her to make a detailed list of the missing items. In fact, she gave me her list just yesterday morning at that café in Athens while we were waiting on you."

"Do you still have it?"

"Yes. Billy Jack made a copy this morning. I did a little checking after you stood me up for breakfast. I think I found a couple of the items on an on-line auction. Billy Jack said he would follow up and get back to me."

"That's why I want to go back to Cowboy's," I said. "I don't think Billy Jack will follow-up on this part of the trail. Besides, don't you want to get your car back?"

Max pushed her plate aside and wiped the condensation from her tea glass with her paper napkin. Her blue eyes told me she was torn.

"Max, I know you too well. What's up?" I said.

She tossed her long hair off her shoulders as she had habitually for many years— an indication she was uncomfortable.

"Well," she began. "I have a confession to make."

"Yes," I said, trying to encourage her to spit it out.

"I have a date, and didn't want to tell you since you're going through a divorce, and already had a rotten day seeing Joe and Birdy together. I realize you don't think men are such a good idea right now. I didn't want you to feel bad."

"Oh, Maxie, come on we've been best friends through worse than this. I'm okay. I'm working through my thing. It's just going to take some time. So, tell me about your new guy, Steve. I really can't believe you kept him from me."

"Well, he's just about as wonderful as they come. You know my whole family was beginning to believe I was destined to be an 'old maid,' but now even they're thinking differently. We laugh and talk for hours. I don't know—"

"Maxine, you're acting like a teenager! Big deal! You'd rather go on a date than snoop around a gas station looking for a pair of dead poets' love letters and your old pink Cadillac. I understand."

"I don't think you do," she said looking me in the eye.

"Maxine Bea Huntington, girl, you're in love, aren't you! How could you keep that from me! Tell me all about him." My final word was lost in the sound of a black and chrome Harley Davidson Fat Boy motorcycle pulling up in front of the Lone Star Café. The rider cut the engine and blew a kiss toward Maxie.

"A biker? You're infatuated with a biker? Your folks will never go for that."

"Jimmie, number one, I'm over thirty years old and number two; my folks are thrilled about Steve."

I looked out at the guy as he took off his helmet and black leather gloves. Max sure knew how to pick the most peculiar guys. Steve was built like a football linebacker. He was about six-feet-five-inches tall. He wasn't fat, but he wasn't slim either. He was muscular. His short, straight red hair was a little darker than Max's and slightly receding. He had light blue eyes and a red goatee. He wore heavy black motorcycle boots, black jeans, and a black short-sleeved shirt with a white-banded collar.

"What, is he for real? Is he dressed for Halloween? He looks like some biker priest," I whispered to her as he came in the door.

"Shhhh!" Max scolded as she waved to him.

He walked over to our table and bent down to kiss Max on the cheek. I hadn't seen her look at a guy like she looked at Steve since Ty Bennett when we were juniors in high school. Maxie was really in love and the biker minister appeared just as smitten.

"Steve Devine," he said holding out his mammoth hand. I noticed he wore two rings—one was a family crest, the other a simple silver cross design.

"You're kidding, right?"

"No, it's really my name," Reverend Devine said with a smile.

"Jimmie Rae," I said shaking his hand. He had a strong, but gentle grip.

"Maxie has told me so much about you, Jimmie. I'm so glad to finally meet you."

I smiled, looking over to my best friend who was literally glowing. "The pleasure is all mine, won't you join us?" I said.

Maxie looked at me. "Actually, Jimmie, I'm sorry, but we have to go over to the Red Cross. We're organizing donations this afternoon before we go over to Round Top for dinner."

"Could I have a rain check? I'd love to visit with you," Steve said. His voice was smooth and his tone comforting.

"I'd like that," I said.

Before she left with him like a giggling teenager on her first date, she warned me to hold off on going back to Cowboy's.

"Jimmie, for once be patient. You're not trained to investigate murders," she reminded me. "Trust the professionals, they'll figure it out. And oh yeah, before I forget, Mrs. Brown brought a yard sale flyer by the Living History office the other day," she said reaching in her shoulder bag for a neon green paper. "Maybe you could go by her place and find out what she told Edna. Who knows? Maybe you'll find some good junk while you're at it. Just promise me you'll leave the real investigating to the professionals, okay, Jimmie Rae?"

I watched her leave arm in arm with Reverend Devine, riding into the late spring afternoon full of sunshine, wildflowers, and love. A lot of help she was.

Chapter Thirteen

"Come hear some of the best bluegrass music in Niceton County! Every Friday & Saturday night down at Floyd's Filler-Up & Opry under the big ole' Texas sky. No cover before 8 p.m.–Five bucks after 8 p.m."

I folded the bright flyer, tucked it into my pocket and decided to check in on The Page Turner before I headed out to the yard sale. Despite the brilliant flowers spilling over in the Garden Club's containers at each of the corners surrounding the limestone courthouse, bleakness hung thick in the air on the usually bustling downtown square. As I approached Star's bookstore on the next block, the glumness was even thicker as darkened windows and closed doors greeted me. I stepped around the two small black metal bistro tables and chairs. Safety hazard, hardly-–more likely they invited to customers to soak up a good read and a few moments of Texas sunshine.

I pulled open the worn left-hand side screen door and found a slim yellow slip of paper taped to the one of the ancient oak double doors. I pulled it off. It was Stella's warning the bookstore was in violation of city code and would be penalized if the offensive metal tables and chairs weren't cleared immediately.

I pushed against the heavy right door expecting it to open and to see my favorite cousin, Jen, at the counter. To my surprise the doors were locked. I fished out my keys, unlocked the deadbolt, and pushed on the door again. Inside it was dark and there was no sign of Jen anywhere. I pushed it open further, revealing only the darkened version of the store where I'd grown up surrounded by books and Star's attention. All was not well. The realization caused a cold chill to chase a trickle of sweat down my spine.

It wasn't like Jen to close up shop in the middle of the day without a note, but perhaps she was at the hospital or running an errand. I dropped my bag on the front counter. From the available daylight I could see the east side interior, an exposed brick wall still proudly donning its original Coke Cola advertising from decades past. When Star began leasing the building more than thirty years ago, the plaster was coming off the brick. With the landlord's approval, she hired some guys from Bastrop to finish the job and paint the remaining plaster walls a warm terracotta. Since then years of extreme temperatures had taken their toll on the paint softening it to a hue more like butterscotch.

A worn 1920s hunter-green velvet sofa sat facing the double doors. Beside it stood a large round walnut table, its finish soft as marble. A silk burgundy, fringed shawl was casually draped across it beside the amber antique stained-glass dragonfly lamp Star always left on. I shook off the bad vibe and headed down the main aisle to the fuse box to switch on the overheads. Dark bookshelves salvaged from Niceton's old Carnegie library embraced the long room holding colorful book spines, each patiently waiting its turn to be discovered in a competitive world of high tech and instant gratification. As if greeting old friends, my fingers traced across the book spines on the fourth shelf as I walked toward the backroom. A noise near the back stopped my feet and shifted my brain into high gear. "Hello," I called out to the darkness.

A calico tabby jumped down from a shelf overhead. "Well, there you are Audrey. You scared me for a second. Where's Jen?"

"Mew," she replied, wrapping her tail around my ankles and waiting for a stroke. Suddenly, the old doors creaked and the screen answered with a quick slam.

"Nice to see someone finally opening the place up," said a voice from the front of the store. Like the unpleasant sound of teeth on metal, I knew that grating voice. I resisted my first reaction and let my maturity and good manners take control. "Mrs. Pierce, what a surprise. How are you?"

Stella Pierce was average height and slim. Her white hair pulled tightly into a bun at the back of her head announced her no nonsense sternness. The sound of her cat-eye shaped reading glasses jingled on a chain hitting the dull black broach at the neckline of her white long-sleeved shirt carefully tucked and belted into a black polyester skirt complete with pantyhose and black loafers. Only an ice queen could wear all that on a hot spring day in Texas. Annoyance and anger shone in her small, dark eyes and wrinkled, pointy nose as she approached.

"Not well, I'm afraid. It's very stressful when people like your grandmother don't adhere to rules or laws. It's very selfish on her part—poor judgment and despicable manners—not really the type of citizens, let alone, community leaders, we aspire to have in Niceton," she said thickening the air with her ego and snooty attitude.

"Look, Ms. Pierce, we both know thanks to Star, generations of Niceton children have learned to read and now know the importance of books. Indeed, we both know Star is the first to volunteer for any community need. She's a model citizen as you recall," I said pointing to Star's wall of fame behind the counter. Numerous framed certificates from the Chamber of Commerce to the Boys and Girls Club dominated the space acknowledging, congratulating, and honoring the incomparable Starlene Agnes Spell.

"However, sadly, my Aunt Edna was involved in a serious car accident night before last, and of course, Miss Evelyn Sue Dinsmore was found murdered yesterday at the First Monday Trade Days up in Canton. I'm sure given these tragic circumstances, you'll want to file this yellow slip in the proper round receptacle." I smiled and handed the yellow slip to her.

"Jimmie Rae Murphy, don't be coy with me." She pushed my hand away. "Your Aunt Edna is an alcoholic and had probably been drinking before her car accident. Furthermore, everyone knew Evelyn Sue Dinsmore was the biggest whore in town and deserved a worse death than she got."

Rage coursed through my body. I fidgeted with the yellow slip and finally tucked it into my pocket. With my hands now free, I wanted to slap her or worse, but restrained myself. Instead, I took her arm and moved her physically toward the door. "I guess you would know all about Edna's alcoholism since you met each other at an AA meeting five years ago. Edna has continued her sobriety, which unfortunately, isn't what I've heard about you, Mrs. Pierce."

Stella stopped in her tracks her mouth hanging open with spittle gathering on the left side. Standing firmly, I looked her in the eyes and continued. "As far as Eveyln Sue goes, the dear woman, who I may remind you, was the pinnacle of commitment and devotion to this community was murdered in broad daylight. Your slander against her only shows your own ineptness and hatred." I shook my finger in her face. "You're her only known enemy." I reminded her as I moved toward the doors again. She stood as if her feet were suddenly glued to the worn oak floor. I put my hands on my hips. "Just where were you yesterday afternoon between three and four-thirty? Huh?

How would you know anything about Miss Evelyn Sue's death unless you had something to do with her murder? What about it, Mrs. Pierce?" I moved toward the screen door and held it open. "Don't let the door hit you in the butt on your way out, and by the way, take my advice, don't be thinking about taking any trips out of town over the next few days. I've got a feeling Detective Mitchell will be meeting with you."

Stella stomped toward the screen door pushing my hand away and holding it herself. "Don't be so sure, Jimmie Rae, I heard you murdered Evelyn Sue with a gun you purchased at the flea market." The wicked grin on her face made the Witch of the North look like a prom queen. She shook her head and looked down her nose at me. "None of your family was ever worth pissing on anyway. Why your grandfather, John Spell, was nothing but a gambler--and did Star ever mention all his catting around? I'll bet you've got kinfolk all over the county--perhaps all over the state. You just tell Starlene her little bookstore business is dead and if you're not careful you'll all join that slut, Evelyn Sue, up in Niceton Memorial Cemetery!"

I'd had all I was going to listen to and suddenly didn't really care if I ended up in the slammer. I pushed Stella Pierce out the screen door toward the hot pavement and slammed the wooden door before the screen door had snapped shut. My hands trembled as I punched 'one' on my phone. Star's voice mail answered. I ended the call not wanting or even knowing how I could leave a message after the exchange with Stella Pierce. I had been determined not to let her get to me, only to fall prey to her vicious words. I had to remember she was a conniving old bitty whose lies flowed as freely as the Brazos River after a heavy rain. Trying to calm myself, I sat down on the old sofa in the darkened bookstore and petted Audrey who purred contentedly unaffected by the toxic verbal exchange. The past day had been so emotional I gave into the sumptuousness of the feather cushions and the air-conditioned darkness and slipped into sleep.

My screaming cell phone awakened me. I sat up trying to remember why I was sleeping at The Page Turner. My dreams had been so vivid. Gaining fragile consciousness I realized most of my dreams were merely memories of the events of today and yesterday. I answered.

"Hey, Star."

"Well, it's about time you answered. Do you need to turn up the volume on your phone?" Star asked.

"No. Believe me; it's annoying enough to get my attention. What's up?"

"I'm just checking in. I saw you had called. I've been in with Edna, but Jen came by while ago upset by something Stella Pierce had done. Where are you?"

"I'm actually at The Page Turner. I fell asleep on the sofa."

"You're probably exhausted."

"Yeah, well no more than you. How's Edna doing?"

"She's out of recovery and doing okay. The surgeon was pleased with the way the surgery went. Did you get a chance to do that favor yet?"

"Oh crap! No! I'm sorry, Star. I'm on my way right now."

"That's why I'm calling. I just saw a weather bulletin, we're in a Tornado Watch and there's a line of severe thunderstorms headed your way. The old radio can wait. Just go on to my house and get some rest."

"Oh, Star, big deal! A Tornado Watch is nothing. I'll go and be back before the rain even gets here. By the way, Stella Pierce paid another visit here this afternoon. Suffice it to say, she was as foul as ever and threatening to shut you down."

"Phish-posh! She's been trying to do that for years. You don't worry yourself about it. I'll deal with her. She's such a pathetic, sad creature. Now, listen, go on to the house, okay? I'm staying up here again tonight."

"Are you sure, Star? I mean I'm happy to come up and let you have a break."

"That's sweet, Jimmie, but I'm not leaving here tonight. Maybe tomorrow you can come up here while I run to the house and freshen up."

"Sure, Star. Whatever you want."

"Love you, girl!"

"Love you too, Star. Bye."

"Bye-bye, hon."

I checked on Audrey who was still sleeping soundly on the other end of the sofa. Walking to the back room, I grabbed a cold water bottle from the avocado refrigerator, poured Audrey more dry food, grabbed my leather bag, and locked up. At the sight of the first trashcan I threw away the slip of yellow citation paper, and continued toward Old Blue.

Chapter Fourteen

"Yard Sale: FM 141 RRBox 306, first house past old cemetery. Friday & Saturday. Lots of old dishes, quilts, light fixtures, porch furniture, chairs, tables, too much to list."

As I drove through my Mayberry-like hometown, I saw it from the outside looking in. Years of living away and perhaps a bit of maturity gave me objectivity to see things I hadn't noticed while I was busy growing up here.

Driving through Niceton brought back a cozy blanket of memories. I passed by my former schools from elementary to high school, each quiet in their late spring reverie. People lived simply here. I passed a couple of women rocking on the front porch snapping beans for supper and, no doubt, trading the latest gossip. There were a couple of teenage boys cleaning up T.J. Collin's yard at Third Street, and even a coed sandlot baseball game at the empty field on Fifth and Independence. Exotic Oleander bushes stood tall next to tenacious antique roses and stubborn succulents in gardens throughout town. Flowers of every variety filled old tires, commodes, and old black metal kettles. Niceton had always been the kind of place where folks watched out for each other, yards were kept neat, and patriotic pride was demonstrated year round as American flags waved from most every house. In many ways my hometown was frozen in time, unwilling to let go of its "Leave It To Beaver" mentality.

Yesterday's murder of its matriarch would change that. With the benefit of age and objectivity I feared beneath the Mayberry image hid a lot of wicked deeds both past and present. It was something I didn't really want to seriously consider.

I knew it could be dangerous, but my curiosity had me cornered. I had to find out who really killed Evelyn Sue and what was going on out at Cowboy's Antiques and Gas Emporium. It didn't seem as if the police or anyone else was too interested in the fact there were priceless love letters in a ladies room off a lonely central Texas highway or that a beloved woman was murdered in broad daylight just outside of one of the nation's largest monthly flea markets.

As I steered Old Blue out of town, the sun shone brightly never hinting at the violent thunderstorms expected later. The lack of clouds clenched my decision to head out to Mrs. Brown's house and then over to the Flying W Ranch to retrieve the old radio Star was having repaired for Uncle Keith's birthday.

As I headed south out of town, I checked the flyer Max gave me and took the first left off of Main toward Mary Jayne's place out in the country. It was just after 4 p.m. However, since it was Friday and this sale was about a mile or so out of town, it might still be rather interesting and not totally picked over yet. Besides, I intended to ask Mary Jayne what she had told Edna that night before her car accident. I turned Old Blue and pushed her gas pedal directing us toward Farm to Market Road 141.

Mary Jayne Brown lived in the same two-story house where she and her husband had raised their four children who were now grown with grandchildren of their own. Her white framed farmhouse with its patinaed metal roof and wide wrap-around porch welcomed me as I crested the hill. Like a proud fortress, it stood as it had for more than 120 years with simple, practical Texas prairie architecture. An infusion of pink and red antique roses tangled along the white picket fence and over the old wooden arch way leading to the kitchen garden, already lush with Early Girl tomato vines, baby lettuces, and lush herbs.

Mrs. Brown sat in a worn wicker rocker drinking a glass of iced tea on the long covered front porch. She waved as I parked in her graveled driveway. I noticed the careful organization of items for sale didn't yet have the "pawed through" look they would tomorrow morning.

"Jimmie Rae Murphy!" she said as she sat her glass down and came down the wooden porch steps to greet me, hugging me warmly. "What in tarnation are you doing out here, girl?"

Mrs. Brown's smile and rosy cheeks rivaled her flower garden in cheerfulness. She was petite and had a slight hunch to her back. Unlike most of her peers, Mary Jayne Brown had a youthful bounce to her step and was still able to keep up with her small farm, great-great grandbabies, and still go Saturday night two-stepping with her husband of sixty years. She wore a pair of white jeans rolled up at the cuffs with a pair of worn red Keds and a navy polka dotted cotton blouse. Her short, wavy white hair was hidden under her baseball cap that read, "*Life is Good.*" She was the type of person who just gushed with positive energy and her lemon chiffon cake was legendary in Lee County, Texas.

I returned her firm hug and smiled. "Coming to your yard sale."

"Well, girl, if you can find anything out here, I'll be surprised. The weather fellows are saying storms are headed this way, so I was just going to start getting all this stuff put up, but you just go for it. I haven't had too much traffic yet. Are my signs still up?"

"Yes. You have great signage. I'm sure more folks will make their way out tomorrow. Fridays can be a little slow, I guess," I said as I made my way to a pile of old hooked rugs she had priced at five dollars each.

"Miss Mary Jayne, may I make a stack over here?" I said pointing to a spot on the ground beside her rocker.

"Sure, honey. That'll work. You shop. I'm going inside to get another glass of iced tea. Do you care for any?"

"Sure, that sounds great. Thanks!"

When she came back a few minutes later, next to the stack of hooked rugs, I had placed a small white primitive table priced at fifteen dollars, a stack of Homer Laughlin Apple Blossom dishes marked ten dollars, a wonderful seventy-five dollar pastel wedding ring quilt, and a pair of metal and crystal sconces for ten bucks.

"Good Lord, girl! Are you sure about all this junk?" She asked as she handed me a glass of tea and settled back into her rocker. "Say, didn't Star mention you and Maxine have a booth at that antique mall in the old First Baptist Church? Now, what's it called?"

"Blessings From the Past," I answered, slightly worried it might have an impact on what she wanted to be paid. I took a sip of tea and settled into the wicker chair next to hers.

"Well, if you're buying all this junk for your booth then, you go, girl! By the way, how's Edna? I couldn't believe it when Star called to say she'd been in a terrible car accident and was going to have surgery. Edna and I had just had lunch on Wednesday for Pete's sake."

The opening couldn't have been better timed. I set my tea glass down, leaning toward her slightly. "Yes, Mrs. Brown, as a matter of fact, I'm hoping you could help me out there. Edna was trying to tell Maxine and me something you told her when she fell fast asleep at the hospital last night. She seemed upset about something besides her injuries. Do you have any idea what it may have been about?"

"Dear, do call me Mary Jayne—Mrs. Brown sounds so old. Now, let me think." Mary Jayne said looking at me and shrugging her shoulders. "I probably shouldn't have said anything at all to Edna. It's just that it stuck me as so odd that some strange, new girl would just so happen to be around when Evelyn Sue fell and fractured her hip a few months ago. When I asked her how it happened, she looked frightened and changed the subject. I had the feeling someone made her fall and she was covering for them. Then when I heard you found her murdered yesterday I felt so guilty." Mary Jayne's teary eyes looked into mine, causing mine to water up too.

"Why on earth would *you* feel guilty?"

"I thought something like this might happen. I've been afraid for her ever since she told me she thought the new girl working for her might be her granddaughter," she said.

I was caught off-guard by this tidbit. "What do you mean, 'granddaughter'? I didn't think Evelyn Sue had any children— let alone grandchildren."

"Well, now that she's gone I don't imagine there's any harm in my telling," Mary Jayne said. She took a sip of her iced tea, sat it back down on the metal side table, and settled back in her rocking chair.

"Back after the second world war Evelyn Sue and I were just young women. The boys were back home after the awful battles they'd been in over in Europe and the Pacific Rim and everyone was ready to have fun. Evelyn Sue and I would sneak out after the kerosene lamps were turned down and we'd head over to Cooter Smith's Honky-Tonk. Well, we didn't drink, but we loved to jitterbug and dance with the young men.

"One Saturday night, we got there kind of late on account of my baby brother, Ricky, got sick and Momma was up with him. Anyway, a new band was playing down at Cooter Smith's. They called themselves, the Texas Prairie Boys. They were from San Antonio. Well, don't you know we'd fall for the two brothers playing the fiddles, Jerry and Jimmy," she said rocking gently, lost in another time and place.

"It turned out everyone loved their music and Cooter Smith gave them a year-long contract. Well, we were really in love with those boys. I'd cover for Evelyn Sue and she'd cover for me. Sometime about four months later, Evelyn Sue began to get sick every morning. We thought maybe she had some terrible disease until my older, married sister, Bess, told us she was probably pregnant. Bess knew a thing or two about having babies since she had two already and had just found out number three was on the way.

"We were horrified at the thought of Evelyn Sue being an unwed mother. Evelyn Sue was especially devastated since she had planned to begin classes at the University of Texas in the fall. There was also the dilemma of her daddy who was very strict with her. As mayor of Niceton, bank president, and head deacon down at the First Baptist, we knew he'd be furious if he found out."

"What about her momma?" I said. "Surely she would understand and help her."

"Well, if she'd been alive I'm sure she would have. She passed before Evelyn Sue began grade school," Mary Jayne said softly.

"So, what happened?" I said picking my glass up for another sip.

"So, she and I packed our bags and went to Houston to look for jobs. We worked at the Fluffy Biscuit Diner with a nice lady named Flo. That is until Evelyn Sue was six months along and was just starting to show. Flo's sister, Ethel, ran a coffee shop down in Galveston. She offered us room and board if I'd waitress for her and Evelyn Sue would keep her books. Evelyn Sue was always so good with numbers."

Mary Jayne took another slow sip of iced tea; she stared ahead lost in 1948 Galveston, Texas.

"Miss Mary Jayne?" I urged. "That can't be the end of the story. What happened?"

She looked at me as if contemplating what to say next. Realizing she had said too much already. "Oh, fiddle! It's a good and bad ending. Bess knew where we were and came to see us late in February. She was very upset because she had lost her baby. Then it occurred to us what had to happen.

"Evelyn Sue would have her baby and Bess would take it as her own. Bess had brought her other two children and she called her husband, Clyde, and told him she was going to visit our cousin, Ruthie, in Rockport since there was a bad flu going around back home. Clyde was working long shifts at the steel plant and as long as his momma cooked for him he was happy to have some peace and quiet when he got home at night.

"So, a month later, Evelyn Sue had a baby girl. We all agreed to name her Patricia Sue. She went home with Bess and Clyde never knew the difference. Why, out at the cemetery Baby Thurston's grave sits in a quiet corner near a huge white blooming rose bush Bess and I planted there so we'd never forget. She went on to have five more healthy young'uns."

"Wow," I said quietly.

Mary Jayne smiled and set her tea glass back down on the metal table. So, what all you buying today?"

Obviously, she was finished with her story. Yet, questions jumped into my mind like kernels in one of those giant, whirling theatre popcorn machines. "All this stuff," I said pointing to the stack. "I think I owe you about one hundred twenty-five dollars, but you check me."

She stood up and moved each item I had in my pile over to another pile. "Sounds good to me. You could actually make it an even hundred."

"Sorry. No can do, Mary Jayne."

"Why in tarnation not?" She said tipping her ball cap back, adjusting her wire-framed glasses, and putting her hands on her hips.

"Let's just say it's a karma thing – your prices are more than fair." I handed her exact cash.

"Well, okay, darlin' if you say so." She grabbed a cardboard box and some packing paper from a wrought iron shelf near her porch swing. "I can hunt you up some more boxes if you need them," she said, her green eyes still glistening with unshed tears.

I dropped the packing paper and stood up to give her a hug. "Oh, Miss Mary Jayne, I'm so sorry if I caused you bad memories. Are you going to be okay?"

"Of course, honey," she said returning the hug. She straightened her blouse and took a daisy-patterned hankie from her pocket to wipe her eyes. "Here, I'll help you pack," she said sitting down on the porch steps next to the box, wrapping one of the sconces. I sat next to her and began wrapping the items I had just purchased in the paper while she spoke.

"Those days are older than this most of this stuff. It was actually kind of nice to tell someone what really happened."

"What happened to Evelyn Sue after all that?"

"Oh, well, Evelyn Sue went off to UT and became a teacher. I think she fell for a fella there, but she declined his offer to marry her. Instead, she decided to devote herself to teaching children instead of raising them. I don't think she ever really got over the guilt she felt in giving away little Patricia Sue even though she saw her often at Bess and Clyde's and watched her grow up."

"What happened to Patricia Sue?" I asked leaning over to grab another stack of packing paper for the delicate floral dishes stacked up beneath the metal table.

"Oh, she was a hellion, that child was! She gave Bess and Clyde such difficult times as a teenager. She ran off to California before she finished high school and became one of those 'hippies.' Bess didn't hear from her until she got a Christmas card from her in 1976. There was a picture of her but no letter. She got one other short letter and a picture of a baby in 1985. She had married some guy and they had a baby. We got news Patricia Sue died about fifteen years from the last time we'd heard from her."

"What happened to her baby?"

"I don't rightly know. We never even learned her name. I guess she went to live with a friend of Patricia Sue's.

"The funny thing is, this young woman dropped by on Evelyn Sue about three months ago just before she fractured her hip. The woman was all friendly and said she'd been working on genealogy and discovered she and Miss Dinsmore were distantly related. When Evelyn Sue asked her how, she was vague. Shortly after that, Evelyn Sue, who dances nearly every Saturday night down at Floyd's, supposedly tripped on her own two feet, fell, and lo and behold, fractured her hip. It still doesn't make any sense to me." She lowered her voice. "Personally, I think that young woman may have caused Evelyn Sue's fall, but I've no proof."

Mary Jayne picked up a piece of crumpled packing paper and smoothed it on her lap. "That's when I began to have a bad feeling Evelyn Sue was in danger. I just couldn't put my finger on it. Anyway, Evelyn Sue told me this young woman offered to help her out around the big old Dinsmore place up on Yellow Rose Hill. Evelyn Sue agreed to let her clean and help out and was paying her. Then, last week she told me she thought she was losing her mind because some of her family heirlooms were missing. I told her to tell that girl to get lost and suggested she call the police and report the missing items."

"Oh really," I said. "She told us the same thing about the missing items yesterday morning before...well, before I found her. Did you happen to catch the name of this young woman?" I asked.

"Kaye Watson. I met her over at Evelyn Sue's a couple of times. She'd just bat her baby blues and Evelyn Sue would give her an extra twenty dollars. But it never worked on me and I warned Evelyn Sue to be wary when that girl was around. I got to where I would show up when she was there, just in case," she said lifting her eyebrows.

Mary Jayne looked out across the fields and took another sip of tea. As if she suddenly remembered something else, she looked back at me. "Evelyn Sue told me she thought there was something familiar about Kaye—like she had taught her in school or seen her around town before. She was always so good with faces—I guess from spending so many years in the classroom."

"Kaye has blue eyes? Is there anything else you can tell me about her appearance? I'd like to talk to her."

"She's a little thing. You'd think with Maria's great cooking no one could stay so slim, let along down right skinny around Yellow Rose Hill. But this girl is really thin and I'd guess in her mid-twenties. I guess it must be her smoking habit that keeps her so thin."

"Hmm, that's weird. I work with a woman at the Armstrong Browning Library who sounds just like the one you described only her name is Kate Wilson. Let me do some checking around and I'll let you know what I find out."

"Okay, darlin', but you be careful. There's something odd and even haunting about that Kaye Watson," she said with a frightened look in her clear green eyes.

I hugged Mary Jayne Brown, assuring her I'd be careful and loaded the stuff I'd just bought from her into Old Blue's cab. My head was swimming with this new information as I loaded my new purchases, waved good-bye to Mary Jayne, and started out once again to fulfill Star's request to pick-up the old radio at the Flying W Ranch. Despite her insistence I wait until tomorrow, I wanted to get it done while I was thinking of it. With all that was going on, there was no telling what tomorrow would bring. My plan to pick-up the radio was too late though – there was already a hitch in my plan.

As I glanced into the rear-view mirror another concern took precedence. It was a black four-by-four super-cab pickup with a heavy metal grate like giant, sharp teeth across its hood headed straight for my tailgate. Unfortunately, I recognized it. I'd seen that truck before. It was the boys from Cowboy's and it didn't look like they wanted to talk about my purchases from Mary Jayne Brown's yard sale.

Chances were these boys wanted to discuss the letters I had carefully replaced in the archives of the Armstrong Browning Library.

Chapter Fifteen

"Estate Sale: Flying W Ranch, 1001 FM 619, Saturday & Sunday. Household items, tack, saddles, 1973 Chevy Farm Truck, and more."

I reached for my cell phone while trying to keep Old Blue on the road. I opened it and looked down. Naturally, it indicated, "NO SIGNAL." I slapped it shut, and pushed Old Blue's gas pedal to the floor. The black truck only continued to gain on me as we wound through a smooth black ribbon of road alongside farms, ranches, and open fields.

I had to be a couple of miles from Floyd's Filler-Up or any kind of help. By the looks of it, they were quite intent on catching up with Old Blue. Although she was a show-stopping classic old Ford, she didn't have the horsepower of modern pick-up trucks and escape from the black truck closing in behind me seemed hopeless.

I came up to a stop sign and saw two cars approaching from opposite directions. There was no way Old Blue could beat them across unscathed. I stopped, locked my doors, leaving the driver's side window cracked open at the top for some air. The black Dodge Ram dually pulled up behind me. Cowboy stepped out as the opposing cars came closer to the intersection.

He lit a cigarette as he approached the driver's side of Old Blue. He inhaled deeply releasing a lungful of smoke as he spoke to my driver's side window. "I was beginning to think you and this old piece of junk you drive were going to have to take a tumble down that ravine back there. But, that would be a shame. Bet no one knows where you are. Maybe no one even cares. All I want are the documents you lifted at our place of business yesterday."

"I have no idea what you're talking about."

"Oh, I think you do. You're smart and you'd better figure it out fast or your granny will be joining the others."

The two cars passed in front of me. Seizing the moment, I threw the shifter into second and gunned the engine. I felt a soft bump as Old Blue lurched forward.

Next thing I knew, Cowboy was holding his left foot, cursing loudly. Glances at the side mirrors showed him hopping around on one boot looking like he was doing some type of Cowboy yoga. I took the opportunity and shot across the road. *That'll teach you to threaten my grandma, buddy*! From the small rearview I could see Lonnie trying to help him. I patted Old Blue's dash gently. "Good girl," I cooed.

As my normal heartbeat returned and I thought I'd lost the bubba brothers once and for all, my rearview indicated a different story. The black truck was moving up fast behind me despite it being an uneven, freshly graveled road.

I needed no more incentive. I shut off the air-conditioner, pushed Old Blue's accelerator to the floor, and turned at every opportunity, twisting and winding as fast as Old Blue could move on the dirt and limestone graveled roads.

While there was some amount of satisfaction I'd been right about the Browning letters and other items, it was overshadowed by a growing sense of deep fear in my gut--uneasiness unlike any other I'd ever felt. For now Cowboy and Lonnie had every reason to pick me off like a duck at a midway shooting gallery. As far as I knew, I was the only one to suspect they had some type of black market ring going on out of Cowboy's Antiques and Gas Emporium.

My feet were dancing on the pedals: pushing, clutching, and braking around the bends, over bridges, past houses, and pastures dotted with cattle. My arms were getting a workout too. With no power steering, I had to turn hand-over-hand to steer the old girl around each bend hoping the next would be familiar territory or better yet, Floyd's Filler-Up. It seemed I had lost them, but I was moving so fast I didn't see the debris in the road. Old Blue's tires sent the grayed boards crackling like a roaring bonfire. I patted her dashboard.

"Sorry old girl— just get us to Floyd's or to help as quick as possible."

I was perspiring as if I were the one running through the woods and up the hills of the wide, open prairies instead of my truck. The fuel dial was stretching closer toward the "E", but fear of what the bubbas might do if they found me kept my lead foot heavy on the gas pedal. I switched directions so many times I might as well be blindfolded and spun in circles. I was undeniably lost. A new sound took precedence over knowing where I was. Old Blue was crippled. Something must have pierced through at least one tire.

The good news— I was alone on the back roads somewhere between Austin and Houston. The bad, I was alone on the back roads somewhere between Austin and Houston— and running out of options fast. Now, as I looked around at the cattle dotting the pasture, I realized a new threat in the blackening skies. Dark clouds like the icing on one of Star's chocolate cupcakes swirled, piling higher and higher. Old Blue veered wildly as I tried my cell phone again. Still "NO SIGNAL" was its answer. I slapped it shut in disgust. There were no metal cellular towers visible across the sprawling Texas terrain. Instead, gentle hills full of grazing longhorn cattle and the occasional grove of ancient live oaks filled the broad horizon. I checked my cell phone for the time (at least it was good for something). It was 4:33.

As interesting as my visit with Mary Jayne Brown had been, I was regretting my impulsive decision to follow her signs instead of heading directly out to the Flying W Ranch to pick up the radio.

Steering Old Blue was proving to be next to impossible. I'd never get anywhere at this rate. Determined to move on down the road before the bubba brothers found me, I got out of Old Blue, lowered the tailgate, and jumped up into the bed to unscrew the spare tire. As the sky grew darker, my hands worked fast, releasing the tire from the metal bracket. Freed from its spot at the head of the truck bed, I pushed on it only to realize it was flat too. This was definitely turning out to be a day I should have stayed in bed with the covers pulled over my head. Between the lack of sleep the night before and all the hub-bub today, I was worn out and frustrated. And now it seemed my only option was to get help or at the very least find shelter as the now threatening clouds began to drift my direction. There had to be a house or something nearby. There had to be an end to this whole thing.

Leaving the spare in the bed of the truck, I grabbed my leather messenger bag off the floorboard. After locking the truck doors, I began to move quickly down the dirt road. The deep drumming of thunder punctuated by a couple of dancing bolts of lightening to the north quickened my step. While the thunder and lightening might mean an inevitable storm everywhere else, I'd learned that it wasn't always a given in Texas. The sun continued searing down, fueling the clouds with even more electric potency.

I picked up the pace nearly jogging down the road rushing toward nothing and everything when out of the corner of my eye I noticed the metal fence beside me. There was a double wide opening crossed with a black metal gate topped with a "W" with wings wielded on—the Flying W Ranch. I knew it didn't necessarily mean the main house was close since the ranch took in over five hundred acres, but it was better than nothing. I jumped the fence willing to take the risk. A zigzag of bright light divided the sky overhead. Finding shelter would be my next priority.

I stopped to readjust my leather bag so I could move better. My brain sifted through the information shards I'd collected in the past twenty-four hours. I kept trying to put the mental vase back together, but each time vital missing pieces left me only more puzzled. I remembered Cowboy shouting into the cell phone yesterday—something about screwing up the plan. What plan? It seemed those two were a couple of enchiladas short of combo platters. I didn't believe either of them were mentally capable of an intricate plan to steal the Browning items and get rid of them on the black market. No, that was way over their brain capacities. So then, to *whom* was Cowboy screaming at on the phone yesterday morning? Obviously, the person working with them—someone with more brains than brawn, but who could it be?

It had to be someone who could both mastermind a black market ring and shoot someone in public in broad daylight—someone so evil, so sinister with no regard for anybody or anything. A truly scary person was at the root of this. The only evil person I could think of as was two-timing Joe, but his evil ways had more to do with his overactive libido and lack of morals than a killer instinct.

Regardless, these boys were just plain up to no good and since I was now their new target, I wondered if they had anything to do with all the other freaky things going on like Edna's near fatal car accident. I also wondered where Daryl Ann fit into it all. Where she was anyway?

And what about Stella Pierce? Could she be involved with the likes of Cowboy and Lonnie? She had publicly threatened Evelyn Sue on numerous occasions throughout the years and all but threatened Star's life only a few hours ago. Then, there was Mary Jayne's revelation about Evelyn Sue's love child and Kaye Watson, the strange young woman who had mysteriously appeared at Yellow Rose Hill and offered to help Evelyn Sue. Did she fit into all this? Did any of this fit together?

Back down on the road I heard gravel sputter as a diesel truck engine reverberated through the intense pre-storm silence of the countryside. Looking through the leaves and developing fruit of a stand of wild plums, I saw Cowboy's truck pull up beside Old Blue. Hidden by the brush, I watched as Cowboy and Lonnie walked around my truck. Their voices lost in the increasing north wind. Seeing the flat tire, I hoped they would figure someone picked me up. Before returning to their truck, Cowboy spit on Old Blue and ran his key down the length of her glistening blue metallic side much like I had on Joe's truck just this morning. Insistent lightening kept him from doing more damage to Old Blue.

"Bastard!" I screamed into the wind.

Incensed fear and anger got my feet moving and kept me sprinting through the field, not caring about what other dangers lurked on the prairie. I just didn't want those two thugs to catch up with me. I didn't want to know what would happen if they found me. The increasing wind seemed to be racing me across the prairie. Through the wind and booming thunder the storm built higher and higher like giant wands of gray cotton candy on the northern horizon. The super-cell thunderstorm brewing would certainly catch the attention of every high-tech radar and weather guru from Austin to Norman, OK.

Over the wind and thunder, I never heard the hooves as a large quarter horse came up beside me. A man in scuffed cowboy boots, torn Levis, a worn sleeveless western shirt, and tattered straw cowboy hat held the reins.

"Back for more, huh?" Thomas yelled through the wind.

It was another of those out of context moments for me. My first sense was relief, then I remembered the mixed emotions I felt earlier this afternoon: distrust laced liberally with intrigue. "Hurry, grab my hand and swing up here before you end up getting us both zapped by lightening!" he said over the wind. Small pellets of ice began to shoot down from overhead. I looked up at the sky and back at him. "Get up here, now," he demanded. I put my foot in the stirrup, grabbed his hand, and pulled myself up behind him. I was intimately squished up next to the same man I'd been sitting on a few hours before.

"Put me down. I'll just walk," I said feeling distinctly uncomfortable with being so close to Thomas.

"I don't think so," he answered. "You'd best hang on tight. Jack Daniels isn't the most reliable when it's storming." I did as he instructed, letting go only to adjust my leather bag across my shoulders. I wrapped my arms around his waist and took in a deep breath. The raw smell of rain, grass, leather, horse, and man were oddly reassuring.

He kicked and we were speeding off across the pasture. Against the wind, rain, and occasional small pellets of hail. I closed my eyes and clung tight. About fifteen minutes later we were dripping wet in a huge red metal barn. "Whoa," he said to Jack Daniels. The dark horse obeyed, shaking its mane. "Thanks a lot, Jack," Thomas said. "You can let loose now, unless you'd just like to sit on top of Jack Daniels for a while."

"Oh, sorry," I said.

"You first," he said offering me his left hand. "Can you swing down?"

"Of course I can, it's been a while, but it's like riding a bike," I said as I turned and pulled my leg over the horse and down to the straw strewn concrete floor. Thunder and wind roared beyond the barn porch sending bits of hay swirling in circles. "See."

"Good job. Now, let me get down, and I'll find us some towels and maybe water or a beer if you'd prefer one. What in the world are you doing running around a field during a storm?"

"I ran into some trouble. Maybe I could use your phone?"

"Ahh, well that is a problem. I've left my cell phone at the house on the charger and we never had phone service down here. We used to use the walkie talkies, but those are in a closet somewhere. Why don't you just relax and I'll get you a towel."

I stood looking around the barn and stroking Jack Daniel's mane while I waited. After being chased by those thugs I found the barn to be warm and comforting. Okay, I'll admit it. I found Thomas Williams to be warm and comforting too. Minutes later I had a giant blue and pink beach towel wrapped around my shoulders.

"There's a bathroom down that way to the right. Just be warned it's rather primitive," he said while wiping Jack Daniels down. "You do whatever you need to. I'll get Jack Daniels more comfortable," he said pulling the straps of the intricately tooled leather saddle free from the horse's back. He placed the wet saddle on a wooden frame and led his horse toward a stall full of fresh hay. I took the opportunity to freshen up.

I walked down a long hallway separated from the stalls and main barn area, passing a bedroom with a four-poster bed and white matelasse bed coverlet. I stopped to peek in. In the defused sunlight, I could see an old oil lamp wired for electricity sitting atop a mission style dresser beside the bed. Near the old lamp, other items were grouped including a stack of books, a small cobalt blue vase of hot pink zinnias, and assorted black and white pictures. Like a page from a country-decorating magazine, the entire room was too feminine to belong to a man or a barn. Perhaps Thomas had a significant other?

I continued down the hallway stopping again outside a darkened room. My hand fumbled along the wall for a light switch. Frazzled curls and my damp face stared back in the mirror over the sink as the florescent flickered on. I took a comb out of my bag and did the best I could without my defrizzing hair product. I found a towel in a small red cupboard next to the sink. I noticed the bathroom was rather nice for being "primitive" and in a barn. There was also a commode and stone tiled shower.

Back in the stall area Thomas brushed Jack Daniels pulling the coarse brush expertly over the large animal as he fed on the pale yellow straw in his trough. Lightening flashed beyond the open barn door, resulting in a loud crackle and instant darkness.

A sound of surprise escaped my lips as I involuntarily jumped at the sudden sound and darkness.

"No worries," Thomas said. Muted grayness shone through the open barn doors. "Jimmie, I can assure you this barn has stood longer without modern conveniences than with them. My great-great-granddaddy established the Flying W back more than a hundred thirty years ago." He lay the brush down and walked over to a wooden bench lined with old lanterns. He took a lighter from a nearby shelf and seconds later warm light glowed.

"Here you may need this," I said handing him a folded white towel. In the lantern's light, his dimples shone along with his large dark eyes. His hair dripped around his neck as his wet western shirt clung to his upper body. The sleeves appeared to have been cut out ages ago.

"Gee, thanks." He paused and took a long look into my eyes. "This is quite a change from our introduction this morning." In a smooth motion he unsnapped his wet shirt, took it off, and hung it on a hook next to the stall where Jack Daniels was eating oblivious to the humans. Without hesitation he dried off his chest and arms. He was lean with only the slightest of love handles developing. The deep "Z" scar from his stomach to below the top of his Levis drew my attention. I quickly looked away.

Content with being somewhat drier, he tossed the towel on the second hook below his shirt. He caught my eyes and leaned down toward me continuing to watch me. I smiled and grabbed the towel back off the hook. Intoxicated by the moment, I rose to my toes, removed his hat, and dried his damp hair and wet face. Then I touched the deep scar on his cheek tracing a streak of water to his lips where my lips met his in a gentle kiss. He folded me closer into his body, his arms wrapped tight around me, drawn to his strong torso. I tossed the towel and his cowboy hat to the barn floor and drew him sharply against my body. His naked chest and arms felt warm as my body flowed with lost desire. Devoid of intimacy for longer than I cared to remember, the clean sensual smell of this man awoke my sleeping senses. They tempted me to linger as my increasing sexual appetite longed for a more passionate kiss—a more intimate moment.

My tongue teased his and he answered taking my mouth fully with his and kissing me with a force equal to the storm raging outside the weathered barn doors. His hands searched for skin beneath my wet blouse. An intense thunderous boom snapped us back to the moment. I stepped back. We looked at each other awkwardly and smiled. He reached out to a wooden table and pulled a Texas A&M T-shirt over his head covering the places I was just getting to know. I realized my heart was racing as fast as it had earlier when I'd been running across the field. This time I didn't mind though. This man opened a place in me I didn't know I had. I wanted more; yet practical sense took control of my libido.

"You're never going to think I'm a gentleman now," he said with an easy grin. "Sorry, Jimmie, you just look so incredible. I lost it for a minute. I usually know at least something about the women I kiss before I let loose like that."

I touched his lips with my finger. "Shhh. Don't spoil it. I usually know more about the men I let kiss me—but I have to confess that was the most incredible thing to happen in a long time."

"Yes, I'd have to agree. Still, maybe we should know a little bit about each other before we get to know each other if that makes any sense."

"Oh, if you insist, but I can tell this won't ever work out," I said returning the grin.

"And just why the hell not?"

"Well, for starters you're an A&M man and I'm a UT woman."

His grin invited banter. "As long as it's in the same state, who cares? You'll have to come up with something better than that Miss Jimmie."

"Okay. So, Thomas, what brings you to these parts?" I couldn't resist adding, "Or do you just wait for damsels in distress, sweeping women up in a moments of passion during summer storms all the time?"

"Hey, I'm wondering the same thing about you," he returned. "Why don't I grab us something to drink and we'll take this out to the porch and watch the rain. I think the worst part is over, and maybe the best part has just begun," he said with a wink. "You can explain how you happen to be trespassing on our ranch. Do you want a bottle of water, soda, or a Shiner?"

"Actually if you could give me a lift down to Floyd's, I'll treat you to a Shiner. I had a flat and the darn spare is flat too."

"Okay. Just give me a minute to get Jack Daniels settled, then we'll grab your tires and head over to Floyd's."

"I can't help but notice this barn is nicer than most homes," I said.

"Yeah, well that's thanks to Julie. She spends a lot of time here when the horses are foaling or if there is need to stay with the animals for a period of time. She insisted on a decent bathroom with a shower. There's even a decent bedroom," he said as he placed the harness and lead ropes back up on hooks near the barn door. "Wait here and I'll come around in the Jeep."

As he opened the door to the chalky day outside, I was left to think and thinking was leading to getting angry. Julie? At the sound of another female name from the lips I had just kissed so passionately and the body I longed to be closer to, I suddenly lost my thirst for a beer or this man.

Chapter Sixteen

"Yard Sale: Saturday only, 501 McKinney. Many kitchen items, old gas stove, dishes, tools, clothing."

I stood and looked for my leather bag. Now, I wanted to get out of here fast, but I wasn't going anywhere without Old Blue. What a fool I'd been! Like it or not, I had to depend on Thomas for a ride to Floyd's to get my flats fixed. Men! I knew it was too good to be true. Why would it be any different now? I should just get used to being single. After all, I did have a life and I'd be getting back to it as soon as I could figure out who killed Evelyn Sue and stole the Browning letters and if the two events were related. *Yeah, right! As if.*

Moments later Thomas and I were in the front seat of a 1950s topless Willies Jeep, his tool chest clanging in the back seat. As we pulled up to my truck, I hopped out before Thomas came to a complete stop. I could see Old Blue's deep metal gouge from a distance. I ran over to Old Blue and traced the scratched paint down the length of the driver's side.

Thomas followed close behind. "Damn! What the hell?" he said quietly. "Let's get this tire off and get these flats fixed. We'll worry about who did this later."

"Oh, I know who did this."

While we took the tire off, I told Thomas about Cowboy and Lonnie and the rare letters I found in the disgusting ladies room. This man drew me to him even though I wanted to slap him silly. I couldn't help but notice the way his muscular arms moved in the tight Texas A&M shirt across his strong shoulders. He tossed the tires in the back of his Jeep and started the engine.

"What thugs!" Thomas said. "Now I understand why you wanted to use the phone. I'll make a call when we get to Floyd's. Let's go get the tires fixed and you can tell me more about yourself, Jimmie. I can't believe we've never met before."

"Yeah, me either. Sorry about inconveniencing you like this," I said as we headed toward Floyd's Filler-Up.

"You're not," he answered. "Like I said before, I'd like to get to know you better. In fact if you'd like to go parking, I know a great little spot –"

"I'll just bet you do. No thanks. Let's just focus on getting the tires fixed."

"You're no fun, Jimmie Rae. All I know about you at this point is that you're a hell of a kisser and you know a thing or two about the martial arts."

"Yeah, well, just drop me off with the tires at Floyd's and you can get back to whatever you were doing before. I really need to be on my way too. My grandmother asked me to pick up an old radio she had repaired. She wants to give it to my Uncle Keith for his birthday next week. I was supposed to pick it up from someone at the Flying W Ranch."

"Yeah, I know. That would be me. My hobby is messing around with old radios and electronics. Your grandmother is Star, right?"

"Yeah, Star, right. So how did you get into old radios?"

"My daddy collected them for years. That's how I came to have a booth at Blessings Antique Mall, I'm selling some of the hundreds of old radios and Victrolas we have in our barns. Tell you what, promise to stay and have a beer with me at Floyd's and if you really want, I'll try to forget this afternoon happened and we can go our separate ways."

I rolled my eyes in reply. He really was tenacious I had to give him that. My gut told me not to trust him, but my aching libido had other plans.

"Don't take this personally, but you sure do a lot of eye rolling, you know that?" he said.

"Yes. Star reminds me quite often that they're going to stick that way someday."

We pulled into Floyd's gravel driveway. The smell of mesquite smoke from the BBQ pit hung heavy in the humid air.

"I'll take the tires over to Hank and you go get the beers. We can sit outside at the patio now that the storm's over or we can sit over on the porch rockers. That's Julie's favorite spot at Floyd's."

Was he kidding me? What kind of idiot did he think I was?

"So which one— patio or porch?" he asked.

"Patio, I guess. Just remember one beer then we forget about everything. Okay?"

"Sure," he said pulling the tires from the back of the Jeep.

I opened the red screen door and entered Floyd's. Even the best interior designers in Austin could not replicate the authentic ambiance of the old olive green car-sided walls covered in longhorns, antlers, and decades of colorful Texas license plates. No, Floyd's was the real deal. A gas station, convenience store, beer, and BBQ joint, and on Friday and Saturday nights, an Opry-like venue featuring some of the best Texas blues, bluegrass, and country music around. Only Luckenbach and a few clubs in Austin pulled in bigger local talent.

At the large refrigerated chests, I selected two amber Shiner Bock beer bottles, and grabbed a bag of sunflower seeds at the cash register. Outside, I took a seat at a table with a bright yellow and blue Corona umbrella. Several people were unloading musical equipment to the left side of the raised stage. This was the Opry side of Floyd's. Tonight this place would be filled with folks who eagerly paid the five dollar cover charge to listen to some of the best local music around. Strings of small clear light bulbs crisscrossed over the brick patio and wooden tables. Behind this area a garden path laden with every color of iris and spiked with creamy crowns of Queen Anne's Lace led the way to the facilities an amenity Floyd's wife, Betty, had insisted on.

Floyd's patio was built around an ancient huge live oak, like an awkward ballet dancer, its lower limbs spread wide, sweeping them toward the earth. A few late bluebonnets and orange Indian Blankets dotted the rolling land beyond the stage.

"The tires will be ready in thirty minutes or so. Hank's got a couple of folks ahead of you," Thomas said as he pulled a wrought iron chair out, mopped up the remaining rain drops with his bandana, and sat down. "Now, where were we? Oh yeah, getting to know each other a little better."

Even across the table from me, his magnetism drew me. My mind wandered to what would happen if, Julie or not, we returned to his barn, passion taking over, our clothing strewn along the hallway leading to the old poster bed—I looked down hoping he couldn't read my thoughts. *Stop it.* The last thing I needed was another two-timing snake.

He twisted the top off his bottle watching me. "What ya thinking about?" he asked, his chocolate eyes engaging mine. Thick brown hair, tinged by a few gray strands, framed his tanned face. I longed to touch the scar on his face again and to hear how he got it. Obviously, he'd been involved in something awful I couldn't begin to fathom.

"Jimmie, I'd just like to understand what just happened back at the barn. I thought things were getting interesting between us. Why the sudden change of heart?"

"It's nothing too important—just an old festering wound."

"Oh. Guess you don't want to talk about it."

"Not really."

"Come on, you'll feel better if you do," he urged.

I contemplated my words carefully as my finger traced the label on the beer bottle. "Okay—Just so you know, I caught my soon-to-be ex-husband shacked up with some college coed this morning, so I'm not looking to be in another stinkin' relationship any time soon," I said daring myself to look him in the eyes.

"I can understand that. That happened to me too. It's never easy to find your lover with someone else."

"Not that it's any of your business, but he's not my lover nor has he been for some time," I snapped before I could stop.

"Oh. Well, I'd be more than happy to help you remember how sweet love can be."

"No thanks! I've got to go now."

"Wait! I'll be damned but you are the most confusing woman I've ever met."

"I'll bet." I took another long drink trying to finish the bottle so I could leave.

"What's that supposed to mean?"

"I suppose I'm more confusing than Julie," I ventured with caution.

"Well, as a matter of fact, yes, you are."

I sat the bottle on the table and stood up. "Okay, that's enough for me. I'm done. I'm leaving now whether you like it or not,"

He took my hand and gently caressed it. "Look, I know we just met and this is crazy, but I'd really like to know everything about you. Please stay. I'd like a second chance at first impressions."

I closed my eyes and drew a deep breath feeling fatigue rush into my body, and all I wanted to do was relax. Without opening my eyes I sensed his presence. I looked at Thomas. I wanted to hate this guy. I wanted to tell him where to get off. Yet, when I opened my eyes and looked into his, I melted like a pat of butter on one of Star's hot buttermilk biscuits.

I closed my eyes again willing myself to relax. I had to admit there was something engaging and intriguing about this guy beyond physical attraction.

"Come on, Jimmie. Let's try this again, please. Come on, sit, and let's just talk. Tell me about yourself besides the fact you've got a son-of-a-bitch ex. I know you and Max have an antiques booth at Blessings. What else should I know?"

My noisy cell phone interrupted the uncomfortable silence.

"Great, *now* I have service," I said reaching for the phone my front pocket. "Hello?"

"Hey, Jimmie— It's Billy Jack. Don't forget you owe me a Shiner at Lucky's. How about we meet in an hour? Hell, I may even splurge on dinner!"

I looked over at Thomas and shrugged my shoulders. Billy Jack sensed my hesitation. "Jimmie, are you there? You aren't planning to stand me up again are you?"

"Yes, I'm here. But I don't think tonight is going to work out."

"Hell, yes. It sure is! Trust me lady, you want to talk to me. I got a little ole ballistic report back a couple of minutes ago. Yes, sister. You're gonna want to drop whatever you're doing and meet me."

"Gee, you're still as smooth as a broncing bull, Billy Jack."

"Does that mean you want a ride?" he asked provocatively.

"Billy Jack, is this business or not? I'm not really in a dating mood this evening."

"Don't get your panties in a wad, sister. Just be at Lucky's in an hour."

"Okay, but give me a couple of hours. My truck has a flat tire and I'm at Floyd's getting it fixed."

"Do you need help? I can be there in a few minutes."

"No, thanks. I've got plenty of help," I said looking over at Thomas. "I'll see you at Lucky's at let's say around eight."

"Done. See you then, Jimmie."

Thomas looked at me waiting for answers. I liked this guy but could only think about his wife or girlfriend or whoever Julie was.

"Look, I really have to go. This was fun, but I think figuring out who killed Evelyn Sue Dinsmore is more important," I said as I gathered my bag and looked for a quick exit. "Detective Mitchell needs to meet with me. Can you take me back to my truck now?" Seeing his expression, I sighed and adjusted the shoulder strap of my bag across my chest. "Look, just forget it. My uncle will help me out. Thanks for the ride, Thomas." I turned to leave.

He grabbed my forearm. "Not so fast. I figured out what pissed you off— Julie. You got tense when I said her name."

I feigned disinterest, fumbling with my leather messenger bag. I closed my eyes again. I was so tired, but there was so much to find out before things could be normal again. I opened my eyes, stretched my neck, and tucked wayward curls behind my ears. Could I stand hearing the truth about who Julie was?

Thomas sat his beer bottle down next to mine and stood up. His large hand took the leather strap off my shoulder and pulled it over my head, laying it down on the table. He looked at me, his hands on my shoulders. "Now that I have your full attention, you should know that Julie is my kid sister. I'm not married nor have I ever been. That's not to say I haven't had a 'significant other' or two. I've been gone from here for more years than I lived here. Julie, her husband, Lloyd, and son, Everett, have been running things around here with our ranch manager, Eddie, since our dad died a few years ago. When Eddie passed away six months ago, Julie and Lloyd asked me to come back and help with the ranch."

I could buy that. The news about Julie's relationship to Thomas was a relief. I sat back down and he followed my lead. "So where were you before that?"

"Where wasn't I? I've spent a good part of my life as a navy officer and the last few years doing…let's just call it 'security consultations' in Europe."

I took a sip from thc tall bottle. The beer was smooth and cold. Beyond the stage, the sun shone like a bright jewel on the turquoise horizon. I drank in the moment as much as the beer

"Hmm, sounds mysterious. So how long have you had a booth at Blessings?"

"About four months now. My father was one hell of a rancher, but messing with old radios and Victrolas were his passion. He had me hooked before I was ten. I was working in his shop by the time I was a teenager, about the same time my mom died."

I looked at his face and touched his hand. "Oh, I'm sorry I didn't know. My folks died when I was young too."

He met my gaze and gripped my hand in his. "I guess what doesn't kill us does make us stronger, huh?"

"That and a lot of loving care from family and friends. So, did you meet Maxine at the antique mall?"

"Actually, no," he said, releasing my hand and taking another long sip.

I raised my eyebrows hoping to encourage more explanation.

"Actually, I met Max in a professional capacity when she and Edna realized several Living History Museum items were missing."

"So, you're a private investigator?"

"No, not really. I'm more like a security specialist."

"Oh," I said realizing I sounded disappointed. A forty something security specialist was okay. It's just he gave off an exotic aura of adventure, travel, and life experience. Maybe I was reading him wrong. I looked at Thomas again. When he looked back at me, I shyly turned my attention to peeling the label off my brown glass Shiner bottle. He was definitely good-looking, but I was undeniably drawn to him in a deeper way.

My voice was low and apologetic. "I mean there's nothing wrong with being a security guard."

He smiled and shook his head. "I didn't say I was a security guard," he said defensively. "In fact, far from it."

"Okay, explain."

He took another long sip, finishing his beer and sitting the empty bottle on the table. "Let's just say I've consulted for some of the world's most renowned museum collections," he said with a smug smile. "When mom died, I couldn't get away from the ranch fast enough. I graduated high school early, loaded up on classes at A&M, joining the Navy as soon as I graduated. I did several tours in Asia and then Afghanistan in the first Gulf War. Finally, I got a post in Italy with the U.S. Consulate and discovered the civilian world paid a lot better. So, I retired from the Navy after twenty-two years and was offered an opportunity to stay in Europe. That was, until Julie asked me to consider coming home to help her figure out what to do with our ranch."

"Oh," I said in a more impressive way. He was clever—seemed like he had really done a thorough self-disclosure, but I still didn't know what type of 'consulting' he'd done. I decided to let it go and changed the subject. "So did Maxine tell you I work at a library with the world's largest collection of Elizabeth Barrett and Robert Browning's writings and personal belongings?"

He shook his head. "No, Max never mentioned that, but that's quite impressive. Guess that explains why you're so worried about those old letters you found yesterday."

"Yeah, I just hope we can get all those items back to their rightful place at the Armstrong Browning Library. Anyway, how did you meet Max in a 'professional capacity'?"

"Oh, well, we were talking one Sunday after church and I told her I planned security systems for high dollar collections. She asked if I could help her figure out how and why items were disappearing from the Living History Museum.

"Last week was the first time I'd heard Miss Dinsmore was also missing items. Then, I found out one of Max's volunteers had taken a liking to Miss Dinsmore and gone to visit her several times a week up at Yellow Rose Hill. Miss Dinsmore told me herself she was suspicious of her, but didn't have any proof she had taken anything."

"By any chance is her name, Kaye Watson?"

Thomas sat his bottle down. "Yes, I believe that's the name I wrote down. How did you know? Are you playing detective now?"

I proceeded to tell him what Mary Jayne Brown told me. He sat back and raised his eyebrows. "Well, now, that *is* interesting. A couple of quick searches on the Internet ought to tell us all about Patricia Sue and what happened to her kid. It would be interesting to find out if this 'Kaye' could be Patricia Sue's daughter."

"Hey, Thomas, I'm all done. Eddie's got the bill inside," a man's voice called from over the waist-high gate.

"Thanks, Hank!"

I stood up, placing the leather strap of my messenger bag back over my head and across my body. Thomas grabbed his straw cowboy hat and followed.

I paid the bill and we hopped into his Jeep and headed out to my truck. He reached for my hand as we bumped along the graveled back-roads. "Thanks, for the chance to redeem myself. Let's get your tire back on your truck and then you can come up for dinner. I'm sure Julie wouldn't mind. It would give you two a chance to meet. She's got some dry clothes she'd loan you too."

I immediately patted my hair realizing I probably looked a mess. "Oh, no thanks, maybe next time—for dinner, that is. I'd better get back to Star's and get cleaned up so I can see what Billy Jack's got up his sleeve."

"You want me to go with you to meet Billy Jack?"

"No, that's not necessary. I've known Billy Jack most of my life. His bark is always worse than his bite."

Thomas looked over at me. "Sounds like the voice of experience."

As stupid as it was, I couldn't help but feel my cheeks heat up as the cool wind rushed past. "We dated in high school—end of story," I said looking straight ahead.

"Ahh, teenage romance! That makes me think I definitely need to go with you to meet Detective Mitchell."

"Believe me; I can take care of myself—especially around Billy Jack Mitchell."

"Okay, but how about the two of us getting together later. We can work on the case some more. I've got the feeling we're close and just need to put everything together to figure out if all this information is connected or not," he said as he pulled up behind Old Blue. He stopped the Jeep and turned off the key. "I'll change your tire, ma'am, but it'll cost you," he said turning to embrace me.

I felt for the door handle. "I've been changing my own tires since high school," I said escaping.

I unlocked my truck door, threw my messenger bag in the cab, and rolled the fixed tire to the back axle. As I changed the tire, Thomas looked down offering me the jack, then the tire iron.

"How about another ride then, Ms. Jimmie Rae Murphy?"

"On Jack Daniels, of course," I said as he lifted the spare back into the bed of the truck and fastened it down.

"Not necessarily," he said with a wink as he jumped down. He pulled me to him and reminded me what I'd been missing.

I pulled away, straightening my shirt, and getting into my truck before my libido tricked my common sense. I rolled down the window. "I'm not interested in romantic interludes, but I think you may be right, Thomas, there's a slight possibility this is all connected." He leaned against the truck window and smiled. Before I let his charms work on me again, I offered my hand to him thinking he'd shake it. "Well, thanks for everything. It's been a little strange but maybe I'll see you again."

He took my extended hand and gently kissed it working his way to my lips. "Oh, you'll see me again Jimmie Rae Murphy. I'm not letting you go that easily."

This guy was tenacious. Irresistibly so. "Fair enough," I said with a slow smile. "You know even after all we've shared today, I don't remember catching your last name."

"Williams. Thomas Seth Williams, at your service, ma'am," he said, patting Old Blue's side. He began to whistle as he walked back to his Jeep.

As I drove away from Thomas, his scent still sweet on my lips, an unnerving thought crossed my brain as I remembered Evelyn Sue Dinmore's dying voice whispering, “William.” It was at that moment I realized I may have just passionately kissed her killer.

Chapter Seventeen

"Carport Sale: Friday only. 2011 Ash Ave. Early birds shot on sight. Misc items—kitchen table, workout equipment, toys, and lots of stuff priced cheap."

Standing naked under a warm shower couldn't wash away the uneasiness I had inside. Had I lusted after the man who killed Evelyn Sue? Perhaps even worse, what had I told him of my discoveries today? I felt nauseous and my head ached. I had to meet Billy Jack and tell him everything. He wasn't my favorite person, but at least I knew I could trust him.

I selected a pair of jeans but changed tops several times—finally, I settled on a plain black v-neck t-shirt and a turquoise cross necklace Star had given me last Christmas. A pair of low-heeled black leather sandals finished my outfit.

Star's house was quiet since she was still at the hospital with Edna. I patted her tabby cat, Darla, lying asleep on the emerald velvet covered piano stool. She kept her eyes closed but gave a "mew" in response to my touch.

While the rest of the house was a comfortable mix of Victorian Texas Ranch style, Star's pride and joy, her chef's kitchen, gleamed in twenty-first century technology. The stainless steel refrigerator quickly filled my glass with cold water. I checked the time on the old blue neon wall clock. I had about twenty minutes to get to Lucky's. Billy

Jack could just wait. I wanted to sit down, drink a glass of water, and think.

As I headed out to Star's screened-in porch, a high-pitched ring tone called out from its place on the marble topped table in the foyer. *Now what?*

I sat my glass down and hurried in to grab my cell phone. "This is Jimmie," I said heading back out to the screened-in porch and settling on the familiar porch swing.

"Hey, girl," Star answered. "I had to call from Edna's room phone because they won't allow cell phones."

"How is she?"

"She's asleep—they just gave her another pain pill. It looks like the yesterday's surgery did the trick. No more internal bleeding and her vitals are stabilizing. She even ate a little bit today. Her doctor told me she should be able to get back to light activity in a couple of weeks."

"That's great."

"I'm sorry we haven't had much chance to catch up, Jimmie. I just need to be here with Edna."

"Star, don't start with the guilt thing. Of course you need to be there. I'm okay. I'm so glad you called because I'm worried about you."

"Oh, I'm fine. I can tell you just about anything you ever wanted to know about the latest Nashville gossip. I've read every country and western publication out there, and my head is full of new recipes from the latest issue of *Gourmet* magazine."

"You are eating aren't you?"

"Yes, but you know how hospital food is. I'd give about anything for a bowl of fresh pesto penne and a salad with balsamic dressing."

"Why don't I relieve you tomorrow so you can take a break?"

"That's sweet, Jimmie, but I want to be here with Edna the next couple of days. I can always walk over to the HEB deli and get something fresh. By the way, did you ever go talk to Billy Jack? He sounded madder than a hornet this morning."

"Yes. In fact, I'm on my way to meet him again."

"Oh. Well, you two always did make a nice couple."

"No, Star. It's not like that at all. Billy Jack just wants to meet with me again. All I want is to do is find out who killed Evelyn Sue. Did you hear they found Daryl Ann's Lexus at the Hillsboro Outlet parking lot today?"

"Was she in it?"

"No. She's missing. Personally, I think she might be involved somehow."

"Jimmie Rae Murphy! Shame on you! You've gotten in over your head. You don't know anything about solving murders and now you're suggesting someone we've known for years killed our dear friend. Really, Jimmie! What you need to do is back off and let the police take care of everything," Star declared. There was a pause then a more maternal tone. "At least you took my advice and went back to the house for a nap, right?"

I knew she would sense something amiss if I hesitated. Yet, I had never gotten away with lying to her.

"Right?" she asked again.

"Not really."

"Jimmy, now I can tell from your voice something's wrong. What happened?"

"Well, I went out to Mary Jayne Brown's yard sale to see what she knew about something Edna tried to tell Max and me last night."

"Uh-huh. Go on."

"Turns out the story about Evelyn Sue having a child may be true after all."

"Jimmie Rae, that's just tacky gossip. Besides it's bad luck to speak ill of the dead."

"Yeah, I know, but I don't have a choice at this point. Besides if it's true, it's not ill spoken, is it? Anyway, Mary Jayne Brown told me everything. I won't go into all the details, but I believe her. The upshot of it all is Mary Jayne thinks the young woman who has been helping up at Yellow Rose Hill may actually be Evelyn Sue's long lost granddaughter.

"Hmm. Really?" Star said in her concerned voice. "It begs more questions than it answers."

"Look, Star, I realize it sounds crazy. It's a convoluted story, but there's definitely something peculiar going on, and I'm determined to find out what it is." I paused for a sip of water before continuing. "So, after I saw Mary Jayne, I headed over to the Flying W, and well, I ran into some bad luck with Old Blue."

"I thought—wait, in fact I *know* I specifically insisted you go back to my house. Were you out in that awful storm this afternoon, Jimmie Rae? As if I don't already have enough to worry about with Edna—."

I could tell from the way her tone changed that Star was getting royally riled up. "Now, calm down, Star. Everything's okay. However, I didn't get to pick up the radio. I promise I'll pick it up tomorrow."

"I told you not to worry about the radio. You haven't mentioned him, but have you had a chance to meet that handsome Thomas Williams yet?"

I hesitated before answering. "Sure, we met earlier today. What do you know about him?"

"Well, just that he's polite, handsome, a decorated military veteran, and quite the world traveler. He came back here recently to help out with his family's ranch. I know his sister, Julie, from church. Their daddy, Ramsey, was a good man. He and John used to be in Kiwanis together. They're a real nice family. Why do you ask?"

"No reason," I brazenly lied. "I'm just trying to figure out this whole Evelyn Sue and Daryl Ann thing," I said trying to avoid an explanation about the whole afternoon episode with Thomas and admittance of having impure—

well, downright sexual thoughts about the man who might just be Evelyn Sue's killer.

"Jimmie, you've got to be extra careful. Really. Just let Billy Jack and his uncle up in Canton figure out this whole Evelyn Sue mess."

"Sure, Star."

"Good girl. Well, then honey, I'll let you go so you can meet Billy Jack. Remember just let he and his officers figure this all out. Don't get any more involved, dear. Now, I've got to go, the nurse just came in. Remember what I said. Stay out of it! Bye-bye now."

The line was dead. That was classic Star— she always managed to have the last word. I took my water and eased back against the swing—the slight weight shift stirred the wooden swing into a gentle rocking motion. I lifted my feet and let the slow creaking sway that so often comforted me when I was troubled carry me back and forth. I relaxed for a moment and took in the sweet honeysuckle smell of a warm Texas evening. It would be easy to pretend nothing had changed and all was well in my little world. Dusk was settling in turning the sky to a soft peach glow through the trees on the west side of Star's street. Cicadas and crickets began their nocturnal symphony as fireflies sparkled across the green grass and tiny pink antique roses tumbled over the small white picket fence my grandpa built when I was ten.

The screened-in porch was a Southern necessity, and Star's was one of Niceton's best. But of course, I might be biased. A relatively recent addition to her Victorian cottage, the large screened-in porch was built to take in the views on both sides of the house, including the ancient live oak sprawled across the front yard. Old Pecan and magnolia trees guarded the spacious backyard, where between the native plants and the vegetable garden, green-blue pickets enclosed an outdoor shower, its bright mosaic floor a summertime project Maxine and I created when we were sixteen.

In the distance a fire truck siren broke the silence of the early evening, droning closer— never a welcome sound in an historic neighborhood of turn-of-the-century wood-framed houses. My phone rang again. In one motion I saw caller ID and answered.

"Hey, Max! I thought you and Steve were off having dinner. By the way, you owe me some details about him."

"Jimmie," she interrupted. "Come quick, The Page Turner is on fire!" Without hesitating, I jumped up from the swing, leaving it to lurch precariously sideways. I grabbed my leather messenger bag, locked up, and headed Old Blue toward the downtown square.

As I drove down Cherry Street and turned at First there was no denying the thin, steady line of black smoke coming from the Square. I parked haphazardly and ran toward the crowd of people, pushing my way through, trying to get closer to Star's beloved bookstore.

From the front of the store it didn't look so bad. No flames or smoke pouring through the doors or windows. "You'll have to stay back behind the yellow tape," a fireman informed me as he motioned me to move back.

"This is my grandmother's business. What happened?"

"I don't have time to explain. Why don't you go on over there and wait with those folks. They're related to the owner too."

My eyes followed his pointed finger to my Uncle Keith and cousin Jen standing arm in arm watching anxiously.

Keith released Jen's arm and hurried over to me. He hugged me as if he hadn't seen me in a long time. "Jimmie, you okay?"

"I'm fine. What about you two?" I asked as Keith stepped back closer to Jen.

Although her boyfriend, Todd, stood a few steps away talking to some other people, Jen was visibly shaken. She reached for my hands and took them in hers. "Oh, Jimmie, this is so awful. The fire is out, but just look at everything. Star's bookstore has been around forever."

"Nothing's going to change that, Jen," I answered with more confidence than I felt. "What happened anyway?"

"I'm not sure. Todd and I were paying for dinner at the Lone Star Café when we saw folks running this way and we followed. The Chief told dad the backdoor was open when they arrived. He said it could be arson, but they'll have to investigate it to be sure. You don't suppose Stella Pierce paid us another visit, do you?"

"I don't know. She was sure juiced up this afternoon. Surely, she wouldn't incriminate herself so obviously. Besides, how could Stella be strong enough to pry the door open? She's a little wacky, but I just can't believe her notion of a supposed code violation would motivate her to set the place on fire."

Uncle Keith stood behind Jen listening. He moved toward me and patted my shoulder. "Jen told me Stella had come by a couple of times today. What's her problem anyway?"

I shook my head and shrugged my shoulders. "Beats me. She was all fired up about Star adding the tables and chairs to the front of the store without asking permission from the city, better known as her 'Downtown Merchants' Aesthetically Correct Committee.' Stella handpicked the three other members who are either like-minded or too afraid of her to speak their honest opinions. Personally, I believe the tables and chairs are a nice touch and enhance the downtown ambiance—or at least they used to," I said pointing to the metal jumble pushed off the sidewalk and into the two parking spots to the right of The Page Turner's front doors.

The fire chief walked toward us. "You folks know any reason why Stella Pierce would be in Star's place?"

We looked at each other, shrugged our shoulders, and looked back at him. "No, why?" Keith said.

"The boys just found her under a bookcase."

I winced. "Is she alive?"

"Yep, but she's pretty banged up. We'll know more once the EMS guys get here."

Maxine and Steve made their way past the on-lookers toward us. Max greeted me with a firm hug. "Thank goodness you're here."

"What happened?" I asked her.

"We were on Steve's bike headed to Cinda's Soda Shop for an ice cream cone, and saw the smoke. We headed down the back alley, saw the door was busted off, and called 9-1-1. You don't suppose this has anything to do with all the other crazy things that have happened, do you?"

My family and friends surrounded me with looks of concern. I remembered Cowboy's threat to Star this afternoon. Why if he mistook Stella Pierce for Star? I wasn't ready to share this with everyone, but it reinforced my commitment to later return to Cowboy's and get the proof necessary to lock those two creeps away before they could do anymore harm. Maybe I should make sure Billy Jack was following up on the information I gave him earlier. Perhaps by getting them put away, the path to Evelyn Sue's killer would be clearer. Regardless, I couldn't afford to hang around the Square speculating on who started the fire at Star's bookstore. I needed to make a graceful, hasty departure.

"I have no idea, but I've got to go meet Billy Jack. Keith, you suppose we can wait to tell Star about the fire? It's really the last thing she needs to worry about right now."

"I'm in no hurry to break the news," he said. "Where are you headed? Maybe you should stick with us."

"I appreciate it, but Billy Jack's waiting for me out at Lucky's. Don't worry. I'll be with Niceton's finest. Keep me updated, okay?"

"I don't like it, Jimmie. Just call him—heck, he probably already knows and is on his way here."

"Keith, come on. I'll be fine."

"Okay, but check in when you get back, hear me?" Keith said in his best fatherly tone.

"Yes, Uncle Keith," I said in a condescending tone. "I hear you. Hey, remember, I'm a big girl now. Really, don't worry about me. Look, the fire chief is on his way over. I hate to ask, but did anyone think about Audrey? I'd just fed her a few hours ago."

"Fortunately, she's okay. Scared, but okay. I'm going to take her home with me while Star's busy with Edna."

"Good. Let's just hope Stella Pierce will be okay and the damage to the bookstore is minimal. Keep me posted."

I was about to depart when Keith grabbed my arm. "Big girl or not—that's not going to save you if there's some creep out to get you," he reminded me.

"Gee, thanks. I'll call you later."

My exit was delayed again as Maxine grabbed my arm. "Not so fast," she said. "Keith is right. Don't worry about Billy Jack. He'll understand if you don't meet him."

"After having his boys escort me to the police station this morning, I'm not about to take any chances on standing him up again. Besides I need to talk to him about the case," I said. "I'll be fine. Billy Jack may play like he's all tough, but you and I both know he's one of our most protective friends. I'll call you later! Promise."

Maxine reluctantly let my arm go. "Jimmie, you stay right with Billy Jack! You hear me? I don't like this."

"Don't freak. I'll be fine." My confidence level was weakening, but I wasn't about to let fear scare me away from the truth. After my meeting with Billy Jack I was even more determined to go back to Cowboy's, but not for the tchotchkes—tonight I was in the market for answers.

Chapter Eighteen

"Memorial Day Weekend Rummage Sale benefiting St. Anne's Youth Group. Friday, Saturday: 8 a.m.-2 p.m. Donuts to Dishes; Bicycles to Bathtubs; Furniture to Flip-Flops — we've got it all! Help us raise $$ for our trip to New Orleans to build Habitat for Humanity houses."

Unfortunately I wasn't dressed for my errand to Cowboy's later. A quick stop at Star's would remedy that. I was upstairs in my room grabbing another pair of shoes when Star's cat, Darla, went darting past my doorway. Being an older cat, Darla seldom moved fast for anything. Her sudden movement down the hallway meant something was up or rather *someone* was downstairs.

Why couldn't Star have adopted a loyal dog with big teeth instead of her fluffy, old cat? I gathered my gear and tiptoed downstairs. As I approached the last step something banged against the backdoor. I dropped my gear, lunged forward to grab Uncle Keith's wooden baseball bat from the umbrella stand, and headed toward the backdoor. I switched on the light with my elbow and opened the door prepared to send whoever it was to the moon.

"Jimmie, my goodness, what are you doing with that?" Thomas said from behind a freshly waxed vintage cathedral radio.

"Thomas? What are you doing here?" My pulse quickened when I saw his face. *Friend or foe? Friend or foe?* The question kept pulsing through my head. For the moment, I lowered the bat, but decided against letting it go completely.

"What does it look like? I brought the radio you were supposed to be picking up out at the Flying W earlier. Uh, may I come in? It's not heavy, but it's a little awkward."

If Thomas were the killer would he bring a radio he lovingly restored back over to Star's? On the other hand, of course, he knew I was alone and it would be a good ploy to trap me in the house. Should I let him in?

I opted for caution and leaned the bat against the wall. "Sure. Silly me. I'll take it, just hand it over," I said pushing the screen door open and extending my arms.

"Why can't I come in? You don't have another guy in there, do you?"

"Would it matter if I did?" The words slipped out before I could shut my mouth. I made brief eye contact with Thomas, and then changed the subject. "Actually, I'm just on my way over to Lucky's."

"Good, I'll go with you."

"Thomas, Billy Jack's not expecting me to bring you," I said standing in the doorway still reaching for the radio.

"Okay, then. Take it," he huffed, letting go.

"Arrgguhh! You didn't mention it weighs a ton!"

"I tried to tell you," he said taking it back and pushing past me uninvited, through the backdoor into the blue neon lit kitchen.

"Cool kitchen. Your grandmother's a great cook, huh?"

"Well, yes, but how'd you know that?"

"When Eddie died your grandma brought us enough food for an army. It was a thoughtful gesture all right, but the casserole and fresh rolls were just lip-smacking incredible. Then a few weeks ago I was fortunate enough to get a piece of her Texas Sheet Cake at the church potluck," he said sitting the radio down on the round oak pedestal table. "How do you stay so slim with her around anyway?"

"It's not easy," I admitted, then changed the subject, "Hey, nice job with the old radio. I didn't have too much hope for it when Star showed it to me after she found it out in the barn. You really did a great job. It looks beautiful."

Thomas sat down at the kitchen table. "I aim to please," he said between coughing and clearing his throat.

"Are you all right?"

"Yeah, they were cutting hay and I had the windows rolled down on the way over here. I forgot how it chokes me up. Could I get some water or something?"

More likely you're just stalling. I brushed aside my increasing annoyance. "Sure," I said turning to get him a glass from the cabinet and filling it from the refrigerator's water dispenser. "Look, I've really got to be heading out. Thanks for bringing the radio by. I'll see you around."

"Gee, that's subtle, Jimmie. Okay, I get it. I'm out the door, but I'd like to take you out on a real date. What about tomorrow night?"

"Sure. Right after I figure out who killed Evelyn Sue, where Daryl Ann Sumners is, why there were priceless Browning letters in that creepy junk store, and now, who set Star's bookstore on fire and why Stella Pierce was in there pinned under a bookcase."

"What was that last thing about a fire at Star's bookstore?"

"It appears someone set it on fire a few hours ago and the firemen found Stella Pierce, still alive, thank heavens, inside pinned under a bookcase."

"That's not good. Jimmie, you may be in a lot of danger. Why don't I take you over to Lucky's? I'll drop you off and Billy Jack can bring you back to Star's."

I took a deep breath. My annoyance with everyone's overt concern mounted. Screaming seemed a bit too dramatic, so I walked over to the backdoor and opened it. "Thanks, but I work solo."

"Here's my cell number in case you change your mind and decide to stop being so obstinate," he said stepping onto the back porch and handing me his business card.

I reluctantly took it. I didn't even know this guy when I woke up this morning and I sure as heck didn't need him getting mixed up in my life now. While the romantic barn scene was the hottest thing to happen to me since my air conditioner went out during last summer's heat wave, acting like it meant anything would only lead to even more trouble. Something I had an abundance of lately.

"Don't hold your breath." I let the screen door slam shut. He stood on the porch looking through the screen.

"That would be hard to do since you take it away, Jimmy Rae Murphy. Ciao!" he said blowing a kiss my way.

Chapter Nineteen

"Estate Sale. Friday and Saturday only, 9-3. Numbers available at 7:30. No early sales or previews. Cash only. 856 South Collins St. Lots of dishes, some furniture, vintage clothing, musical instruments, full garage."

From the outside, Lucky's Tavern didn't appear to be much of anything. But regulars knew its rather scruffy exterior kept a lot of newcomers from summoning up the courage to enter. They also knew Lucky's had a reputation for its locally brewed beer, fork-tender chicken-fried steak, and showcasing the best musical talent around. The parking lot was filling up fast. I parked Old Blue and waited in line to get inside. Eight dollars and a hand stamp later, I was surrounded in red neon glow. The place was alive with music, laughter, and loud end-of-the-week conversations.

A raised wooden stage overlooked a worn, oak dance floor complete with a twirling mirrored disco ball. At the opposite end, the bar took precedence. About thirty square tables separated the two ends to seat diners. High-backed, brown vinyl booths lined the walls. I figured a quick trip to the bar might overshadow the fact I was late.

"Bartender, two Shiners please."

"Longnecks or draft?"

"Draft, please."

"Jimmie, over here." I heard Billy Jack's voice above the strains of the band's cover of Stevie Ray Vaughn's "Texas Flood." Billy Jack had selected a booth lit by the soft glow of an art deco wall sconce and a lit candle in a red glass holder. His familiar black cowboy hat hung on a hook separating the booths.

"You're late. Better be a good reason," he said pushing aside an empty beer glass as I approached the table.

"Would you believe anything I said at this point?" I sat the full pilsners on the table.

He scooted out from the booth, stood up, and looked down at me with a tainted grin. "Now why would I go and do that?" I could smell his warm beer breath and his spice scented aftershave lotion as his lips brushed my cheek gently. "My, but you're lookin' mighty good tonight, Jimmie Rae."

The intimacy of the moment caught me off guard and I could feel my face flush shamelessly. His gentle kiss sent me back to the familiar comfort of his old truck with its fogged up windows parked so many years ago on a country road beneath a mischievous Lone Star moon on a chilly autumn night. It warmed far more in me than I cared to admit—or remember.

"Thanks, Billy Jack. You look great too," I said trying to stuff the memory back to the far reaches of my mind. I needed to keep it light with Billy Jack. I had to admit though he really did look great. His black Harley Davidson t-shirt showed off more taut muscle than beer belly. His Wranglers were pressed and even his Lucchese alligator boots were highly polished. His belt was an eye catcher—black tooled leather with a huge gold buckle won in the 1995 National Finals Rodeo. I hoped my attention to the year he won the buckle didn't lead him to think I was thinking about him below the belt. The heat of that thought caused me to blush again. *Time to concentrate on the beer.*

I slid into the booth opposite him and took a sip. He shrugged and sat back down.

"So, what kept you this time, Jimmie?

"There was a fire at Star's bookstore. I'm surprised you didn't get a call on it."

His expression changed making his eyebrows look knitted together and creating deep crevices on his forehead. "Really? You'd best not be shittin' me, Jimmie Rae."

I frowned at him. "I can't believe you'd think I'd lie to you. Unfortunately, it happened earlier tonight."

"Oh, crap, Jimmie! I told my guys I didn't want to be bothered unless it was a super high priority call. What happened?" His left hand reached across the table to take both of mine, gently caressing them. It was impossible to keep from looking directly into his blue eyes. I squirmed, uncomfortable under his intense scrutiny.

I cleared my throat and forced myself to ignore the warmth of his hand. "Maxine called me a couple of hours ago and told me The Page Turner was on fire," I continued choosing to ignore the sensations his caress stirred in me. "I hurried down to the Square. They wouldn't let me get too close, but it looked like it was mostly smoke damage since the firemen got there so fast. Unfortunately, Stella Pierce was pinned under a bookcase and the fire chief believes the fire was suspicious." I wiggled my hands free and took a long sip of cold beer.

"Did Rick indicate why the hell Stella was in there?"

I didn't recognize the name. "Who?"

"Rick Bernard, ya know, our fearless fire chief."

"Oh. Well, no. Honestly, I don't know Billy Jack." I said wiping thin foam from my lips with my forearm. My lack of etiquette erased the intense concern from his face. He leaned back taking his glass with him as I continued. "Stella's been pretty riled up about a couple of metal bistro tables and chairs Star has in front of the store. She's been ranting they are a code violation. Today she paid both Jen and I a visit at the store to make sure we let Star know she was going to lose her business license if she didn't remove them immediately."

"Still that doesn't explain why she'd be in there pinned down under a bookcase. Stella Pierce is a lot of things but an arsonist doesn't come to mind."

"I know. I have a theory though."

Billy Jack raised his eyebrows and took another drink of beer. He sat his glass down and smiled. "Go ahead, I'm all yours Jimmie."

"What if those creeps I told you about this morning were responsible for Evelyn Sue's murder?"

"You mean the thugs with the old poet stuff?"

"Yes," I said meeting his eyes directly so he'd know I meant it. "Yes, the Browning items. Did I mention that I think I saw one of them at Canton yesterday before I found Evelyn Sue? Then today those two idiots chased me on a back road. Old Blue picked up a nail and since it didn't seem as if they were chasing me down to ask me to go to the movies with them, I left my truck and hid behind a plum thicket. I watched as they keyed Old Blue's paint."

"Whoa! Wait one-cotton pickin' second. They did what?" Billy Jack leaned toward me intent on my every word.

"You mean the part about them scraping Old Blue's paint?"

His curled his right hand into a fist and hit the table shaking our glasses. "The friggin' bastards!"

I wanted to slap this man here and now. The intensity in his eyes and face told me he wasn't kidding. "Billy Jack Mitchell, REALLY? Come on and tell me murder in broad daylight DOES trump a screwed up paint job on my old truck. RIGHT?"

He looked at me ashamed and reached for my hands again. "Of course, Jimmie. It's just that, well, that's a damn shame. Your grandpa's truck is such a classic, but of course you're right. We can fix the paint job— bringing Evelyn Sue back is…well, a little harder. So tell me more about your theory."

I ignored the way his warm hands continued to send a tingle down my spine. Was I so desperate for a man's touch? *Get a grip, girl.* I took a deep breath and continued. "So what if those two creeps started the fire at The Page Turner and thought they were getting Star instead of Stella?"

"Okay, that's an interesting theory. And just why would they be after Star?"

"Because just maybe they figured out that I may know they have stolen property and just maybe they saw me at First Monday too."

"Hmm, sounds like you could be in a whole mess of trouble. I'll give Rick a call later and see what he says about the fire. You'd best keep your theories between us until I can make some calls and investigate this a little further. Now what about it?"

"What about what?" I said loosening my hands once again and reaching for what beer was left in my glass.

"A dance—let's take a spin," he said tilting his head in the direction of the dance floor. "You know, for old times' sake."

"Billy Jack, I told you this is business tonight."

"No, it's business *my* way. Don't you want to know if you and Maxine are implicated in Evelyn Sue's murder? You want something I have and the only way to get it is to dance with me," he said with a wink and a little shoulder shimmy. "You always loved dancing with me in high school, and I'm a much better dancer now, Jimmie Rae."

I sighed deeply. I should have known Billy Jack wasn't sharing information so easily. I should have known there would be a hitch. "Look, Billy Jack Mitchell, I already know we're not implicated. We didn't kill her. Besides, if we were implicated I don't think you'd be sitting so relaxed asking me to dance. So let's get on with it. How many dances do I have to dance with you to get the results of the ballistics report?"

His brows furled in disgust. "Well, Ms. Snarky, I didn't know you hated me that much. I was just suggesting a dance for old times' sake. No strings." He looked down at the table.

I'd forgotten how sensitive he was. Just when I was about to give him a verbal slap in the face, I remembered what a rough time Billy Jack had been through over the past year. While he did have a propensity to be overly dramatic, I still considered him a good friend. I touched his big hands. "Hey, Billy Jack, come on. I didn't mean it like that. All kidding aside, I know you've been through a lot lately. You know I love you, maybe not in the same way, but I do love and care about you."

"Like a friend," he said sarcastically, looking up at me.

I smiled demurely. "Yes, like a friend."

"Well, that's something anyway," he said as he raised his almost empty glass for the last sip.

I realized that beer probably wasn't his second of the evening. If I was going to get information, I should distract him from drinking before he got too sloshed to move or talk.

"Hey, Billy Jack, no hard feelings. How about I buy us dinner? Remember what a good chicken-fried steak they make here?"

"Do they still make twice baked potatoes with those little bacon pieces too?" he asked a little slurred.

My plan seemed to be working. The way to a man's ballistics report was through his stomach not his pants.

Half an hour later, with our plates scooted to the edge of the plastic gingham tablecloth, and Billy Jack working on another beer, I reached my hand across the table toward him. "Okay, ready for a spin?"

"Don't do me any favors, Jimmie. I'll tell you what you want to know," he said. "Like you thought, of course, the report cleared you guys. The gun Max found was not the one used on Evelyn Sue. On the other hand, it leaves a lot of questions."

"Yes it certainly does," I agreed. "Seems to me there are several potential suspects."

Billy Jack never took his eyes off mine. "What? Are you a detective now, too?" he said, dimples at full alert. "This I've gotta hear. So solve the murder, Ms. Murphy. You'll save the cities of Canton and Niceton a lot of time and tax-payer money." His tone was playful.

"Never mind."

"Oh, come on. I'm listening."

"Tell you what, if I come across some hard evidence, you'll be the second to know. Now, Officer Mitchell you owe me a dance."

The band was playing a slow ballad so we waltzed—a little clumsily at first then smoothly. Billy Jack was still a good dancer. He held me close—too close. I tried not to think about how his scent stirred my sweet high school memories. *Good grief, he's a friend, nothing else. I'm not in the market for a relationship—even with an old friend*, I reminded myself like a mantra. *Especially not with this old friend.*

"Excuse me, sir. It's time."

Billy Jack stopped abruptly. "Sorry, Jimmie. Duty calls." He followed a young man in pressed jeans and a white western shirt sporting a brass shield bearing "Niceton County Sheriff's Dept., Lamont."

I was left in the middle of waltzing dancers shuffling around me as pink lights cast a romantic glow and the disco ball spun glittery reflections around the room.

I moved through the crowd to look for Billy Jack and Officer Lamont. They were gone. I reasoned only something of vital importance would cause Billy Jack to abandon me on the dance floor. I checked the time on the lighted Shiner clock over the bar: 10:15. If I left now, I could be at Cowboy's by eleven, get what I was looking for, and get home to a decent night's sleep.

Time to get answers. If all went well, I'd have some news for Billy Jack, some answers for myself, and maybe even enough evidence to point to Evelyn Sue's real killer.

Outside Lucky's, as I neared Old Blue, I heard Billy Jack's voice yell out. "Hey, Jimmie Rae, wait up!"

Ignoring him, I got in my truck and slammed the door. He ran over and knocked on the window. I rolled the window down. He held a steaming travel mug wafting a strong coffee smell in the other hand.

"Hey, girl, I'm sorry I left you like that. Something's come up— it may be the break we are looking for. I'm glad you're headed back to Star's place. I'll catch up with you tomorrow morning." He reached in the truck and touched my hand resting on the steering wheel. "Tonight was good, Jimmie. Thanks for dinner and everything. I really needed that." He grinned. "Thanks for being a friend." His words hung awkwardly in the warm night.

I looked at him. "Yeah, about that—"

"Hey, Mitchell! Hurry!" A voice called from a group of men, some in uniform, and some in padded vests with "NPD" printed boldly on the back.

"See ya!" Billy Jack said patting my hand.

As I looked in my rearview, I noticed he never saw me turn left instead of right back to Niceton. The evening was young and I had work to do back at Cowboy's Antiques and Gas Emporium.

Chapter Twenty

"Garage Sale: Thursday and Friday, 9 a.m.–3 p.m., 317 Woodvine Dr.—Fine home décor and accessories, designer clothing and shoes, many other marvelous items. Don't miss this sale!"

A dusty half moon floated among bright stars in the chalkboard sky as I traveled down the now familiar road to Cowboy's. Listening to Miranda Lambert erased my fatigue and gave me the confident kick-butt attitude I needed to carry out my mission. I saw an old barn a short distance down from Cowboy's and parked Old Blue out of sight.

Once my truck was hidden, I prepared, trading strappy sandals for my action-ready white and neon orange cross-trainers. I tucked a small digital camera in my left jean pocket and my cell phone in the right—not that it would do me any good as I recalled it was out of my carrier's service zone the day before. My faithful tiny book light lit a narrow path along the shoulder of the two-lane road. As I approached the dark building my hands began to sweat. I was far from my comfort zone. A field mouse scampered in front of me causing me to jump before it raced off into the field.

As I neared Cowboy's Antiques and Gas Emporium, the menacing sound of dogs barking stopped me in my tracks. *Where did they come from?* I didn't remember any dogs yesterday. *Please let them be tied up.*

Undeterred by the tall grass and thoughts of possible creatures residing and even slithering in it, I made my way to the back of the cinderblock building. Rusty appliances and car relics littered the area behind the building. A lone yellow bug light glowed at the back door. The window I recalled at the back of the building near the ladies room was unlocked. Years of filth kept it from moving. I gritted my teeth and leaned into it, slowly inching it up. I refused to think of the all the cobwebs and grossness as I crawled through in a less than Hollywood smooth motion. Let's just say I was glad no one saw me.

The sound of angry barking dogs greeted me inside the junk store. I scoured the darkness, assuring myself they were in the garage bay.

Like stepping on warm marshmallows, I tiptoed across the sticky floor toward the Dutch door praying it was securely shut. Beyond the fact the glass half of the door was full of paw prints and dog drool, the door seemed to be holding the vicious mutts in for the time being. I peered through the glass to be sure. Suddenly a snarling Rottweiler sprang up, pressing its flaring nostrils against the darkened half-glassed door. With teeth bared, it looked ready to break through at any moment. I noticed there were no cars visible in the half-lit garage. What had they done with the pink Cadillac? I backed away praying the door was strong enough to hold the dogs back until my work was done.

Returning to the main aisle, I made my way to the back of the building where I hoped to find the mysterious boxes I'd seen yesterday. Cold metal met my touch as I wiggled the vintage doorknob in my hand and opened the ladies room door. I remembered a light chain over the pedestal sink and reached up to turn it on.

Illuminated by an orange incandescent bulb, the teal and black tiled bathroom was empty except for the paint-worn table, dingy toilet, and cracked sink. Spiders and scurrying roaches were the only inhabitants. No boxes. No nothing. I stood there in shock until a few moments later a distant voice caught my attention. I reacted by pulling the chain to complete darkness.

I'd always heard one's senses are sharper when one of the senses is missing— in the blackness I heard a woman crying. Outside the ladies room I couldn't hear her. Back inside, she was clearly sobbing. Not knowing whom or what I was looking for, I called out, "Hey! Are you in there?"

The crying stopped. "Help me," the voice answered.

I switched on the ladies room light again and saw a vent high above the toilet. "Keep talking," I encouraged her.

"Help me," she said again. "I'm tired and hungry, and oh Lord, could I use a bath and a manicure."

"Daryl Ann Sumners? Is that you?"

"Jimmie Rae Murphy! Is that you? Girl, get me out of here before those thugs get back!"

"Oh my gosh! It is you! Where are you?"

"How should I know? They gave me some kind of pill and I just woke up a little while ago. It's pitch black in here, and darlin', I'm trying hard to be calm, but I hear the scurrying of nasty little bug feet in here—so, move fast!"

"Okay, Daryl Ann, breathe slowly and think about your trip to Paris last month. You know you've been bragging—I mean telling us all about it for weeks now."

"Paris? Think about Paris in HERE? I'll try Jimmie, but it'll be tough."

"Focus, Daryl Ann, you can do it. Keep talking as loud as you can and tell me about your trip."

"Okay. This time though, it's first class all the way, and they better have Ozarka Spring Water."

I shook my head. Oh yes, indeed, no doubt about it, it really was Daryl Ann Sumners. She's the only person who would insist on the locally produced Ozarka spring water over any number of fine French mineral waters available on a flight to Paris.

"Stay focused Daryl Ann. Think Paris brocante markets." Her taste in water aside, I needed to finish my mission and get the two of us the heck out of here. Who knew when those buffoons would be back? I looked back up at the vent and contemplated where they could have hidden her before I returned to the main room. With my book light I could see there were four other wooden doors along the same wall as the ladies room.

I tried the knob of the one closest to me. It swung open easily. "Daryl Ann?" I inquired into the darkness. I reached my hand into the room hoping to feel a delicate metal pull chain. The six legs climbing up my arm were not what I had in mind. "Ewwwehh!" I said brushing the bug off. Quickly withdrawing my hand, I bumped a switch plate on the wall and flipped the light on. Roaches scurried across the floor around the open toilet lid and up the walls. No Daryl Ann.

I willed myself to continue, but my impulse was to forget the past thirty-six hours and head south as fast as possible to the closest Mexican beach resort. I took a deep breath and tried the next door. I jiggled the metal handle and it popped off in my hand. "Daryl Ann, keep talking! Tell me what you found at the flea markets in Paris. Be loud! I'm trying to find you!"

The dogs began a new round of ferocious barking and were now throwing themselves against the half glass door separating the store area from the garage bays. I was beginning to regret not having a partner for this adventure. It wouldn't have taken much to get Billy Jack to come with me. However, my pitiful regrets weren't doing Daryl Ann or myself any good at this point. I needed to find her and get us out of here fast. I wished there was a phone or that my worthless cell phone had a signal. Wishing wasn't solving anything though. I continued my search for Daryl Ann.

I nearly tripped over a vintage tricycle and then scraped my leg against the sharp edge of a metal sign sticking out from behind a table. The next door stood behind a big pile of dusty tchotchkes littered with brittle bug carcasses balancing precariously on a warped drop-leaf table. I couldn't hear Daryl Ann's voice, but she was kicking the bottom of the door vibrating the table in front of it.

"Okay, good! I think I found you," I said as I began unloading the table. I picked up a pair of souvenir aluminum ashtrays only to have some type of sticky goodness-only-knew-what stuff cling to my fingertips. For the second time in the past ten minutes a disgusted sound unconsciously escaped my lips. This situation was nearing ridiculous.

I went back to the ladies room, which was only slightly less offensive than the mens room, and washed the sticky stuff off my fingers. It took a few seconds of scrubbing with a melted Ivory soap pat and ate up time, but gave me the courage I needed to finish my work in this creepy place. As I made my way to Daryl Ann's door I thought I heard the faint sound of a vehicle engine outside. It was difficult to tell since Daryl Ann was screaming incoherently only to be out done by the fierce barking Rottweilers. Just to be on the safe side I hurried back to the ladies room and shouted into the vent. "Daryl Ann! Daryl Ann! Hush! Someone's here! It might be them. Hush NOW!"

She began to sob again. "Don't worry!" I said more to reassure myself than her. "We'll be out of here in no time."

"Sure, we will," said Daryl Ann. "In pieces! They'll kill us!"

"Paris brocante markets! Breathe and go to your happy place. I'll get us out alive, I promise!"

I went back out to the main room and ducked down until I could be sure we didn't have any company. A doorknob I hadn't noticed before on the opposite side of the building began to jiggle. The ancient metal innards dropped to the wooden floor and the door opened. A path of light emerged from a flash light. *Great, my luck, of all nights in all places, this joker is breaking into Cowboy's!* My nocturnal "to-do" list was increasing the longer I was in this dump. I had to get rid of this guy so I could bust Daryl Ann out and we could escape. Now, would be a good time for my cell phone to have service, but fat chance of that happening.

The light went out as the man entered the room and headed toward where I hid. I was tired, impatient, and getting this side of pissed off. I decided to take matters into my own hands. This time we're on my terms. I picked up the closest item within reach. A heavy cast iron Alpine cowbell would work just fine. Silencing the clacker between my fingers, I slipped from my hiding spot and followed the intruder. He was tall, slim, and moved with care across the wooden floor.

He knelt down, examining a box of sheet music on the floor near the front counter. I took the moment to force the cast iron cowbell across the back of his head. The clacking of the bell joined the dog's barking hysteria and Daryl Ann's cries for help. The man fell over— knocked out cold. I quickly dropped my knees to his gut and pulled his arms over his head determined to keep him from reaching for his weapon if he came to. A small silver flashlight rolled from his right hand. The thin light stream revealed the intruder's face.

Thomas Seth Williams was laid out like road-kill in the center of Cowboy's Antiques and Gas Emporium. I had mixed feelings. I was glad to see him, yet what if he were somehow involved with all this? How did he know Daryl Ann was here? I really didn't know this man at all. A passionate kiss, an exchange of come-ons, and a shared moment over a beer were hardly thorough background checks. He could have easily lied about being in the Navy or working in Europe. Come to think of it, what a great cover story to orchestrate a black market ring from South Central Texas to an international clientele out of reach of the United States judicial system. He was clever enough to pull a job that size and he seemed to know a lot about it all. What a big fake! I ought to slap his face while he was passed out. Instead, I carefully removed a pistol from his shoulder holster and laid it down beside my knee.

His eyes fluttered open and closed as if he were trying to regain consciousness. He looked at me. "Not you again." He moaned and closed his eyes again.

As I sat there trying to figure out what to do next, a red light flashed from the top of Thomas' black jeans. Billy Jack's voice joined the chaos, "Charlie Brown to Linus. Charlie Brown to Linus. Do you read me, Linus? What's your twenty?"

I freed one hand, removed the radio and responded, "This is Lucy. Hey Charlie! Linus is down. Sally needs out of the doghouse. And the Snoopys are royally pissed off! Get in here now!"

Above all the racket, Thomas looked up at me. "We've really got to stop meeting like this," he said, and passed out again.

Chapter Twenty-one

"Garage Sale: 501 Tyler St., Th/F only— 7:30 a.m.–5 p.m.—furniture, dishes, linens, light fixtures, brass décor items."

Silence and static traded places on the hand-held radio as Thomas tried to come to. I shifted my weight across his mid-section, using one hand to use the walkie-talkie and the other to hold Thomas' arms above his head.

"Jimmie Rae! What the hell are you doing there? You could have been shot. Where's Linus— I mean Tom?"

I grimaced at the walkie-talkie. "Me? What are YOU doing here? Look, there's no time for this—Thomas needs an ambulance. I knocked him out. Get in here now!" I threw the device on the floor and focused on making sure Thomas couldn't move.

The walkie-talkie sputtered and I heard a faded "Oh hell! Why the crap did you do that? We'll be right there—and Jimmie, do me a favor and try not to kill him. I'm bringing the EMTs in."

The door flew open as a several men with weapons drawn entered. Billy Jack followed, his pistol drawn surveying the situation. He lowered the gun and raced to where I sat on Thomas. His black Lucchese boots stopped by my extended elbows. I looked up to see Billy Jack looking down in his black cowboy hat. He put his gun back in its holster. He was shaking his head. "My Lord,

Jimmie Rae, get off the poor man! I think you've done enough detective work for one night," he said sarcastically as he bent over to retrieve Thomas' gun and tucked it into his waistband.

I jumped up. "Just what in the world is going on Billy Jack?"

Three men in blue uniform shirts and jeans raced around us to check on Thomas. "Where's the overhead lights in this rat-hole?" one of them asked.

"Not now, Jimmie. We've got real detective work to do. Go over there somewhere," he said as he walked back to the wall near the open door and pushed the switches up. The eerie glow of fluorescent lights shone like a 1950s sci-fi movie.

I watched as the EMTs checked Thomas out. A small pool of blood formed on the dirty floor beneath his head. I was torn between feelings of tenderness and suspiciousness toward him. I didn't trust him, but like Star's bread and butter pickles the enticing combination of sweet and bitter could be a good thing.

Suddenly I remembered what I'd been doing before Thomas distracted me. I lifted the drop-leaf table still full of items not caring now what noise I made or what broke. The door behind the table wouldn't budge, even though Daryl Ann was still kicking it while she yelled. "What's happening? Hurry and get me out!"

"Hey, Billy Jack! Over here! I think Daryl Ann Sumners is locked up in there," I said as I continued yanking on the doorknob.

"Nicky, get over there and do your thing!" Billy Jack said to one of his men.

"Jimmie, move over and let Nicky work it. He's a magician with locks. While he's doing that, why don't you show me all that stolen poet stuff."

"Yeah, about that," my voice trailed. I stepped away making way for the police officer headed toward the door.

Billy Jack stood surveying the scene, his hands on his hips and head shaking. "For crying out loud, who can think in here? McQuaid shut those dogs up now!" he ordered as I approached him. "I'll call animal welfare to come pick them up, but calm them down in the meantime."

I stood next to Billy Jack. "You okay, Jimmie?" he said touching my shoulder. I flinched.

"Yes. I'm good."

"So, some night, Jimmie Rae. You sure know how to screw up a good bust."

"What's that supposed to mean?"

"When my guy came and got me at Lucky's we had just busted one of these thugs. He spilled about Daryl Ann, but said he didn't know anything else. We were hoping to catch the accomplices back here. At least, we've got the contraband."

I looked at him puzzled. "Huh?"

"Show me the letters and crap you found yesterday."

"Billy Jack, that's the thing. I came back here to take pictures of the Browning items to prove I'm not crazy, but when I got here it was all gone."

"Shit! This day just keeps getting better!" He took a deep breath. "Okay, at least show me where they were."

I walked to the ladies room and kicked the wooden door open with my shoe to reveal the empty black and teal tiled bathroom. My stomach was queasy and my head began to throb. "Billy Jack, you've got to believe me! This place was piled up with cardboard boxes yesterday morning. There were so many, I had to move them off the commode to use it. There were letters and an oil painting of Robert Browning I wrapped for an exhibit next month."

"How valuable is that stuff?"

"Oh, well, I never really considered that. If they have the original letters and who knows what else, I suppose to a collector they could be quite valuable—perhaps several hundred thousand dollars—maybe closer to a million? It makes me sick to think about it honestly." I remembered I still hadn't heard from Dr. Gifford and she was scheduled to leave for Italy.

Someone tapped my shoulder bringing me back to the current crisis. I turned around to see Daryl Ann more disheveled than I had ever seen her before. Her normally perfectly coifed blonde hair was matted and smeared make-up caused her eyes to look even more tired and haggard. I didn't know if she would slap or hug me.

She reached out and hugged me tight. "Jimmie Rae, girl, you are a sight for sore eyes. Thank you for finding me and getting help." An officer approached her with a thin green army blanket and a water bottle.

"Mrs. Sumners, I need to get your statement while it's still fresh on your mind."

"Can't I do that in the morning? My little FiFi needs her momma and her momma needs a proper bath and some beauty sleep," Daryl Ann said as tears formed in her puffy eyes.

"Daryl Ann, go with them. I'll take care of your dog," I told her as she still clung to my hand.

"My neighbor was supposed to take her out for a walk until I got home, but I don't know if she would have noticed I'm not home. Would you really go check FiFi for me?"

"Sure."

She released my hand. Turning away from the officer she removed a key from her bra. "I always keep an extra hidden here. FiFi's food is in the utility room pantry. Be sure to tell her mommy will be home soon."

As the officer led Daryl Ann out of the building, I looked around for Thomas. Billy Jack stood by as technicians continued to monitor him. His eyes were wide and pained. My heart ached for him. Yet, why if Thomas was the killer?

Billy Jack was yelling for me. “Hey, Jimmie Rae, get over here!”

I walked to where Thomas was stretched out. “They’re taking him to Niceton General for observation. Could you follow them and help him out since you got him into this mess?”

“What? Uh, no, I can’t go with him.”

“Oh really. And just why the hell not?”

I glared at him. “Well, I can think of about a hundred reasons why not.”

“Look, Jimmie, you hit the man on the head with a cowbell for crying out loud.” He pulled me close and said, “I’d make nice or he’s liable to press assault charges on you. It would be your story against his.”

“You’re threatening me? Really? Good grief! What about your inept so called bust? I could go to your supervisor and tell him how much you had to drink before your big mission tonight. So find someone else, Billy Jack. I’m checking on Daryl Ann’s dog then I’m hitting the sack.”

Billy Jack’s demeanor changed. He reached out and took my hands. “Now, darlin’ ain’t anyone here that likes the idea of you in the sack more than me, and we both know you got no reason to tell any tall tales on me. Let’s work together on this, Jimmie. I think we’re getting close. You go to the hospital with Tom and I’ll get this thing solved. Yes, ma’am, tomorrow it will be a done-deal then I’ll take you out on a real date. Can ya do that for me, Jimmie?”

“Sir, telephone for you,” an officer said handing a cell phone to Billy Jack. He took it but covered the speaker. “So, are we good? You’ll go to the hospital with him?”

I sighed deeply in reply. “Yes, I’ll go. I stopped and turned around. “Hey, Billy Jack?”

“Yeah, Jimmie?”

"Don't suppose you've ever considered Thomas a suspect, have you?"

Billy Jack laughed from the bottom of his heavy rodeo belt buckle.

"Ya mean Tom? Oh, Jimmie, you are funnier than those redneck comedians!" he said laughing deeply. He grinned widely, his blue eyes dancing. "Oh, girl, you are a hoot!" he said slapping my shoulder and trying to hold the cell phone in his large hand at the same time.

"Go on, get outta here. I'll see ya tomorrow," he said with a smile.

Well, so glad I could give you a laugh. I wanted to reply in some way, but it was way too late, and I was way too exhausted. Instead I let it go as one of Niceton's finest motioned me toward Thomas. I walked over to where Thomas was situated on a gurney. "Says he wants to talk to you before we load him up. Hurry, please," the paramedic said to me.

I knelt down on the floor near Thomas' head. "You sure know how to have good time. Have you always been such a knock-out, or was that just for me?" His voice was low and serious, but he managed a smile.

His brown eyes like melted chocolate chips should have been angry or at least miffed, yet they were gentle and held no grudge. He reached his hand out toward me. "You're following us right?"

"Sure, Thomas. Sorry about the cowbell. You relax and go with these guys. I'll be there as soon as I can."

He squeezed my hand. "Good, I've got something to tell you."

"Sir, we really need to get going," said a man with "Bobby" embroidered on his blue uniform.

"I'll meet you there. I've got a few questions to ask you too," I said patting his shoulder.

"Jimmie Rae, over here!" Billy Jack boomed across the store. "Any idea why these two knuckle-heads would have booked flights to Italy?"

Chapter Twenty-two

"Getting Married Yard Sale: Saturday, 9 a.m.–3 p.m. only; 517 McKinney St. Hot plate, beanbag chairs, futon, mini-fridge, towels & sheets, and more."

"No. Those two don't really seem like the traveling for pleasure type. Unless—" I hesitated. My mind was whirling like Star's stainless Kitchen Aid mixer.

"Yesss," Billy Jack said motioning his hand in a circle.

"Unless they were planning to sell some one of a kind Victorian poets' letters and art," I said realizing the pieces were sliding together to form a picture I didn't want to see.

"Yesterday, Lonnie told me their deceased mother had incurred all kind of debt. He told me his brother had a plan to get them out of debt and on Easy Street. At the time, I didn't think anything about it. Where are the tickets to, exactly?"

"American Airlines from DFW to London to Rome, tomorrow night, first class."

"Well, the geniuses aren't going too far without their confirmation numbers. Suppose they were smart enough to remember their passports?"

"My greater concern is what they planned to do and what they might do next. Jimmie, you could be in real danger. For once, please do exactly as you are told. Go to the hospital and I'll send my plain-clothes guy, Greg

Fowler, to keep an eye on you. Now, scoot. I'll keep you posted."

I reluctantly left the building and headed toward Old Blue. As I approached, the ambulance driver rolled the window down and asked, "Ma'am, are you about ready?"

"Yes," I answered. "I'll be right there. I've got to make a quick stop, and then I'll be on my way to Niceton General."

"Thank-you, ma'am," he said politely. He kicked up gravel pulling away from Cowboy's Antiques and Gas Emporium and headed south to Niceton with the red lights flashing.

As I drove down the blacktop road, fragments floated through my mind like ice in a hot drink. Daryl Ann seemed less a suspect and more a victim now. Her car was found in Hillsboro, some ninety miles west of Canton and almost a hundred miles north of Niceton. Lord knows she didn't kill Evelyn Sue. The mere thought of blood would send her to the floor. Besides she wouldn't want to muss up her manicure or hair. Murder was a messy business. Nausea threatened again as I recalled Evelyn Sue's last moments of life.

It must have been sometime after midnight when I pulled up to Daryl Ann's house. Lights wired high in the twisted branches shone down on a pair of ancient live oak tree trunks in the front yard. Cast as if they were on stage they appeared as natural sculptures in the front yard. I parked Old Blue, found the key Daryl Ann had just given me, and headed toward her house. Thanks to Daryl Ann's feng shui savvy designer, a cherry red front door with two Provincial garden urns each holding a carefully manicured six-foot topiary offered an inviting welcome.

The key slid in easily, and the door opened revealing Daryl Ann's toy Boston terrier, FiFi, who barked in equal parts of fear and happiness to see me.

"Hey, FiFi! Want to eat something?" I said, petting her coarse black hair. She jumped up my leg and licked my outstretched hand in response.

I had been to coming to Daryl Ann's with Star for various social events for years. I made my way to the pantry to get the dog food when a slip of paper with a local phone number and initials "K.W." on the front of her black refrigerator caught my eye. After I got FiFi fed, I copied the number onto a memo pad, tore off the page, and stuck it in my front pocket. I checked the digital clock on the electric stove—1:27. No wonder my eyes felt so heavy, I'd been up for almost twenty-four hours, and it wasn't over yet. I still needed to go to the hospital to see about Thomas.

A short drive later, bright lights and a heavy antiseptic smell awakened my exhausted senses at Niceton General. I walked up to the empty ER desk. A nurse walked by and slid the glass partition open. "Yes? May I help you?"

"I'm looking for Thomas Williams. An ambulance brought him in awhile ago."

"Come on back," she said pushing a button automatically opening the heavy steel door. He's in the second cubicle to the left," she directed.

I stopped at the curtain partition, wondering whether or not to enter. Conventionality insisted I knock first or somehow announce my entry. Exhaustion encouraged me to cast manners to the wind and walk in on him. At this point, formality seemed a joke after ending up on the floor on top of him at Blessings Antique Mall, sharing a passionate kiss in his barn, and then whacking him with a cast iron cowbell. What did I really have to lose now? After all, I still wasn't too sure about how he fit into this whole scenario.

The lights were dimmed except for the florescent near his bed. He rolled his head and opened his eyes as I walked into the room. "Oh, hey. You're not going to hurt me again, are you?" he asked in a low voice.

"You never know with me. It kind of depends on what you say."

He looked at me. "I'm never too sure when to take you seriously, Jimmie Rae."

"Believe me, the feeling is mutual, Thomas Williams."

A male nurse entered the curtained partition. "Oh good. Your wife is here," he said coming toward me with a clipboard.

"I'm not his wife."

"Ohhh," the nurse said. "So that's how it is, huh?" he said with a wink. "Well, Mr. Williams is being released by the attending physician. Here is a list of what you need to watch for through the night."

"What do you mean 'through the night'? You expect me to stay the night with him?" I couldn't believe what I was hearing.

"Mike, it's okay. I'm fine," Thomas said trying to sit upright. "Eww!"

"Lay back down, Mr. Williams, that's an order. The doctor doesn't want you to strain yourself. Ma'am, are you taking Mr. Williams home or not? The EMS guys said you were planning to come up here to be with him," Nurse Mike said impatiently.

"Oh, okay. Yes, I'll take him home," I said. At this point I was willing to do what ever it took to get back to Star's and sleep till Labor Day.

"Good," Nurse Mike said. "Here, sign these releases. Mr. Williams has already signed his part and we've gotten his information. Call us at this number if he begins to have any symptoms. It will reach one of us directly at the desk tonight. Do you have any questions?"

"No."

"Okay then! Mr. Williams, you are all set. Go ahead and put your clothes back on and be sure to take your medication, and rest. You should feel much better tomorrow."

"Thanks, Mike."

Thomas barely got the words out before Mike disappeared behind the blue striped curtain again. An awkward silence filled the small cubicle.

"Umm, could you hand me my clothes?" Thomas said pointing toward a mound of clothing hanging out of a plastic hospital bag.

"Sure," I said handing the bag to him. "Do you need help?"

"Well, I think I can manage the skivvies, but you may have to help me with the rest."

I reached in the plastic hospital sack and grabbed a pair of black cotton boxers, and handed them to him. He flinched in pain as he sat up and put his feet on the floor.

"Umm, you might want to avert your eyes despite the fact you've already taken our relationship to a more physical level," he said raising his eyebrows. "I'd like the chance to find out your favorite food before we get anymore intimate."

I smiled. It was hard not to be charmed by him. He was handsome, tough, smart, and had a decent sense of humor. I turned my back as he struggled around his hospital gown and into his boxers. "Okay, it's safe now. Hand me my jeans and let's see if we can get them on without you finishing me off."

I stuck my tongue out as I tossed his jeans to him. I couldn't help but notice his developed chest again just as I had earlier in the barn. Desire stirred as I remembered our passionate kiss and Thomas holding me firmly against his bare chest. In the florescent lighting the purple zigzag across his taunt abdomen seemed to glow. He stepped into his jeans and zipped them. He looked up at me, motioning for his shirt and caught me staring at the jagged scar.

"Believe me, you don't want to know. Suffice it to say tonight was not my first screwed-up bust."

"Let's go," he said, pulling a silver cross necklace over his head. He pulled his black t-shirt over his head next. "Wow, my head hurts. I'm not sure staying with you all night in a dark room is a good idea. You've got to let me heal before you attack again, okay?"

"Would you rather I drove you out to the ranch?"

"No. You look like hell and I feel like hell. We'd better lay low for a while."

"Gee, thanks. Do I need to at least call Julie and let her know where you are?"

"No. She knew I was working with Billy Jack tonight. Phone calls in the middle of the night only give her nightmares about her big brother."

"Right."

After I got him loaded into Old Blue we made our way back through downtown past The Page Turner which looked unnaturally dark and forlorn. Tomorrow, I would help clean up and salvage whatever was left. Something Thomas said earlier nagged at me. "I hate to ask this, but what were you going to tell me?"

"Oh, that. I was going to tell you good-bye. I'm catching a flight to Rome late tomorrow night.

Chapter Twenty-three

"Multi-family Garage Sale: Th–F, 8 a.m.–2 p.m., 509 Independence Drive. For Sale: clothing, dishes, toys, baby items, furniture, more. Something for everyone!"

"Oh? Interesting. And may I ask why you're headed to Rome?"

Thomas looked over at me. "I'll tell you everything tomorrow. All I want to do now is lie down and sleep. You look like you could use a little shut-eye too."

"Yeah, you already mentioned that. Considering it's been almost twenty-four hours since I last had any real sleep, yes, I could definitely use some shut eye."

With Star still holding vigil at the hospital, the driveway was empty when we pulled up in Old Blue. I managed to get Thomas in the house and helped him upstairs to my room. I planned to give him my bed and sleep on an antique chaise near my bed in case he got sick.

We never said a word to one another as I helped him pull his t-shirt back over his sore head and traded it for one of my late grandfather's soft, v-neck cotton t-shirts. I helped him pull his boots and jeans off and turned back the covers so he could slip in. Handing him a glass of water and pain pill, he looked up at me and smiled. "Thanks, Jimmie Rae Murphy."

Before I could reply, he had drifted into a deep sleep. I literally forced myself down the hall to Star's bathroom and showered. I thought about the case as I washed the vermin and filth from Cowboy's out of my hair and off my skin. It seemed we were close to figuring everything out, but something was missing. Something big. Dried off, I pulled a pink cotton camisole over my head and pulled on pink polka-dot drawstring pajama bottoms. As I was combing through my tangled, wet curls, I remembered finding a phone number at Daryl Ann's house. I set the comb down and removed the slip of paper from my jean pocket. The initials K.W. taunted me, but if my theory was correct, this case would be closed by this time tomorrow.

Thomas slept soundly. I turned on the ceiling fan, reached for a cotton throw, and lay down on the chaise watching him sleep. His deep rhythmic breathing was oddly comforting. Since Joe moved out, I'd learned to sleep alone, but I had to admit Thomas was growing on me. I'd only just met him, but felt like I'd known him forever. *He'd better have a darn good reason to be headed to Rome tomorrow*. I curled up beneath the cotton throw and let sleep wash over me like high tide at Galveston Island.

"Jimmie Rae Murphy, wake up!" Star's stern voice whispered loudly through my dream. "You have some explaining to do, missy!" I hoped I was having a nightmare. I was in such a deep comfortable sleep, hearing a steady strong heartbeat so contented I wanted only to be left alone to sleep for days. Then I heard Star's voice again. "Jimmie Rae, wake up now!"

I opened one eye and saw Star glaring at me. Her hair was in its usual single braid down her back. She wore a crisp, white linen short sleeve blouse and denim capris. As I shook the mental cobwebs from my head, I realized there was a man's arm draped across my shoulder and his body spooned close to me. For a suspended moment in the cosmos I thought I was still dreaming, but the lingering fragrance of Star's lavender soap was too real. I struggled to open my eyes and remember what was going on. Light escaped from behind the wooden shutters covering my south facing window.

"Star, it's not whatever you're thinking. I can explain everything," I said moving out from beneath Thomas' warm, sleeping body. "I'll be right down. Just give me a few minutes, okay?"

"You bet you have a lot to explain. Billy Jack's on the screened-in porch waiting on you. Dr. Gifford left a message wondering why you'd signed out on several Browning artifacts. And when were you or anyone else around here going to tell me there was a fire at The Page Turner last night? Or that Stella Pierce was found at the scene?"

"Oh, yeah, I wonder if Stella is okay," I mumbled trying to come to.

Star's expression was serious. "Yes, thank heavens she's okay. I already called her and checked to see if she was all right. She's cranky as usual, but luckily she had no broken bones just some scrapes and bruising. She said she noticed the back door was open and thought I was there so she went in and someone shoved that empty bookcase over on her then she smelled smoke." Star gave me the *look*. "Wait a cotton-pickin' minute— that's not the point. The point is you've gone too far this time, Jimmie Rae! Now get dressed so you can explain yourself!" she said before pulling the door shut.

After she left, I got out of bed, vaguely remembering getting up in the night and climbing in bed beside Thomas when he cried out in his sleep. As I moved across the oak floor, he shifted and rolled to his other side, still sleeping soundly. My head felt like a margarita-induced brain freeze without the buzz. I grabbed clean clothes from my bureau and headed toward the bathroom.

Minutes later Star handed me a cup of coffee without saying a word. "Thanks," I said, breaking the silence. "I promise to explain everything. Right now, let's go out to the porch and see what Billy Jack wants."

Humidity made the morning air thick while mosquitoes buzzed beyond the mesh screen. "So, what the hell were you thinking sleeping with the guy?" Billy Jack asked in a dejected voice.

I looked at Star. She raised her eyebrows letting me know she had told Billy Jack where she'd found me.

"First of all I didn't *sleep* with him. Secondly, remember you are the one who insisted I go to the hospital with him. The nurse told me someone needed to be with him through the night in case he got worse. It seemed the only choice at the time, okay? Besides I was so exhausted by then, I didn't care anymore."

"All in the line of duty, huh?"

I starred at him and took a sip of coffee. "Nothing happened Billy Jack, and I doubt you came over here to reprimand me. What's up?"

"I wanted to check up on you and return your cell phone. You left it at Cowboy's last night. Is there anything you want to tell me?"

"Like what? Help me out. My brain is still waking up."

"Like maybe why your boss would be calling you at dawn this morning wondering why you've signed out for the Library's rarest letters and other Browning stuff?"

I looked over to Star. "I think that's what we'd both like to know. Answer him," she said.

"Star, are you insinuating I had anything to do with the missing Browning items?"

"Jimmie, just answer Billy Jack's question."

"Okay. No, I have absolutely no idea why Dr. Gifford might think I would sign out for any Browning items. I've never taken anything out of the Library ever. Wait a minute. You two hang on, we've got a phone call to make."

I raced upstairs, stepped into my darkened room, and grabbed the slip of paper I found at Daryl Ann's.

Downstairs I grabbed the cordless phone and headed back to the screened in porch. "What in the world are you doing, Jimmie Rae?" Star said. "Now's no time to make a phone call."

"Shhh, you're both my witnesses," I said pressing the numbers and then "SPEAKER."

"This is Kate. You know what to do."

"Aha!"

"What the hell, Jimmie Rae?" Billy Jack asked, clearly not amused by my phone skills.

"I got this number off Daryl Ann's refrigerator last night. I think it may have something to do with Evelyn Sue's murder. Don't you see?"

"Nope, not following. Enlighten us, Jimmie," Billy Jack said.

I looked at Billy Jack. He was giving me one of his serious police glares. I took a deep breath and began to explain, "I work with a woman at the Armstrong Browning with these same these initials, her name is Kate too. Kate Wilson. She was in the Library when I went in early yesterday morning. I thought it was weird, but attributed it to her doing some extra work for Dr. Gifford's trip to Rome. Now, I'm beginning to wonder if she could have anything to do with the stolen items at Cowboy's or even Evelyn Sue's murder."

"Who's the murderer?" Thomas said from the doorway. He was dressed in his clothes from the night before, holding a cup of coffee. "Mind if I join the party or is it private?"

"How are you feeling?" I said sitting my coffee down and standing up to move a newspaper off one of Star's rocking chairs for him.

"Thanks, Jimmie. I've got a bit of a headache, but I've survived much worse. Although I have to admit my perpetrators aren't usually as pretty or feisty as you," he said as he sat and took a sip of coffee.

"Well, that is so just so damn sweet, you two," Billy Jack said bitterly. "Jimmie, could you stop coddling your boyfriend long enough to finish your sentence, please."

"Oh, yeah," I said ignoring Billy Jack's tone and taking my place back on the porch swing. "Unless, the person who signed my name has big plans for the Brownings' items and was working with the same two jerks who left their tickets for Europe at their shop."

"Okay," said Billy Jack. "You have my full attention."

"Bottom-line is we need to find Kate Wilson and have a chat with her. I think she has the answers we are looking for. Besides I think Dr. Gifford may be in danger. I'm going to Waco to get this straightened out."

"Now, wait a minute. Your accusations are just that. You don't have any proof and the story about the stolen Browning items didn't pan out, remember? You can't just go off half-assed, Jimmie. It doesn't work that way."

"You heard the man, right?" Star said from her wicker rocker. "Let Billy Jack do his job. He's a professional, Jimmie."

"I agree with Star, Jimmie," Thomas said over his steaming mug of coffee.

Billy Jack's cell phone rang. He looked down at the caller identification. "Okay, I'll get one of my guys to do a little research on this Kate Wilson. Jimmie Rae, leave this to us. Stick with the old poet and junky stuff, okay? Hang close in case we need to contact you. Comprehende'?" He stood. "I've got to get back to work. Star, thanks for the great cup of Joe. Tom, meet you at the office. And Jimmie, for once, do what I say, okay?" Billy Jack said sitting his cup down and making his way out the screen door to his brown Ford pick-up truck. “Mitchell here,” he said answering his phone and while opening his truck door.

“Don’t suppose you could run me by the police station? I need to pick up my truck. Maybe I can meet you later.”

“Whoa!” Star interjected. “Sorry to cut you off, Thomas, but no one else leaves until my biscuits are out of the oven and eaten.”

“You heard her, better plan on staying for Star’s breakfast first.”

“Throw me into that briar patch,” Thomas said following us to the kitchen.

“Thomas you did a fabulous job with the old radio. I don’t think it ever looked better. Keith is going to be so happy to get it. He’s been hounding me for years.”

“It was my honor, Star. It’s a great specimen. Your husband took good care of it. It just needed a couple of new tubes and a little cleaning. You want me to move it so we can eat at the breakfast table?”

“Sure, just sit it in that front bedroom off the stairs. Thanks, Thomas.”

As soon he left the kitchen, Star shot me a barrage of questions.

“Hey, give me a chance for a second cup of coffee first,” I said.

“So, what’s up with you and Thomas?”

“Nothing.”

“Sure, that’s why he’s in your bed wrapped around you like plastic.”

“Well, maybe something. But nothing either of us necessarily wants. I’m sure not looking for a relationship right now. Yesterday, I found my ex out with another woman. Actually, come to think of it, he was ‘in’—playing house with Maxine’s twenty-something cousin, Birdie. You should have seen his face after I threw that pitcher of orange juice on him.”

“Oh, Jimmie Rae, you didn’t, did you?”

"Oh, yeah, I did. It felt good too."

"Well, you know what I've always thought about Joseph." Star said shaking her head while she stirred the scrambled eggs. "Still, Thomas isn't Joe by any stretch of the imagination. He's a gentleman and comes from an honorable family. Billy Jack told me he's been working with the Niceton police department to help break up a group stealing historical items from local museums and selling them on the black market. Isn't that what Edna and Maxine were talking about a couple of days ago?"

"Yes, I guess so. But how well do you know Thomas?" I moved beside Star and whispered, "What if he murdered Evelyn Sue Dinsmore?"

Star answered with a laugh as she removed the large cast iron skillet of hot biscuits from the oven. "Jimmie Rae, you know better than to make me laugh when I'm hauling a hot pan of biscuits out of the oven. What would ever possess you to say such a thing anyway?"

I got out of her way to place the silverware and plates on the table. "Sorry. I wasn't actually looking for a laugh. I'm serious. I remembered just before Evelyn Sue died, she said the word, 'Williams.'"

"Are you sure?" Star asked reaching into the pantry for the honey bear bottle and a jar of Mayhaw jam.

"That's what it sounded like to me."

"Sure it wasn't more like, 'Wilson'?" Thomas asked as he walked back into the room.

"How long have you been standing there eavesdropping?"

"Long enough to assure you both, I'm not the murderer. Believe me, I've seen enough violence to last me more than a lifetime. Besides, didn't you just tell us your theory about Kate Wilson? I'm thinking you may just have something there. She may be the connection we're looking for. I want to check this lead and compare the information with what Billy Jack's guy finds out this morning. You may have solved this case, Jimmie."

"Oh, Lord. Please don't encourage her, Thomas," Star said as she poured each of us another cup of coffee. "Okay, the biscuits are hot and I don't allow talk of murder at my table, so you two can take a seat if you promise to eat and make more pleasant conversation."

We talked about Edna's recovery, Julie's quilting business, and my cousin's new baby. However, the elephant in the kitchen refused to be ignored. "Have you been over to the bookstore yet, Star?" I asked reaching for the juice.

"Not yet. I'm meeting Keith and Jen later this morning."

"I'll go with you too," I offered.

"That's sweet of you, honey, but I'd appreciate it if you could take that cake over to Evelyn Sue's place. I told Maria to expect my Texas Sheet Cake this morning. Besides, I want you to see if she and Tony need anything else. She's not very good at asking for help, but I know Evelyn Sue used to give her extra cash to help her buy groceries for her grandkids. She's probably a little stressed out. I got a call while ago telling me Evelyn Sue's funeral is set for Monday afternoon. The viewing is tomorrow."

I sat my juice glass down as I felt tears threaten. "Oh, goodness. It just breaks my heart, Star. I sure hope we get this thing solved before then." I dabbed at my eyes and got up to take my dishes to the dishwasher. I placed them in the top rack and walked back to lean over and hug my grandmother. "Of course, I'll take the cake over, Star. I've got to drop Thomas off at the police station first, but I'd be happy to swing by on my way back."

"That would be a big help, thanks, Jimmie," she said as she patted my embracing arms.

Thomas cleared his throat and gave Star a big grin. "Well, on that note, Miss Star, I can honestly say that was the best pan of biscuits I've ever had. Thank you for such a great breakfast and for your hospitality. Unfortunately, I should be getting over to the police station. We've got a lot of information to check out." Thomas followed my lead, picking up several dishes and handing them to me to load into the dishwasher.

"Thomas and Jimmie don't worry about the dishes," Star reprimanded from the table. "It feels so good to be home for a few hours. I just want to relax, drink another cup of coffee, and read the paper. You kids go on. Jimmie, be sure to tell Maria to call me if she needs anything else. Patty over at the church office has several folks bringing more food this afternoon."

"Okay, Star. Don't worry about the shop. I'll meet you guys over there later and help clean up," I said.

"Okay, darlin'. Don't forget to call Dr. Gifford," Star called after us.

Chapter Twenty-four

"First Methodist Church Yard Sale and Car Wash@College and Brazos—Saturday, 7 a.m.–2 p.m.—Proceeds go toward Youth Mission Trip to El Salvador. All kinds of great stuff (including the kitchen sink!) Don't miss it!"

"Oh yeah. Thanks for the reminder, Star. Don't worry. I'll get it straightened out with Dr. Gifford, and see you over at The Page Turner later," I said sliding on a pair of lime green flip-flops.

"Want more coffee or something?" I asked Thomas as I grabbed my bag and keys off the entryway bureau.

"No, I've had more than my fair share and it doesn't even seem to be fazing my headache," Thomas said following me to Old Blue.

With Star's cake wedged in the seat between us, I started Old Blue and we made our way over to the police station. Heaviness hung between us like a velvet theatre curtain. I had so much to say and yet, felt strangely reserved.

"For what it's worth, I'm really sorry about hitting you with that cowbell last night," I said breaking the silence. "I've got a headache too and no one banged me over the head. Maybe it's just this crazy murder thing."

"Yeah, it's crazy all right. But some good has come out of it all."

"What's that?"

"I finally got to meet the infamous Jimmie Rae Murphy in all her glory. I've got to say it's been my pleasure in every way—even with a lump on my skull. Guess you could say you left your mark on me in more ways than three."

"L-O-L," I said pulling into a parking slot at the police station. "Hey, before you get out, you could at least tell me why you're headed to Rome."

"Oh that. I'll trade you information for a kiss."

"Are you kidding me? I don't think that's a good idea."

"Okay, suit yourself. See you later."

I was trying to think of some sassy remark but Thomas had already hopped out of Old Blue and was headed toward the back "Official Entry Only" door at the rear of the small station.

Your loss. But I realized I was the one who regretted not taking the opportunity to kiss him good-bye. I remembered to call Dr. Gifford. She must be beside herself thinking I was the one responsible for the missing Browning artifacts. She picked up on the first ring. "Jimmie, I've been trying to reach you. I need to talk to you. Can you meet me after lunch?"

"Of course, first you have to know I didn't take the Browning artifacts, Dr. Gifford, but I think I know who did."

"I'll be interested in hearing all about that. Can you meet me at the Coffee Grounds at 3:30?"

"Yes. I'll see you then."

"Thanks, Jimmie Rae. Bye."

"Bye." I wanted to add more in my defense but the dial tone in my ear couldn't care less.

As I drove around the town square and past the new library out toward Evelyn Sue's family home, Yellow Rose Hill, I thought about Thomas. I'd only known him a day so far, but it felt like we'd known each other for years.

Conversation, even under the duress of the last twenty-four hours, was easy with him. After so many years with Joe and his constant condescending attitude it was nice to just be myself with Thomas. Despite our strange introduction and the mayhem that followed, Thomas was a guy I wouldn't mind getting to know better. Perhaps when this case was solved we could try an actual "normal" date— if Thomas was still around. By the sound of it, it didn't seem like he planned on hanging around Niceton for too much longer.

Minutes later I arrived at the Dinsmore Estate. As I pulled down the long driveway lined with yellow roses blooming like little orbs of sunshine, I could tell something was not right. With her daughter, Anna, kneeling beside her, Maria sat on a front porch rocker holding her face in her hands. I parked Old Blue and carefully lifted the metal pan of Star's renowned chocolate-cinnamon scented Texas Sheet Cake off the middle of the narrow bench seat.

"Hi, you two! Star's sent a cake out. She's already cut it so it's ready to serve," I said kicking the truck door shut. "Hey, what's wrong Maria?"

"Oh, let me take that to the kitchen. Star is too kind to send this," Anna said meeting at the porch steps and taking the cake. "Mama is a little shaken up. Last night, someone broke into Miss Evelyn Sue's house and wrecked it. The police just left, but told us not to touch anything yet. She's worried because whoever broke in left a huge mess and she won't have enough time to make it nice for Miss Evelyn's funeral reception."

As Anna took the cake in, I leaned over and hugged Maria. "What happened?"

"I'm so upset. I've never let Miss Evelyn down in all the years I've worked for her. She was such a wonderful person and now this. I should have stayed here last night, but I was so upset about her death. Tony finally suggested we go stay with Anna and Ben and the kids to get our minds off her horrible murder."

"Did the police say what they think happened? Was it random? Or do they think it could be related to Evelyn Sue's murder?"

"I don't know mi muchacha dulce," Maria said with a deep sigh.

"Don't worry about this mess. I'm sure we can figure out something—we'll just change the venue to St. Anne's parish hall or even Star's place. You really don't need to worry about this, Maria. You've had enough to think about with all this nasty murder business.

"Do you mind if I take a look around inside?" I said. "I promise not to touch anything."

"Si," Maria answered with sad eyes. "I tried to tell Miss Evelyn that young woman was bad. I could sense she was up to something. I think Miss Evelyn was paying money to that woman to keep a secret— how do you say?"

"Blackmailing?"

"Si, blackmailing Miss Evelyn. She wouldn't tell me anything when I asked, but I saw her write that woman a check for mucho dollars. It was enough to buy a small house."

"Really? Interesting. Do you remember the young woman's name?"

"Kaye Watson."

"Can you describe what she looked like?"

As a gentle breeze sent the porch's wind chimes and whirly-gigs singing, I listened to Maria describe the same young woman I knew at the Armstrong Browning Library as Kate Wilson. I still planned to take a peek inside the house, but didn't expect to find anything new since the police had already gone over the scene. Maria's information confirmed my suspicions. One woman with more names than good sense seemed the best way to describe Kate or Kaye or whatever her real name was.

Regardless it seemed she was on a mission and it didn't involve mercy just murder. I hoped Billy Jack and his team would find her before anything else happened.

"Maria, let's get you a glass of water or something, okay?" I said reaching my hand out to help her up.

Once inside the old mansion, despair hung thick in the air like the stench of burnt toast. I'd been in Evelyn Sue's home on many happier occasions through the years. Though the house stood in nineteenth century grandeur with lead glass windows and transoms, the décor reflected retro seventies brown shag carpet and orange Formica in the kitchen. As we walked through the marble tiled foyer into the long dark paneled hallway, overturned furniture, scattered papers, and broken glass were apparent in the formal living area, den, and the room Evelyn Sue had long used as her office. "Mind if I take a peek at Miss Evelyn's office?"

"Go ahead, Amiga, I'll get us some tea," Maria said.

Evelyn Sue's office was painted a delicate shell pink and had a large bay window overlooking the antique rose gardens with a pretty pond beyond. Ancient live oaks framed the scene. Inside, cotton candy pink and mint green striped taffeta curtains draped the bay window. Matching cushions on the wide ledge provided a comfortable reading niche. Walls full of books and early twentieth-century German porcelain figurines hugged the cozy room. Drawers from Evelyn Sue's large oak teacher's desk hung open and files had been carelessly strewn across the room like the aftermath of a tornado. Evelyn Sue's teaching and good citizenship awards lay smashed in one big glass and metal glob on her antique French rose Aubusson rug. What I kept noticing was the trail of pink-tinged cigarette butts throughout. I broke my morning's promise and carefully retrieved a couple of cigarette butts in a tissue from the box on Evelyn Sue's desk. I placed the bundle in my messenger bag and headed toward the kitchen.

Once in the kitchen, I noticed there was no evidence of vandalism. It appeared to be untouched by the violence that littered the rest of the house. Maria was putting ice in glasses as I entered. A large green pottery jug full of iced tea sweated on the bright orange counter. She gave me a weak smile as she poured the tea into the glasses.

"Thanks, Maria. I'm so sorry about all this. It really will be okay." I took a sip of tea. "As always, the best tea in Lee County. That hits the spot," I said as I followed her back out to the porch and sat carefully on the wooden swing. "You know Maria, I couldn't help but notice cigarette butts on the floors. I didn't think Evelyn Sue let anyone smoke in the house. What's up with that?"

"Si, true, but that Kaye smoked, even though Miss Evelyn repeatedly asked her to keep it outside and even got her pretty ashtrays for the porch. The odd thing is I just cleaned house on Thursday while Miss Evelyn was—" Tears welled once again in her eyes.

"Oh, Maria, I know. We've lost a good woman and great friend."

"Si," she said as I patted her hand.

I spent the next thirty minutes sitting with Maria and Anna on the front porch catching up on what Anna's children were doing, trying to get Maria's mind off the murder investigation and Yellow Rose Hill vandalism. All the while, my mind kept considering the cigarette butt I found near the murder scene and the ones now in my bag. Did the same person carelessly leave behind a trail of lipstick stained butts at the crime scenes?

I said my good-byes to Maria and Anna and walked down the mansion's expansive steps toward Old Blue. As I waited for the air-conditioner to kick in, I called Star to tell her about the vandalism. Although she was on her way to The Page Turner, as soon as I described Maria's dilemma, Star assured me she'd call the church office and make arrangements for the reception to be held there.

As I turned back onto the blacktop road to Niceton, it occurred to me I had my own dilemma. Should I take the cigarette butts to Billy Jack? Or should I even bother since I'd promised to not interfere anymore? After his tirade this morning, I decided against taking the butts to Billy Jack—I certainly didn't want any more grief from him today. I reasoned Billy Jack's guys were smart enough to have taken some of the cigarette butts for evidence.

Instead, I chose to go to Star's house and pick up the items I'd purchased yesterday at Mary Jayne Brown's yard sale. I needed to get them in my booth anyway. Taking the stuff to Blessings Antique Mall would keep me busy with my antique business and off the murder case.

After a quick stop to retrieve the yard sale items, a few minutes later I pulled Old Blue into the back parking lot at Blessings Antique Mall. As I was removing a small crystal chandelier out of the truck bed, Maxine drove up beside me in her brother's beat-up red Volkswagen van.

"Hey, Jimmie! What's going on?" she said sliding the side door open, and retrieving several 1950s vintage silk parasols. "Look what I scored this morning at the Methodist Church yard sale. Sweet, huh? That's a pretty little crystal chandelier. Where'd you get that?"

"At Mary Jayne Brown's."

"Oh, good. Did you get any other stuff—like information?"

"Yeah. You were right. Evelyn Sue did have a child years ago. Mary Jayne's older sister raised the girl as her own. She left as a teenager and they never really heard much from her."

"I guess that would make her in her sixties now?"

"Well, not exactly, she died several years ago. All they know is that she moved out West and had a daughter sometime in the eighties."

"That's interesting, but doesn't sound like much to go on," Maxine said draping brightly colored tightly woven Mexican serapes over her arm.

"Oh it gets better. I found Daryl Ann locked up in a roach-infested bathroom. Of course, that was only after I kinda knocked Thomas out with a cast-iron cowbell. Actually, I kind of knocked him out cold. So he had to sleep in my bed, and Star wasn't too pleased to find us together and wondered why Dr. Gifford was calling my cell which Billy Jack brought by early this morning because I'd lost it last night at Cowboys and he was waiting impatiently on Star's screened-in porch before I got up."

"Whoa! Time to breathe, sister! Let's take a deep breath and try this again. This is too good not to savor. You just sit that back down in the bed, and I'll sit this stuff next to it. Now, just hop up here and take a moment for a proper visit on Old Blue's tailgate," she said patting a space beside her. I complied. She smiled and lifted her eyebrows as encouragement to continue. "There, nice and comfy?"

I nodded in agreement.

"Good! Now, tell good ole Maxine all about it and don't you dare leave out one morsel. Remember, Jimmie Rae, I've been your best pal forever."

I couldn't help but smile. I must have sounded crazy even to my best friend of twenty-seven years. I took Maxine's advice and took a deep cleansing breath. "Okay, I'm calmer now. Are you ready for all this?"

"Oh I'm ready if the real meal was anything like the appetizer, sister, this is gonna be a steak dinner with all the trimmings," my vegetarian friend said.

I explained what had transpired with the murder case and the stolen Browning letters, but she seemed transfixed on the whole Thomas episode. "So he rode up on a horse during that rainstorm yesterday and just whisked you to the old barn and had his way with you?"

"No, girl. Were you even listening? It was a great moment—but really just a simple little kiss," I said not willing to make eye contact with Maxine.

She punched my arm playfully. "Yeah, right, Thomas Williams rocked your world. I can tell by your expression. It's okay, Jimmie. You deserve a good guy for once. I just can't believe you slammed the guy to the floor yesterday afternoon, kissed him passionately in a cozy barn, laid him out cold with a cowbell, and then topped off the day by sleeping with him. It's all so romantic! That makes dating a red-headed, Harley-riding minister seem pretty lame by comparison," Maxine said as she hopped off the tailgate. "Enough chatting! We'd better get this stuff unloaded so we can go help Star clean up over at The Page Turner."

Before I could clarify my story, Maxie grabbed her serapes and silk parasols and headed through the mall's backdoor. I rolled my eyes and began moving my stuff in too.

As I was carrying in a box of glassware and the cool bluebonnet painting I'd found yesterday morning at the Waco estate sale, another mall dealer, Lori Appleton, tucked a neon pink flyer into my box. "What's this, Lori?"

"I don't know. A kid stopped by early this morning and asked if we could distribute these flyers to all the dealers. He said he was in trouble because he'd been asked to deliver them yesterday and forgot. It looks like it might be a good sale. Too far out for me, but you love a good barn sale, huh, Jimmie?"

"Of course my reputation precedes me and that question is rhetorical," I answered with a smile.

"Hey, tell Star we've missed her at Bridge Club. How's Edna Jean doing?"

"You heard she had a car accident, right?"

"Yeah, I heard she was coming home and hit a deer or something. When did it happen?"

"I don't know about the deer, but she definitely hit something or something hit her. It was late Wednesday night. Why do you ask?"

"Well, I was coming home from church Wednesday evening and thought I saw Maxine's old pink Cadillac but it didn't look like her driving it."

"Did you recognize the driver?"

Lori closed her eyes in concentration. She opened them. "Yes, I think it was the same young woman I'd seen in here helping Evelyn Sue recently—Kaye something."

Chapter Twenty-five

"Living estate sale, Saturday only, 9 a.m. to 3 p.m. at 1001 Crestline. Cash only. High quality antique furniture and art. No children please. Line numbers distributed at 8 a.m."

As I walked down the sidewalk toward Star's bookstore, I contemplated the conversation with Lori. *So much for getting my mind off the case.* I was sipping on an iced tea when my cell phone let out its screeching ring.

The caller's voice caught me off-guard. "Jimmie, hey, thanks for answering. I figured you were still madder than a hornet after our surprise meeting yesterday. Talk about awkward."

I grimaced. "What do you want, Joe?"

"Listen, sweetheart, I've been thinking about us and I now realize I've made a big mistake. Until yesterday, I'd forgotten how beautiful you get when you're fired up. Why don't we get together and see if we can work things out. How does that sound, honey?"

"Like your usual load of crap, Joe. I'm busy. Good-bye."

"Wait, sugar. You always were such a good kidder. Really let's give 'us' another try. Please?"

His tone was as sincere as he ever sounded, I thought as I listened to his empty words. Then, as I rounded the corner and headed toward The Page Turner, yesterday's unsure future transformed into today's intriguing certainty.

With one look I knew all bets with Joe past, present, or future were off.

Down the street I watched as Thomas Williams carried four huge trash bags to the alley dumpster—his hair damp with perspiration and his biceps flexed. My breath quickened and my heart danced in my chest. The annoying voice yammering on from the object in my hand continued begging, pleading, and trying to get my attention without any success. I took a deep breath and raised the cell phone back to my face. "Gotta go, Joe. The divorce papers are final. I'm okay with it. Have a good life."

Minutes later, my step quickened as I hurried to open the metal door for Thomas. "Hey, what are you doing? Aren't you supposed to be convalescing?"

"Yeah, oh well. When I got back to the ranch, Julie and my nephew, Everett, were eating an early lunch so they could come into town and help Star get her place cleaned up. It seems Everett really admires Star."

"Well, that's not too surprising; most everyone admires her. She has always had a way with people. It's really nice of them to want to help out though."

"It's more than that. Star has made a huge impact on Everett. You see he had some learning challenges when he was a little kid. Julie was so worried that he'd never learn his letters or how to read. She began bringing him to Star's story time and getting him involved with the summer reading contests. Star made the stories come alive for him and always helped him choose a new story to tackle. Later, as a teenager Star's bookstore was his favorite place to hang out and play chess with some of the older fellas during the summer. Now, he reads incessantly."

"That's pretty cool. So how old is Everett now?"

"Oh, he's twenty and will be graduating from A&M in a couple of years with a degree in Chemical Engineering."

"Says his proud uncle," I teased.

"Well, yeah." He smiled, and crossed his arms across his broad chest. "Anyway, when Julie and Everett heard what happened, they weren't about to sit around and do nothing. I caught a ride with them, hoping maybe I could catch a ride back with you," he said with a half smile and full wink.

Whatever you wanted to call it, a magic spell or just his pure charm, it was working on me. Anyone willing to help one of my favorite people clean up from a personal disaster when he could literally be doing anything else on a Saturday afternoon definitely got brownie points on the old scorecard of life in my book. I offered him my iced tea.

"Thanks," he said taking it. "I suppose it's no worse than kissing."

"As I recall, you didn't mind that too much yesterday."

"With you, Jimmie Rae Murphy, I'll never mind." He proved his point with a quick kiss on the lips. "Right now, there's a lot to do. It seems that in the midst of cleaning up, your grandma has had a revelation about a new business opportunity."

"What do you mean?"

"Come ask her yourself."

As we entered the shop I was prepared for the worst. The stench of smoke still lingered inside on the brick walls, but there wasn't as much actual fire damage as I feared. The double front doors were wide open and the door at the rear was also wide open. In between, down the narrow bookshelf aisles, industrial sized fans blew forcing the smoke stench out of the building. Inside as many as twenty people were busy talking, laughing, and working on cleaning the shelves, floors, and books.

Star stood at the smoothly worn oak counter hunched over a piece of drafting paper with Uncle Keith and Marcus Hamilton, Niceton's architect.

"Hey!" I greeted everyone as I walked up to the counter. "What's going on?"

Star's face looked elated—happy, in fact. "What's going on is that these great folks are helping me clean up so we can open again before the Niceton Celebration Days in a couple of weeks. As for what the three of us are doing, Marcus here is showing Keith and I how we can add some additional space from Glen Spade's old place next door and build a new area for a bar."

"What? Are you serious? A bar in Niceton?"

"Of course, I'm serious, but not a bar like you're thinking—a coffee bar. I've been playing with this idea for months now ever since Edna Jean and I met Mayleen up in Seattle last October. We visited every bookstore and coffee house we could find. It turns out there's quite an art to making a proper latte. But, of course, you know that having traveled extensively through Italy. Now that we're doing repairs and clean-up anyway it seems the right time to really consider both Marcus' plan and Glen's offer."

"What offer is that?"

"Well, a few weeks ago Glen told me he and Martha have decided they want to sell their old space and retire to San Miguel, Mexico. They're giving me first crack at buying their place next door. They're willing to work out a deal and sell it to me at a more than fair price. Sometimes opportunities come along and you just have to be smart enough to know to grab the right ones. Even though everything else seems wrong now, this feels right, Jimmie."

I couldn't think of one reason to tell my grandmother who'd always been there for me why it was a bad idea to buy Glen Spade's shop next door and add a coffee house to her bookstore. Actually, it seemed the most logical thing I'd heard in the past twenty-four hours. I pulled a lime green bandana out of my messenger bag. "Where do you want me to start?"

"Why don't you help Thomas?"

"Sure, I can do that, but I won't be able to stay too long. Dr. Gifford is expecting me in Waco in a couple of hours."

"Oh, good now you can get all that business straightened out with her. Since the Fire Chief has all the evidence he could collect they've give us the okay to clean up. They'll let me know if they find out anything. In the meantime, Thomas has taken on the worst of the damage in the back by the bathroom and storage closet. I'd appreciate any help you can give him. Thanks, hon. I knew I could count on you. Love you, Jimmie."

"I love you too, Star."

As I held the trash bag open for Thomas he updated me on what he'd been able to find out at the police station. There was a search underway for Kate/Kaye Wilson/Watson. Although there was no concrete evidence she was involved with Evelyn Sue's murder, she was wanted for questioning. Thomas explained she was a *person of interest* according to Billy Jack.

"According to many witnesses, Evelyn Sue was known to have given this young woman large sums of money for what appears to have been menial household tasks," Thomas said as I swept the soot and ashes out of what was once a combination small bathroom and broom closet.

I stopped, "You know that Evelyn Sue's place got trashed last night, right?"

"No, what happened?"

"Evelyn Sue's housekeeper, Maria, and her husband, Tony, live in a cottage behind the big house at Yellow Rose Hill, but last night they stayed at their daughter's place. When they returned this morning, Evelyn Sue's family home had been completely trashed, ransacked, and vandalized. As you can probably imagine, Maria was pretty distraught."

"Yeah, I can see how she would be."

"There's more, but I can't go into all that now. I've got to run. Dr. Gifford is expecting me back in Waco."

"Good, you finally got to talk to her," Thomas said tying a knot in the huge black trash bag we'd filled with debris.

"Well, it wasn't exactly a conversation. It was brief. She just asked me to meet her at 3:30."

Thomas checked his wristwatch, "We'd better scoot."

"We?"

"Remember? Julie brought me. I don't have my truck."

"Yeah, well, she's still here. Can't you catch a ride back with her?"

"No, she and Everett are getting supplies for the ranch and meeting Lloyd in Austin for dinner with some of their friends." He touched my arm leaving behind goose bumps on my hot skin. "Come on," he insisted. "I brought fresh clothes. I'll get cleaned up and ride shotgun and you can finish telling me what else Maria told you."

"What about your flight to Rome?"

"Perhaps what you have to tell me will change my plans. I'm starting to get the feeling you don't want my company, Jimmie. Should I take it personally?"

"No. It's not that I don't want your company, it's just that I thought you didn't want me to interfere anymore with Evelyn Sue's case."

"Jimmie Rae, even though we only met yesterday, I believe among other things you're a strong-headed Texas woman who pretty much does what she wants and asks permission later."

"You think you know me, huh? Pretty egotistical on your part, wouldn't you say?" I said playfully punching his arm. "Maybe I'm more assertive than I used to be, but that's only because if nothing else the last few months have taught me it's a rough world and you gotta watch out for yourself and the people you love no matter what."

"You're preaching to the choir, girl. Let me introduce you to Julie and Everett before we tell Star good-bye."

Julie was seated on the floor cross-legged, wiping books and stacking them carefully as Everett handed them to her. I'd seen them both around town numerous times but never had the occasion to meet them formally.

"Hey, guys, take a break for a moment. I want you to meet someone." He held his hand out to Julie who took it and rose to her feet, "This is my beautiful baby sister, Julie, and my brilliant nephew, Everett, who'll be graduating from the best university on earth! WHOOP! And this, my dear family, is the one and only, Jimmie Rae Murphy, Star's granddaughter, who also has a booth over at Blessings."

Julie reached out her hand to me and smiled. She had the same dimple in her right cheek as Thomas, but that's where the sibling comparisons stopped. Her hair was blonder than brown and cut pixie-short. Her brown eyes were spirited and her grip was strong. She wore no make-up, but had the natural look of a woman who worked the land, loved horses, and wasn't afraid of a hard day's work.

"It's a pleasure to meet you both," I said shaking Julie's extended hand. I blushed when I realized how dirty my hand was, but she didn't seem to notice.

"I've heard so many good things about you, Jimmie. Of course, we think the world of Star. I can't believe someone tried to burn down The Page Turner last night."

"Me either. At least Star seems to see it as an opportunity instead of a catastrophe."

"How so?" Julie asked.

"I think she's considering expanding her store and adding a coffee bar."

"Oh, that's a wonderful idea."

Everett scowled. "Well, I don't like it at all. Star's place should stay like it's always been."

I wasn't sure how to respond. Thomas sensed the awkward moment, "Everett, you're about to find out no matter how things in your hometown change, they are still basically the same because the same good people still live here."

"That was before Miss Dinsmore took one and someone tried to burn Star's bookstore down," he said, bitterness tingeing his deep voice.

"Everett—really, son. That's uncalled for," Julie chided. "Well, we had best finish up this shelf so we can meet Lloyd, later. It's so great to finally meet you, Jimmie. You must come have dinner with us one of these nights, okay? Lloyd does a mean brisket. Or are you a vegetarian?"

"No, I'm quite the beef fan actually. It's so nice to meet you both. And Everett, I appreciate your objections to Star's coffee house idea. I'm still thinking it over too. Julie thanks for the dinner invitation. I'm sure I'll be seeing you around."

"I'm catching a ride with Jimmie, Jules," Thomas said over his shoulder as he followed me to tell Star good-bye.

"Sure, bro."

"We're off," I said to Star.

She raised her eyebrows at the "we" but kept her voice steady. "Where to?"

"I'm dropping Thomas off at his place and then going to Waco to meet Dr. Gifford."

"Just remember you promised not to interfere anymore with the murder investigation, Jimmie, right?"

"Yes, Star. I remember."

Keith approached. "Oh, hey, Jimmie. Hey, Thomas. Say, Thomas could you help us carry some of these burnt up shelves out back before you head out?"

"Sure," Thomas answered without a second thought. "I'll catch up with you."

Eager to be on my way, I gave Thomas a thankful, but impatient look. "I'm stopping by the Lone Star first. Do you want anything?" I asked him.

"Whatever you're having. See ya in a minute."

Thomas' smile and wink weren't lost on Star or me as he turned to go.

"Be careful, Jimmie," she whispered as she hugged me good-bye.

I didn't bother to ask with what. Lately every aspect of my life was like navigating quicksand. While Thomas helped carry the blackened bookshelves to Keith's truck, I headed out the door and down the sidewalk to the Lone Star Café for iced teas to go.

One of the many great things about Niceton was nobody cared about the grime, soot, and dirt covering my face or clothes. Instead the Lone Star's manager, Linda Leigh, a former high school classmate with a reputation for rampant flirtation and a collection of ex-husbands, asked how it was going over at Star's place. We exchanged small talk and a smidgen of gossip.

"Wait here while I go make your teas, okay?" she said as she turned to head back to the kitchen.

Thomas arrived through the double screen doors as I waited. "That was quick," I said as he took a seat at one of the counter barstools.

"Yeah, there were about ten of us so it went fast."

"Hey, Thomas seriously, thanks for everything you've done to help out at The Page Turner today. It's very nice of you."

Thomas pulled a bandana out of his jean pocket and wiped his brow never taking his eyes of me. His smile was slow and sure. "Jimmie Rae, before we go any further you should know, I'm not a 'nice' guy. In fact, it's one of my least favorite words in the English language. I don't do things out of pity or to be good. If I believe in cause, I work hard to make it happen. I don't care about what's in it for me. Got that?"

"Sure. You're a man of principles. I respect that. Sorry about mistaking you for being nice. I didn't mean it as an insult or anything." I tried a different subject. "So, what are your plans once you get your father's estate settled?"

"Hmmm," he said carefully considering his words. "That's not an easy question to answer. Prior to our rather intimate introduction yesterday, I'd been seriously considering taking a job overseas. It's a great opportunity and very lucrative, but like I just said that's not the interesting part to me. I'm more fascinated with the collection I'd be doing security for—it's a recent discovery of fifth century art pieces unearthed on a small Greek island."

"That sounds intriguing. So, why wouldn't you jump at the chance and take the job?"

"Now you're being coy too?" he said brushing some soot off my cheek and lifting my chin to meet his eyes. "I think we both know why I'd consider turning it down."

The moment was interrupted. "Here y'all go, Jimmie Rae. Two large teas—I got ya sweet even though ya usually go unsweet. I figured ya needed a little sweetening after all the awful things that keep happening to ya. Ha! Get it?" She handed me the teas and I, in turn, handed one to Thomas. By the way she licked her lips and stuck out her hip, I could tell Linda Leigh had discovered Thomas Williams.

"Why Jimmie Rae, I stand corrected. You've seem to have found something quite sweet after all."

"I don't know about that, Linda Leigh, but put your tongue back in your mouth and keep your hands to yourself for crying out loud."

Thomas laughed as the bells on the front door of the Lone Star Café signaled our exit.

"See, someone thinks I'm pretty incredible," he said as we walked back to Blessings where Old Blue was parked.

"Good," I answered. "Why don't you go back and give her your number. Just be warned Linda Leigh goes through husbands like Lance Armstrong goes through bicycle tires."

As we walked down the alley between the antique mall and the drug store on the other side, I realized something was not right. The back parking lot for the antique mall was full, in fact, I recognized several of the other dealer's vehicles, but Old Blue was gone.

"Where's your truck?" Thomas said reading my exact thought.

"Good question. I parked it right there," I said pointing to where an older model Bonneville was now reflecting the sun's gleaming rays. "What the heck is going on now?"

"Let's go in and see if anyone knows anything. Think anyone cares what a mess we are?" Thomas said.

"Nah, besides who cares? I want to know what the heck happened to Old Blue."

Inside, I saw Daryl Ann arranging crocheted doilies on an oak table in her booth. "Hey, Daryl Ann, you look a lot better than when I saw you last night. How are you feeling today?"

"Oh, Jimmie Rae. Hey! I'm better now that I've gotten a mani-pedi and got my hair done," she said as she stopped to take a look at me. "Dear, pardon me for saying, but it looks like you could use the name of my salon. You look vile and you smell, honey."

"Yeah, I'm a mess. There was a fire at Star's bookstore last night. We were just there helping her clean up."

"And this would be?" she asked looking past me to Thomas and vainly patting her hair.

"Thomas Williams, ma'am," he said extending his hand. "I'm glad you're doing better. I hear you've had quite the experience."

"Oh, Lordy, yes. You could say that. When that Kaye Watson called me and asked me to take Miss Evelyn Sue to the Trade Days I never dreamed there would be such trouble. I just can't believe she's gone. I miss the old girl already. God bless her soul," Daryl Ann said, her eyes filling with tears.

"Wait a minute," I said touching her arm. "Kaye Watson asked you to take Miss Evelyn Sue to First Monday Trade Days? You *did* mention that to Detective Mitchell, right?"

Daryl Ann dabbed at her eyes with a pressed vintage floral print hankie. "Why yes, hon it's not like it was any big deal. We usually go together, but I had to cancel a dental appointment to make it this time. Why in tarnation would I mention it to Detective Mitchell?"

"So you didn't mention it to him?"

"Maybe, maybe not. I can't remember. Why?" Daryl Ann stared at me, nervously twirling her hair under. Then as if someone flipped a switch, she placed her hands on her hips. "Wait a minute, Jimmie! You don't suppose that girl had anything to do with Miss Evelyn's untimely death—do you?"

"I don't know, Daryl Ann, but at this point I don't think we can count anything out of the equation. By the way, do you happen to know where my truck is?"

"I believe it was impounded by the police. I saw them tow it away as I pulled in while ago. I got your spot after they hauled your truck away. Since they've got my car impounded, I'm driving Reggie's old Bonneville. It's a beast to park," she said patting her hair again.

I couldn't believe this. I put my hands on my hips. "Wait just a bloomin' minute! You saw them tow my truck? Daryl Ann, for crying out loud, why didn't you tell me that in the first place? I've got an important appointment and I need my truck right now!" I stomped my foot for emphasis.

Thomas stepped between us. "Jimmie Rae, obviously Mrs. Sumners didn't have anything to do with your truck being impounded. Let's go find out what happened," he said to me. He faced Daryl Ann. "Thanks again, ma'am. Nice to meet you."

Daryl Ann gave me a shrug, but turned on the charm as she reached her hand out to Thomas. "Pleasure's all mine Thomas, and please do call me Daryl Ann," she said fluttering her eyelashes like a teenager.

Oh, brother.

By the time we speed-walked to the police station my blood pressure felt like it had jumped up by fifty points. I was furious. Billy Jack was talking to a uniformed officer and refilling his coffee cup when I stormed up to him. "Where is Old Blue, Mitchell?"

"That's Detective Mitchell. So nice to see you too, Jimmie Rae. Hey, Tom! How's it going?"

"Glad you asked," I interrupted Mr. Congeniality. "That's the reason we're here. I want my truck back, and I want it now, Billy Jack Mitchell!"

"Pipe down, sister. You get that weird twitch in your right eye when you're mad. Looky at that, Tom. Bet you've never seen anyone else get so riled up that their right eye twitches. She looks a mess, but it's kinda cute, isn't it?"

"Come on, Billy Jack; let Jimmie have her truck back. You've got not reason to keep it."

Billy Jack glared at Thomas. He sat his coffee cup down and poked Thomas in the chest. "Remember you're not in charge here, Williams. This is my jurisdiction and I'll conduct my investigations as I see fit. So back off!"

"Billy Jack, cool it! There's no reason to get so testy. Just give me back the keys for Old Blue and we'll get out of your hair."

Billy Jack looked at us both. He shook his head as if to prevent any more hostile words from escaping his lips.

After straightening his shirt collar, he picked his coffee cup back up. "Not that it's any of your business, but my uncle up in Canton requested the impounding just to be sure we've got all the evidence we need for the case. Besides even if I took pity on you and gave Old Blue back, I couldn't. The guy with the keys to the lot is gone for the weekend. He'll be back bright and early Monday morning."

"What the…? You'd best be joking Billy Jack Mitchell!"

He smiled. "Sorry, my hands are tied, Jimmie Rae. Tell you what just to show you no hard feelings, I'll get you a ride back home in a squad car."

"Gee, thanks, but no thanks, Billy Jack. I want Old Blue back in the same condition or better, you hear?"

"Loud and clear, Jimmie. You just better pray we don't find anything to link you to the murder or Old Blue will be the least of your worries."

Rage filled me and it was all I could do to keep my mouth shut and walk away before I said something I knew I'd regret. I spun around and strode out the door, slamming it shut. Anger fed upon exhaustion and my feet responded by pounding as fast as I could run down the tree lined streets oblivious to the humidity, traffic, or sun beating its fierce intensity on the pavement. I never heard him come up behind me, but right there in the middle of Tyler Street, Thomas Williams caught my arm and turned me around to face him. His expression said it all. His kiss was deep and passionate raising awareness in places that hadn't been aroused in too long. I melted into him as he clung to me and hot tears steamed down my face.

Chapter Twenty-six

"HUGE BARN SALE, FM 2958, #3524, 3rd house on left. Tons of great stuff— CHEAP!"

"Slow down! You're as tight as a steel drum. Try to relax, this shouldn't be difficult to figure out," Thomas said leading me by the hand to the sidewalk. "We're almost to Star's. Is there another vehicle we could borrow?"

"No. Now I'm going to miss my appointment with Dr. Gifford and goodness only knows what will happen next. I hate this!" I said turning to walk quickly toward Star's house. Thomas caught up with me as I stepped off the sidewalk to avoid two boys on skateboards. I continued my brisk walk and he kept pace while continuing to brainstorm a solution.

"There's no other vehicle at all at Star's place?" he asked.

"Well—there is one, but he'll kill me if I borrow it," I shouted over a passing ice cream truck's droning music.

"And who will kill you for what?" Thomas said encouraging me to tell him the details.

"It's Keith's car. His first car— his baby, and it's UT burnt orange." Thomas caught my arm, spinning me around again. He wiped his forehead and attempted to wipe a smudge off my face.

"Okay, who cares as long as it runs," Thomas said quietly. "It does run, doesn't it?"

"Of course it runs, it's old, but he babies it every chance he gets," I confirmed.

We turned the corner ducking beneath an overgrown rose bush. "Then here's what we do. We get cleaned up." Before I could object just in case he used the plural as in we'd be showering together, he caught my look and added, "Don't worry, I'll use the downstairs shower. Then while you're getting ready, I'll get the car going. Star has a set of keys, right?"

We turned up Star's driveway as I got my keys out of my pocket, "Yeah, they're on the hook by the backdoor. The one with the UT Longhorns." I said unlocking the door.

"Where's the car?"

"Out in the barn behind the garage. The key for the dead bolt is also on the hook. It's got a blue tag on it."

"Although that smudge on your nose is rather cute, you'd better go get cleaned up and I'll meet you in about fifteen minutes."

Impulsively, I wiped at my nose realizing too late I was probably making a small smudge only grow bigger. I wasn't sure how Keith would feel about us borrowing his car, but I wasn't about to ask either. Once upstairs, I called Dr. Gifford to let her know I was running late. When she didn't answer I left a message.

Never underestimate the wonderfulness of a quick shower. I pulled my wet hair through an elastic band. Leaving the flip-flops, denim shorts, and t-shirt in a clothing puddle on the bathroom floor. I grabbed a brown bandana and walked back down the stairs in a fresh pair of khaki Bermuda shorts, crisp white linen shirt, and leather sandals. I reached for my leather messenger bag, locked the door, and went outside to meet Thomas.

Dressed in a pair of khaki shorts and a clean short sleeve shirt, Thomas stood beside Keith's car staring at it like a he was in a trance. Fortunately, I'd seen many of my boyfriends through the years react the same way when it came to this car.

"Ready?" I called.

"Oh, Jimmie Rae, girl! Do you know what this sweet ride is?"

"Yeah, Keith's sweet old car. Let's get out of here."

I hopped in the driver's side and waited on Thomas as he gently dropped himself into the white leather passenger seat, pausing to wiggle his hips into the grooved worn seat and sigh deeply. "This, my dear Jimmie Rae, is a 1970 Mustang Fastback BOS in Grabber Orange. There were only about 45,000 produced and I'm guessing very few in Grabber Orange. It's an incredible, sweet, sweet machine."

"Yeah, whatever," I said squealing the tires down the driveway onto the hot pavement. "Hang on, this thing moves really fast."

Thomas looked my direction in awe, buckled the single strap across his waist, crossed himself, and smiled. "So what else where you going to tell me about Maria at The Page Turner?"

"Oh yeah, I'd almost forgotten with all the other distractions thanks to stupid Billy Jack. Maria told me she'd seen Evelyn Sue pay Kaye Watson. She believed it was blackmail, but when she asked Evelyn Sue about it, Evelyn Sue wouldn't tell her why. I asked Maria to describe Kaye Watson. She's just got to be the same person who works as the part-time receptionist at the Armstrong Browning Library."

"Why would Evelyn Sue be paying someone else if she already had a long-time, live-in housekeeper?"

"Well, the other day at the Piney Woods Café we chatted for a few minutes before we left for the flea market, and Evelyn Sue told me she hired a young woman to help out because Maria had surgery and there were some tasks she couldn't do yet. Still, that doesn't explain why the huge payments. And there's something else."

Thomas raised his eyebrows encouraging me to continue.

"At the crime scene Thursday I found a pink stained cigarette butt. I didn't think too much about it until today."

"So?"

"So, this morning, I saw the same color lipstick on cigarette butts throughout Evelyn Sue's house. Maria confirmed that Kaye Watson smoked and that Evelyn Sue had asked her to keep it outside. It's a long shot, but why if this Kate Wilson/Kaye Watson person is somehow related to Evelyn Sue? I've got a bad feeling about this."

"Did you tell Billy Jack about the cigarette butts yet?" Thomas asked.

"No, I guess I forgot with everything else going on. It didn't seem as important as it does now.

"Hey, aren't we headed to Waco?" Thomas asked as I turned the opposite direction and headed toward the Flying W Ranch.

"I don't remember saying you were invited to come with me to Waco. I'm taking you home. You've got to be tired and what about your head injury?"

"I'm fine. Just turn around and let's go talk to Dr. Gifford."

"No can do, mister," I said taking the dirt road off the blacktop a little too fast causing the tires to spinout slightly and kick up gravel. The landscape rushed by as I let the motor roar down the country road. I looked over at Thomas and smiled.

"Uh, Jimmie, maybe I should drive you to Waco. This car is obviously too much power for you."

I laughed turning widely through the metal gates of the Flying W Ranch. I pulled up in front of the house and stopped. The car purred impatiently. "Right! Ta-ta,

Thomas. I'll call you later. Don't let the door hit you in the bum on your way out.

He looked at me in disbelief, then opened the door and walked around to the driver's side. Leaning into the open window, his lips brushed mine. "Just remember you promised you wouldn't play detective. I'm going to give Billy Jack a call and tell him what you just told me about the lipstick stained cigarette butts."

"Yeah, okay. I've got to go," I said not liking the way I was beginning to crave his touch.

"Stay safe, Jimmie. And by the way, you owe me a real date. Think Keith would let us borrow his car again?" Thomas said raising my hand to his lips and kissing it gently.

"He just might," I said pushing the clutch hard against the floor, dropping the shifter into first, and letting it go, peeling out of the circle driveway, leaving Thomas shaking his head and laughing.

Down the hill from the Flying W, I stopped to pull my messenger bag into the vacant passenger seat. The barn sale flyer Lori had given me earlier fell out. Since I hadn't heard back from Dr. Gifford yet it didn't seem like there would be any harm in simply stopping by the sale for a few minutes just to make sure I didn't miss anything exciting. I checked the address at the bottom of the page and pulled my well-worn, folded Lee County map from the side pocket of my bag. The sale was only a few miles up the blacktop. Yes, definitely convenient enough for a quick little peek, I told myself. It wouldn't hurt to just check it out; I heard my inner voice drowning out Star's more practical concerns with my stubborn streak, inquisitiveness, and slight obsession for junk.

By the time I arrived at the next intersection, a huge wooden sign for the barn sale reinforced my decision. Although the road to Waco was right, I turned left, and followed the enticement of a good junk haul.

As I pushed the Mustang smoothly down the black ribbon road, the warm wind whipping wisps of hair across my face, I realized I felt great. Although I loved Old Blue's steady ride down the road, there was nothing like a sweet kiss, a fast car, and the gypsy sense of adventure to make a girl's day go from okay to fabulous.

As I headed to the barn sale, I contemplated what I knew about the events of the past two days. Evelyn Sue Dinsmore was dead. Who killed her? Then the true answer hit me like a Monday morning shot of espresso. All the jagged puzzle pieces finally fit smoothly together. I knew who killed Evelyn Sue Dinsmore and who was behind the stolen Browning items. Evelyn Sue wasn't trying to say 'Williams.' Now, I knew for sure she was saying, 'Wilson.'

Three miles past Floyd's Filler Up, I made a hard right onto FM 2958. A yellow tractor mailbox was marked 2300. I was going the right direction.

Elated by my revelation in solving the case, I was energized and ready to hurry through the barn sale and get back to town to wrap it all up.

I pulled the Mustang between a rusty pair of open metal gates, across the cattle guard, and up the dirt road driveway. The house was nearly unrecognizable as a shelter. Its wood structure was wrapped in green vines of wild Cherokee roses and honeysuckle. Beyond it, a large weathered barn sat, the doors wide open welcoming me in with a sign that said: BARN SALE HERE. Tables of smalls held the large metal doors back. No other cars were around. I checked my cell phone. It was on NO SIGNAL, but I had a few minutes and then I'd head back to the Niceton Police Station and let Billy Jack know I'd figured it all out before he did. Might as well bask in the glory of it, after all he put me through the last twenty-four hours. After I gloated—I mean, informed Billy Jack, I'd have him contact Dr. Gifford and let her know that I had nothing to do with the stolen Browning items.

I paused at the outside tables to look over the smalls. There were vintage hankies at a quarter each. I picked up a hand full and made my way into the dark barn. My eyes struggled to focus.

In the next moment I knew I'd forgotten the first rule of martial arts—never let your guard down. In an instant I'd realized my mistake too late.

From behind me, I heard a gun cock and felt its warm metal tip shoved into the back of my head. "You *are* a sucker for a good sale aren't you?" Cowboy said. "Well, now. Be my guest and sit a spell. You won't be going anywhere else for a long time, except maybe to join the old broad up at the pearlies."

Chapter Twenty-seven

"Red Wagon Antique Mall, 1001 Brazos River Road. Closing Forever! Don't miss dealers' clearance sales! Unique & One of a Kind Items at discounted prices for limited time."

"What do you think you're doing?" I asked Cowboy as he pushed me into an old wooden chair and began tying my hands and feet with rope.

"You're not stupid! Now, shut up or neither one of us will have to worry about this. We'll just jump to the part where I leave you for the vultures and rats."

"You'll never get away with it, you know."

"With what?"

"With this."

"That's where you're wrong," he said smiling and hitching the rope extra tight.

"Someone is expecting me. If I don't show up, a whole bunch of people we'll be looking for me."

That got his attention for a moment. Cowboy came from behind my chair and lit a cigarette measuring up the situation. He blew a puff my direction. "More likely they'll think you changed your mind or got side-tracked by some crazy sale you just couldn't pass up. Besides, this place is pretty remote," he said blowing another plume of smoke in my face.

I struggled to retain my composure and not go into coughing spasms. "You left a trail," I reminded him.

"If you're counting on the "Barn Sale" signs my associate removed them all as soon as you showed up in that sweet little ride out there."

I contemplated this. "All of them?"

He inhaled deeply again. "Yes, all of them."

I looked into his scowling leathery face, two veins in his neck bulging. The pain from the tight rope seared into my skin, but I refused to let him have even the remotest sense of accomplishment. "You guys won't get away with this," I repeated again with an edge to my voice.

Cowboy snuffed out his cigarette butt with the toe of his well-worn Justin ropers, "You're starting to annoy me. We've already been through this. Now, shut up."

"I'm not talking about this little side-show. I'm talking about the whole scheme."

"What?" he said.

"What you and Kate are planning. Where is she? Is she your associate? Surely, you're not stupid enough to trust her. You know, she'll leave without you. While you're stuck out here, she's probably already at DFW Airport. Besides, do you realize your brother has already narked you out and you stupidly left your plane confirmations for the police to find last night?" I watched as he reached in his front pocket for an almost empty pack of cigarettes. He tapped one out, and lit it in one fluid motion.

"Actually, she's pretty much in the same predicament as me," he said as he drew in a deep hit of nicotine. "Seems your boss got too curious and began to figure out what was going on, but Katie is taking care of her. Now for the last time, shut the crap up!"

"You mean, Kate Wilson. The one who killed Evelyn Sue Dinsmore in broad daylight? You know you'll go down with her as an accomplice. At least your brother was smart enough to cooperate with the police."

Anger gripped his face turning it red and drawn, his blue eyes almost white. He drew his hand back and laid it across my jaw line.

My head whipped back from the force of his hand. I glared at him. My eyes blurred with tears as drool and blood leaked from my lips. "You're pathetic—hitting a woman. Disgusting filth!" I screamed at him. He could kick the crap out of me, but I wouldn't quit. Too much was a stake now. "She killed her own grandmother, Evelyn Sue! I knew it! You know you can't trust her. She's probably already sold the loot and is sipping lattes in St. Peter's square."

"I told you to shut the freakin' hell up!" he said kicking the back of my chair. I was getting to him.

"You fool! She's leaving you to take the heat. What a jackass she made of you," I said forcing laughter out and tears back.

His twisted face displayed such deep-seated hatred I hadn't ever seen in anyone before and never wanted to see again. He spoke in a low voice. "All I know is it's been pure hell to stay one step ahead and then that damn idiot Lonnie went and sang his damn heart out. Now, shut up or I swear you'll be next, little girl."

He yanked the brown bandana out of my hair and tied it tightly around my mouth. "There! Problem solved. Don't be tryin' nothing or I'll blast you away right now, I swear I will."

I tried to kick at him, but my legs were tied too tightly to the chair. I watched him go into a side door and could hear him swearing presumably into a telephone—one with a landline.

Despite the fact my head rang and the taste of blood mixed with my saliva, the whole thing made sense now. Kate Wilson and Kaye Watson were definitely one in the same. She had to be Evelyn Sue's granddaughter, but why would she kill her own grandmother? Even worse was the way she killed Evelyn Sue, luring her to her favorite flea market—it was blatant premeditated murder.

Then there was Dr. Eva Gifford, my supervisor and friend at the Armstrong Browning. Cowboy just told me Kate was "taking care of her." Whatever was going on, Kate Wilson had nothing to lose now. Somehow, I had to get to Waco to warn Dr. Eva, and stop Kate from boarding that plane. After all, if Kate Wilson made it out of the country, it might be impossible to find her and bring her to justice.

I closed my eyes shutting out the stench of musty hay, manure, and mildew. *Okay, this was bad, but it could be worse.* When events unfolded beyond my control, I closed my eyes and forced myself to breath deeply five times.

Calmer now, my fingers explored the rope burning the skin on my wrists. It was five ply at best. I felt for the end and began working it with my fingertips. Minutes seemed like decades as I paused to breath deeply again, focusing on the task, all my energy forcing itself into concentrating on freeing my hands. I loosened the rope, but it tangled on the back of the chair. I wiggled my shoulders and arms to free it. I thought about Latin music and gave that chair the best shimmy I had ever done, freeing the rope and my hands at the same time. I yanked the bandana gag off my face and wiped my bloody lip on my white shirt. My fingers gently explored the burning place where he back-handed me across the face. It smarted, but nothing would stop me now. I bent to untie the rope from my legs. My next task was reaching the Mustang and getting out of here.

Minutes later, just as I began to think I might be able to somehow escape, Cowboy came stomping out of the office. The phone call hadn't changed his angry demeanor. He actually appeared even more sinister than before. He leaned on the office door, taking a long pull on a half-bottle of cheap tequila. Emptying its contents, he walked over to a table full of glassware on the far wall and placed the bottle on top of a stack of crystal glasses. He pulled his revolver from its shoulder holster, spun it three times, and shot the stack to smithereens. The sound of shooting and glass bursting sent his loud expletives echoing through the straw strewn rafters. I jumped in response knocking over the chair I had freed myself from.

"What are you freakin' doing untied? Damn it! Come on, you and me are taking a ride in that car out there. Give me the key, bitch!"

"It's in the ignition," I replied sarcastically then generously offered, "You take the car and I'll just hang here."

"Ha! You'd like that. Bet I know some other things I could do that a pretty little thing like you would like," he said heading my direction.

I moved behind brown hay bales working my way toward the open barn doors. "In your dreams, creep!"

Shots rang out again. "That's it! Get over here now, bitch!"

I shrank down smaller behind the bales, still able to see where Cowboy stood aiming his gun toward my hiding place. My mind raced for other options, but I was blank. Nothing came to mind. I reassessed. I'd left Thomas at his house so he was probably sound asleep by now. I'd pissed Billy Jack off royally, so he wouldn't be looking for me. Worst of all, Star thought I was safe and sound with Dr. Gifford. Nobody would miss me until it was too late. Nobody would even know where to look for me. I had to think of something.

I found an empty beer bottle on the dirt floor and threw it toward his head. It hit him upside the back of his head and thanks to his taste for cheap tequila; it threw him off balance just enough to trip him up. He hit the ground hard, and I took the opportunity to make fast tracks through the open doors to the Mustang.

As I rounded the corner toward the car I smacked into the table of smalls and got tripped up. Cowboy lunged toward me holding me down with one of his massive legs while he tied my hands behind my back again, this time so tight I could feel drops of blood trickle down.

"Oh no you don't, girlie. I ain't done with you yet. Now, comes the kinky part. I put the bandana back across your big mouth, blindfold you with this, and top it off with this," he said squashing a large hat on my head. I cringed realizing it was probably the filthy gray fake Stetson that had been sitting on the first table into the barn. The hat slid over my ears disguising the blind fold and gag to anyone who might pass us.

With my hands tied and blindfolded any ideas I had about kicking the crap out of him and taking off were gone. He shoved me in the passenger seat and slammed the door shut.

New rounds of fear mingled with terror as Cowboy revved the car's loud engine. His shrieking whistle was loud and pungent with tequila as if he were judging a bikini contest. Keith's car had that weird effect on men. Like a skateboarder on steroids we shot backwards. Cowboy let out a loud "Yippee!" as I heard pellets of gravel rain down on the Mustang's perfect paint job.

I felt nauseous and berated myself over my lack of discipline toward my junking obsession. If I'd just kept my nosy self on the straight and narrow, I'd be in Waco by now and maybe I would have been able to keep Dr. Gifford from harm. Instead, I'd let my bad habit for stopping at every dang sale sign rule my judgment and now I was in Keith's prize vintage car with a fatalistic lunatic. *Great!*

We'd been traveling for about thirty minutes at break neck speed, but I had no idea what direction.

After what seemed like the worst amusement park ride ever, Cowboy slammed on the brakes and killed the engine. I had no idea where he'd taken me.

"Stay here," Cowboy commanded as if I had any other choice. I felt the car shift and the heard the door slam as he got out. I tried pulling my hands apart, but the rope only dug deeper into my skin. I tried again with all my might and I felt a slight give to the rope. A few seconds later it loosened enough to give my poor wrists relief. With complete determination I pulled as hard as I could and the rope fell to the floorboard. I threw the stinky cowboy hat off, pulled the mask from my eyes, and untied the bandana from my mouth. It looked like he'd taken us to an abandoned building somewhere. Time to kick some bad Cowboy ass.

Cautiously, I opened the heavy Mustang door and pushed it closed. A BMW convertible and beat up Chevy truck were the only other vehicles parked in the otherwise overgrown parking lot. It appeared to be the Red Wagon, a defunct antique mall located on the far southeast side of Waco. Crouching down, I hid behind an industrial-sized trash container fragrant with filth in the warm late afternoon air.

I pulled my cell phone from my front pocket. It flashed with a voicemail notification. I listened to Eva Gifford's usual professional voice quiver with disappointment as she told me she'd received my message and would meet me at the Red Wagon Antique Mall. I looked again at the disintegrating building shaking my head. It made Cowboy's gross Antiques and Gas Emporium look like a swanky Turtle Creek hotel by comparison.

I didn't like my odds. I pushed 9-1-1 and waited for the operator. As I was telling her where I was, I heard a gunshot from the old building. "There's gunfire!" I screamed into my cell and crammed it back into my pocket. I had to hurry and get in there. My leather sandals were proving to be a detriment as I tripped and a sliver of glass found a new home in the top of my middle toe. "Ouch!" Blood dripped from my toe. I ignored it, found the rusting back door, and tested the lever to see if it was locked. The handle obliged by lifting easily. Inside, I stopped to get my bearings and let my eyes adjust to the dimness. I heard loud voices and moved cautiously toward them, careful to avoid tripping over the dusty piles of junk.

I crouched behind a tattered pink bunny chenille bedspread hung across the doorway.

"Who's there?" Kate yelled.

I peeked through a hole assessing the scene. From the intensity on their faces, it appeared Kate and Cowboy had been arguing. The flash of a pistol in Kate's hand got my attention. I held my breath.

"Who's there!" Kate yelled louder, stepping away from Cowboy and exposing a body sprawled out on the floor. I peered harder and could see it was definitely Dr. Gifford. She appeared to be alive, but injured. Her puffy eyes hinted at her immediate pain and fear.

"Kate, get away from that damn window! Someone's sure to see ya in here and get all nosey. I done told ya I took care of Jimmie Rae."

Kate swung around toward Cowboy upsetting a tray of green Depression glasses and sending them smashing to the floor.

"Me? You left Jimmie Rae in the car and you're worried about me? What a blithering jackass you are, Ronnie!" Kate looked down at the green glass chunks and kicked at them as she strode back to Cowboy. She stood on her toes and looked him in the eye. "Ya suppose she's still out there?" Kate's voice belted out as she waved her pistol toward the back door. "Guess there's just one way to find out," she said dropping to her knees and aiming the pistol at Dr. Gifford's head.

"Jimmie Rae, if you've joined our little party, get out here now! I know if you're in here you won't be able to stand seeing your beloved supervisor blown away," Kate shouted at the murky light. Cowboy spun around, his gun drawn and ready to blow me away. A mouse squeaked past my foot. "Ick!" I squealed.

Kate let out forced laughter and aimed toward my voice. "Get your ass out here now, Jimmie, or bossy lady gets it right this instant." She cocked the pistol and aimed it again at Dr. Gifford's head. Dr. Gifford began to sob, her body shuddering with each breath. I couldn't stand to watch anymore.

"Stop!" I moved into the patchy spot of sunlight squinting though the small windows of the stuffy cinderblock building.

"Gee, I have to freakin' do everything myself!" Kate stood up and glared at Cowboy as she moved closer to me aiming her pistol toward my face. "I should have just taken care of you yesterday at the Library. I can't believe someone like you is getting between me and my way outta here." She continued to point the gun in my direction, but looked back at Ronnie. "I asked you to take care of one little insignificant pest and you couldn't even manage that, Ronnie! Hard to believe we share DNA."

Ronnie, alias Cowboy, looked hard at me and almost growled his reply. "I can take care of her, Kate. It'd be my pleasure to kill her right here and now."

"Hell no! You've screwed this up enough, Ronnie. Go back to the parking lot and guard the building. I'll do this myself, besides I'm getting good at this now."

"Ya sure 'bout that? This one's slippery," he sneered.

"YES!! Beat it now, before any more unwanted customers show up," Kate shouted, moving toward me.

Cowboy Ronnie shrugged his shoulders. He took out a cigarette, lit it, and stomped toward the front entrance.

Kate twitched and attempted to reach the square outline of her shirt pocket for a cigarette. I took the opportunity to side-step toward Dr. Gifford. “Stop or I swear Jimmie Rae Murphy, I’ll blast you away! God, what I’d give for a cigarette! Damn it!” Kate watched me. “I said, hands where I can see them! What a bumbling jackass Ronnie is!”

“Must run in the family,” I mused as my eyes adjusted to the dim lighting.

“Oh, yeah, you’re real funny, Jimmie,” Kate said as she moved closer to me and jabbed the pistol into my bloody white blouse. I wanted to distract Kate and stall for time until I could figure out a way to get the gun and call for help. I pointed toward Dr. Gifford. “What did you do to Eva? At least let me try to help her then you can do whatever you want to me.” I boldly moved toward Dr. Gifford’s limp body.

A shot went off into the ceiling sending pink bits of insulation raining down on us. “You’re insane!” I screamed into her face without thinking. The hot poke of the pistol to my forehead stopped me from slugging her. Perspiration dripped down my back and fear sent a mouthful of bile up from my gut. I swallowed hard and stared into her cold blue eyes.

“I’m warning you, bitch—don’t think I won’t shoot you! Hands up now or you’ll take the rest of this clip, Jimmie Rae!”

I adjusted my posture, sizing up Kate and for once thankful to weigh more than another woman, I clenched my fists. “Either shoot or kindly remove that thing from my head,” I said in low voice. “If you think you’re going to leave a bloody trail across Central Texas and sashay onto a trans-Atlantic flight, you are nuttier than I thought,” I said purposely spitting into her face. “Face it, Kate, it’s over. Why did you do all this anyway?”

Her laugh was deep and uncontrollable, the sound of jagged insanity. "You want to know why I did it? Money, revenge, and more money— to quote your favorite poet, Elizabeth Barrett Browning, 'let me count the ways.' You see, Jimmie, I'm just taking what is rightfully mine. My mother got ripped off while my grandmother, the high and mighty Evelyn Sue Dinsmore, she sat in her castle on the hill being 'teacher of the year,' my mom worked her ass off trying to keep us off the streets with food in our stomachs."

Dr. Gifford groaned. She drew her legs up into fetal position. "Shut up!" Kate screamed turning from me and kicking Dr. Gifford in the side. Dr. Gifford gagged and began violently wrenching, her moans only getting louder. Not caring what Kate did, I lurched toward my friend and mentor. I wasn't so worried about Kate shooting me. I know that sounds crazy, but I figured that if she were really serious, she'd already have sent me to pick up the mail at St. Peter's gates. Dr. Gifford was my main concern.

I pushed Kate aside and knelt beside Dr. Gifford. She was white as altar cloth fair linen. She looked up at me with swollen teary eyes and tried to speak. The stench of blood and vomit in the warm room nauseated me, but I refused to let it get to me. I had to figure a way out of this one.

As I took Dr. Gifford's pulse, Kate watched, grinning. She jabbed her pistol into the top of her shorts and reached for her cigarettes and lighter. "Okay, you help her, Jimmie. I'll just have a little smoke. Not much you can do anyway, she's dying." Kate proceeded to light her cigarette, took in a deep draw, and continued.

"Now where was I? Oh, yes. My childhood spent in nasty rentals and homeless shelters. When my mom said something about being from Texas, I wondered why her family didn't help us. Then when I was sixteen, mom was diagnosed with cancer and the doctors needed to know her family history. I contacted the woman I thought was my grandma, but she'd adopted my mom at birth and there were no records. As I watched my mom die, I was determined to make her birth mother pay for what she had done to both our lives." Kate dropped her lipstick stained cigarette butt to the dusty floor and ground it out with her tennis shoe. She retrieved her pistol.

I held Dr. Gifford's cool hand, shaking my head and fighting back tears. "So what did the Browning items have to do with it?"

"It was my brilliant idea to expand to the world-renowned Browning collection—as kind of an extra bonus after we blackmailed Evelyn Sue into signing her will over to me." Kate shifted her weight, checking her pistol and moving toward Dr. Gifford and I. "Can't say it's been good to know you, Jimmie Rae. Now I have to shoot you and catch a plane."

Things were looking bleak for us. I had to stall her. "Was Daryl Ann in on your plan?"

"Who?"

"The woman you kidnapped. You left her Lexus in Hillsboro . . ."

"Oh, that bitchy, whiney woman! No, she was just supposed to get Evelyn Sue to Canton, but she didn't even do that right. She muffed up the whole thing. She had bought a bunch of junk and taken it to her car. Boy, was she surprised when she found me waiting for her. I wanted to blast her away, but Ronnie thought we could make some extra cash since she is three shades of rich."

Dr. Gifford was dying. She needed immediate medical attention. A spider dropping a thin opaque strand dangled from the ceiling. It gave me an idea, maybe our last chance. I stood up with my hands on my hips. "Greed will always ruin an otherwise well-thought out plan." I moved toward Kate pointing my finger at her. "Tsk-tsk, Kate, you should have known better than that. If you'd just murdered your grandmother you might have gotten away with it." I stopped and looked up, tilting my head sideways. "Oh, and look at that. A cute brown recluse is about to land on your neck," I said my eyes wide and a smile on my lips.

Her look told me she was trying to determine if my bluff was real or not. She looked sternly at me. "Nice try. You better hope it doesn't jump on me or my trigger finger is liable to react. Game's over, Jimmie. Now, keep your freakin' hands where I can see them."

I ignored her and looked up again, this time pointing. "Well, okay, but don't say I didn't warn you. I lowered my arm, stepping closer to Kate. "I know you're smart, Kate. Why don't you just hand me the gun. Yes, you'll get a murder wrap, but depending on the jury, they may have pity on you"

"Dammit, Jimmie! Don't pull this friend crap with me. Get back down there right now," Kate said, directing the pistol toward the corner where Eva Gifford lay dying.

"Okay, but first there's a couple of things you need to know," I said standing directly in front of her.

Kate gave one of her condescending, jagged laughs. "Like what, the fact you're nothing but a professional college student who sells junk? Ha! I figured that out months ago. You're a freakin' loser, Jimmie Rae Murphy!"

I stood tall and smiled, shaking my head again. "That's where you'd be wrong, Kate. I'm a devoted friend, a fierce protector of precious objects from the past, and most importantly for this particular discussion, a Tai Kwan Do black belt!"

I got in position, and squarely kicked the pistol out of her hand and across the filthy floor. It landed in a box of yellowed celluloid doll heads. We both scrambled for it. She beat me to the box and reached her hands in among the slick plastic doll heads. She found it, but I kicked her legs out from under her. The gun discharged again, sending a bullet into the glass of a vintage picture. Glass from the frame sprayed us.

Undeterred, I forced Kate Wilson a.k.a. Kaye Watson onto the dirty floor, pulled her arms behind her back, and pried the small black Lady's Stetson pistol from her long, skinny fingers. She cried out in pain, but I didn't care. I pulled tighter hearing a snap as her shoulder and arm separated. "That's for murdering, Evelyn Sue Dinsmore, sister," I hissed in her ear. "I'm afraid you won't be making your flight after all. I think you'll be staring at the walls of Huntsville State Women's Prison for some time—that is if you don't get the death sentence. This is Texas after all and bad relative or not, we don't take kindly to killing a sweet retired school teacher in broad daylight at our favorite monthly flea market. Remember that, Kate," I said letting my weight force her into the stained tiled floor.

Kate's face grimaced in agony. "You BITCH!!"

"It is over Kate!" I glared at her and considered doing more harm when I was interrupted.

"That's what you think! Drop the gun!" Cowboy's voice commanded. A feeling of deja vu interrupted my triumphant moment as the sharp thrust of metal poked into the back of my skull for the second time today. I did as he commanded. "For such a pretty, supposedly smart girl, you're friggin' stupid," Cowboy said to me, cocking his pistol once again against the back of my head. "Now hold still, you're actually both in the perfect position to die."

Chapter Twenty-eight

"Moving Sale: Fri.-Sat. 8 a.m.–3 p.m., 1126 Lyle Street. Furniture, kitchen items, exercise equipment, misc. household items."

Kate squirmed under me, trying to use her good arm to work loose. Her voice rasped. "Ronnie! Get her off me! Remember, we're kin! Don't listen to stinkin' Jimmie Rae. This will still work."

"Doubt that. Tough shit, Kate." Cowboy tossed his cigarette butt on Kate's long blond hair, using the tip of his boot to smother it out, but not before the ends singed.

"What the fu -- You burned my hair, you bastard! What the hell do you think you're doing you stupid fool? You don't have the contact information I have, you redneck grease monkey!"

Now, as if there was any question, I knew I was in a bad place between the two of them. The tip of Cowboy's black leather boot kicked me sharply in the side. I took the hint and rolled off Kate onto the grimy floor trying to avoid the glass shards. While they continued to argue, I stood up and hurried back to Eva Gifford, kneeling beside her.

Cowboy bent over to cock the gun against Kate's temple. She glared up at him. "You wouldn't dare. You're nothing without me," she screamed. "You don't have the Browning stuff, you sorry loser!"

Cowboy took a moment to consider her words and spat in her hair. “That’s where you’re wrong. I found the file on your laptop a week ago and copied it just in case you pulled some bullshit like this. I don’t need you at all, Kate.”

“Bastard! I hate you!” Kate fumed trying to get up from the floor. “Why the hell are you letting Jimmie walk around freely?” she asked pointing to us. I was perfectly still, doing my best possum act, hoping they would kill each other.

While they continued their bickering, I felt a shift in the old floor. Behind the tattered pink bunny chenille bedspread I recognized a pair of shiny black combat boots. *Well, it’s about time.* I lifted my head slightly off the floor to get a better view of the scene. Kate and Ronnie were oblivious.

Kate held her shoulder, screaming. “Ronnie, I need help! It hurts like crap! Help me!”

“Hell yeah, I’ll put you out of my misery, Kate!” He aimed his gun at her.

The floor boards creaked again. I looked back toward the bunny chenille bedspread to see multiple pairs of combat boots. I raised slightly to get a better look. No doubt about it, the proverbial cavalry had arrived. Thomas peeked through the apple-sized hole and gave me a quick wink and ‘thumbs up.’ Then he motioned me to get down. A second later a dozen men in black t-shirts and bulletproof vests filed in around the perimeter of Cowboy Ronnie and Kate Wilson.

“Drop your weapon, you’re under arrest!” a voice commanded.

Cowboy looked up from Kate at a circle of semi-automatic weapons.

Shaking his head, Cowboy dropped his gun. Kate began hollering. “Help me! He’s a murderer!” Silently, the police moved in, cuffed, and searched Ronnie, as an officer read him his Miranda Rights. Two other officers were attempting to cuff Kate as she yelled curses about her shoulder. They ended up cuffing her hands pulled to the front and letting an EMT attend to her.

Thomas scurried to me. “Are you okay?”

“Not really, but Dr. Gifford needs an EMT fast. She’s dying,” I said accepting his strong hand up.

“Medic!” Thomas shouted above Kate’s mayhem.

In a flash, Dr. Gifford was surrounded by a team of EMTs.

As I stood up the tiny glass fragments felt like a hundred little needles poking my leg. I looked down at them. “Crap!”

“What’s wrong? Where are you hurt?”

I cringed looking down my blood stained legs. “I’ve got a few glass fragments in my leg.”

In one swoop, Thomas picked me up and carried me to a cane-back chair. “I sure didn’t want you to get hurt in all this. Don’t worry another ambulance is on the way.”

I did appreciate the way this man carried me around. It went against my independent streak, but his sensual scent brought back happy reminders of our passionate kiss in the barn. Still I had questions and needed to focus. I sat in the chair dabbing at the bloody stains on my legs with my bandana.

“So, Mister Williams, you seem to know a lot about it all. Do you know if anything has happened to the Browning letters and other art pieces?”

He smiled down at me then checked his watch. “Don’t worry, they’re safe for now. We have just enough time for you to get those fragments taken care of and grab a bag.”

“Huh?” I said dumbly.

“How do you feel about fresh pasta and a glass of Chianti for lunch? We have to leave soon for Italy. We’ve got to intercept the Browning items. They’re set to arrive in Rome tomorrow. My friend, Nicholas is picking them up."

"Well, good, he can just send them back to their rightful place in good old Waco, Texas."

"You don't understand. Donati, is pretty trustworthy, but his brothers are— well, unsavory."

"Huh?"

"Let's just say they could find buyers on the real black market in one phone call. So it's imperative we go to Italy. I can go alone, but I figured you'd want to be sure we got it all."

I stared at this man. I never knew him until two days ago. However, in the past twenty-four hours, I had attacked him, shared a beer, attacked him again, and spent the night with him. Now he was telling me we needed to head off to Italy together. My head began to pound. My cell phone sent out its annoying high-pitched ring.

"Excuse me," I said to Thomas. "Hey."

"Hey, Jimmie." I knew his slimy voice. He wanted something. I took a deep breath and rolled my eyes. "Joe, what do you want?"

"I made a mistake. I miss you. I don't want a divorce. Let's give it another try."

"I thought I made it clear yesterday. You may not want a divorce, but I do. And I'd bet Star's best china, you only want to get back together because you got fired again. Forget it, Joe. Bye now." I pressed END. Energy like an electrical current flowed deeply within. It felt good.

Thomas had stepped away to give me privacy. "Is everything alright?"

"Yes, let's get out of here. I've got to do some quick packing."

He smiled and bent down to kiss me in a soulful possessive way. I was healed.

Chapter Twenty-nine

"Don't miss Austin's City-Wide Garage Sale at the Palmer Events Center. Antiques, Collectibles and Vintage Market—70 plus dealers—Sat. 10 a.m.–5 p.m./Sun. 11 a.m.–5 p.m."

"So let me get this straight," Max said leaning toward me, her red hair almost curtaining off her face. "Your first date with Thomas involved going to Italy, staying in a top notch hotel, riding around in a red Maserati through the Italian countryside, and ending up at Lake Como at the Grand Hotel Villa d'Este. You've got to be kidding!"

I smiled at my best friend. "Well yes, but we only stayed there because Mr. Gisseppi was delayed in Paris, and insisted we stay there until he could meet with us," I said knowing my justification was a tad on the boastful side. "After all, it was a business trip."

The ruffled collar of Max's cream chiffon dress lightly brushed against her chin as she beamed back at me. "Business, my big toe!" she quipped.

"Well, it's true," I pleaded. "Even though, yes, I admit I'm falling for Thomas and yes, I did wrangle him to the ground twice and yes, one time we did sleep in the same bed, but it was all very innocent! We had separate rooms the whole week in Italy."

Max giggled at my discomfort. She patted my shoulder. "Oh, I believe you, Jimmie. Only you and my grandma would take off for Italy with a guy like Thomas and act like a nun on holiday."

The golden sun was sinking past the trees of the Flying W Ranch leaving a brilliant orangey-peach glow in the sky. A gentle warm wind stirred the leaves overhead in the ancient live oaks. Long wooden tables had been pushed together on the patio. Twinkling fairy lights and candles lit up the summer evening. Lloyd and Julie were bringing out food.

On the covered porch Thomas' friends were playing guitars. Thomas was laughing at something Star was telling him. It made me a little nervous, but I was glad they enjoyed each other's company so much. Beside Star, Aunt Edna sat looking better than I had seen her look in a while. Daryl Ann was chatting with Dr. Gifford and even Billy Jack and Reverend Steve looked relaxed as they talked with the new foreman, Maria's husband, Tony. Maria and Anna were laughing with Uncle Keith who fortunately had forgiven me for taking his car. Beyond, Anna's children along with Everett and his friends were laughing and roasting marshmallows in the outdoor limestone fireplace.

Max touched my hand. "Did you know your divorce from Joe was final before you left?"

"Yes, I knew, but Thomas and I want to take this slow. The next time I say, 'I do,' I want it to last forever."

"So, what did you do for a second date?" Max asked, her eyes twinkling.

"We invited everyone involved in the First Monday case to a party with Lee County's best BBQ and music at the Flying W Ranch to celebrate getting all the Browning letters and paintings back to their rightful place at the Armstrong Browning Library." I looked at Max and smiled. She glanced down at her hand, and my eyes followed. "What's this?"

"It seems I am betrothed to our new minister."

"Oh Maxine! I'm so happy for you! Does everyone else know?"

"Only you and my parents, but I'm hoping you won't mind if we make a little announcement."

I hugged my dearest friend. We both had joyful tears in our eyes. I let her go, giving her a little push. "Well, get going! We've got a lot to celebrate!"

More Good Stuff

- Star's recipe for Texas Sheet Cake

- Jimmie Rae's Junkin' Finds:
    - Italian Mosaic Jewelry

- Road-Trippin':
    - First Monday Trade Days &
    - Armstrong Browning Library

- A few Junkin' Resources

Texas Sheet Cake

Here's Star's (author tested) recipe for Texas Sheet Cake as published in the *Dallas Morning News* a few years ago.

2 cups sugar
2cups flour
¼ pound (1 stick) margarine (or butter)
½ cup shortening
1 cup water
3 tablespoons cocoa
2 eggs
½ cup buttermilk
1 teaspoon soda
1teaspoon vanilla
1 teaspoon cinnamon
Frosting (recipe follows)

Preheat oven to 375 F. Grease a .cookie sheet with sides, set aside.

Mix sugar and flour in a large bowl and set aside. In a saucepan, heat margarine, shortening, water, and cocoa until mixture comes to a rapid boil. Stir or whisk into sugar and flour. Add unbeaten eggs, buttermilk, soda, vanilla, and cinnamon. Beat well. Bake about 20 minutes. Frost while warm. Makes 16 servings.

Frosting: Thoroughly mix ¼ pound softened margarine or butter, 3 tablespoons cocoa, 1 (1-pound) box of confectioner's sugar, 4 to 6 tablespoons milk, 1 teaspoon vanilla and ½ cup pecans.

Jimmie Rae's Junkin' Finds

Italian Mosaic Jewelry

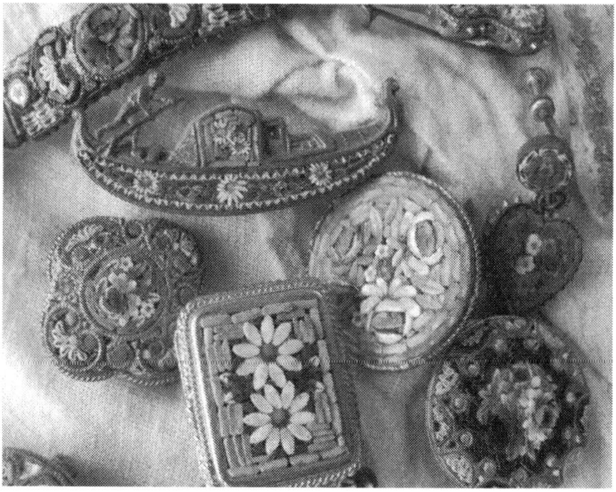

While at First Monday Trade Days, Jimmie Rae finds a piece of Italian mosaic jewelry. As a collector myself, I've seen Italian mosaic jewelry in all forms from bracelets to earrings to pendants to rings. I even have Italian mosaic trinket boxes and photo frames. Italian mosaic dates back to the end of the 18th century when artist studios began opening all over Florence, Italy. The mosaics are intricate glass beads crafted into floral designs. The micro-mosaics are even more impressive as they are literally tiny glass chips meticulously arranged into gold-filled frames.

Clues to the age of a particular piece are often found in the clasp—the more primitive, the older the piece. The patina of the piece is also a good indicator. If the framing is more gold than brass, it's probably a more modern piece. Italian mosaic can be found at antique malls, estate sales, vintage markets, flea markets, and on a very lucky day—thrift stores or garage sales.

Peace, love, and happy treasure hunting!

Road-Trippin'

First Monday Trade Days, Canton, Texas

First Monday Trade Days is an impressive monthly haven for antiques, junk, stuff you need and stuff you didn't know you needed. With more than 7,000 vendor spaces, covered Trade Centers, and an endless supply of every great Fair food, this market should be on every junker's bucket list. First Monday Trade Days is open Thursday-Sunday BEFORE the FIRST MONDAY of every month. It's open from daybreak to sunset. The Trade Centers are officially open Friday-Sunday. www.FirstMondayCanton.com

Armstrong Browning Library at Baylor University, Waco, Texas

The Armstrong Browning Library at Baylor University is Jimmie Rae's place of employment in First Monday Murder.

This fascinating place is remarkable in many respects and most worthy of a day trip. Armstrong Browning Library boasts the world's largest collection of Robert and Elizabeth Barrett Browning's personal items and writings. In addition, it also holds many other collections of Victorian writers, a Shakespeare collection, and a full range of 19th century reference materials.

The architecture of this wonderful Library is also something to behold. It is spectacular, from the awesome custom made bronze entrance doors to the beautiful stained glass windows depicting the poetry of Robert and

Elizabeth, to the 23-carat gold leaf dome sparkling from the light of a two-ton handcrafted chandelier in the Foyer of Meditation.

Armstrong Browning Library is located in Waco, Texas on Baylor University campus at Speight Avenue between 7th and 8th Streets. Admission is free (however, donations are happily accepted) and the hours are Monday through Friday from 9 a.m.-5 p.m. and Saturday, from 9 a.m. to noon. www.browninglibrary.com

Junkin' Resources

Warning--This is not a comprehensive list! There are literally thousands of fabulous shops, markets, boutiques, and vintage shows around the world. These are just a few suggestions to get you started on your own junkin' adventure. I'd love to hear of your favorites.

Post your favorites on my author Facebook wall: Lisa-Love-Harris.

Or email them to jimmieraefmm@gmail.com and I'll list them on my blog and Facebook pages.

Oregon

The Butler Did It Antiques, 124 North Hemlock, Cannon Beach

Monticcllo Antique MarketPlace, 8600 SE Stark Street, Portland, OR 97216

www.monticelloantiques.blogspot.com

Molly Mo's Summer Antique Faire, Sublimity, OR www.mollymos03.blogspot.com

Plucky Maidens Junk Fest, various locations, www.pluckymaidens.blogspot.com

Palmer Wirfs Antique and Collectible Shows, www.palmerwirfs.com

Texas

North Texas

Diggin It! 507 North Tennessee, McKinney, TX 75069 www.thediggintshop.blogspot.com

Antique Company Mall, 213 East Virginia, McKinney, TX 75069

Third Monday Trade Days, 4550 West University, McKinney, TX 75071 www.tmtd.com

East Texas

First Monday Trade Days, Canton, TX www.firstmondaycanton.com

Girls Gone Junkin', Row 46- Across from The Porch In the Paul Michael Bldg. at First Monday Trade Days www.girlsgonejunkin.com

Pandora's Box, 180 North Frankston Hwy, Frankston, TX 75763 www.pandorasboxantiques.com

Winnie & Tulula's, 119 East Tyler Street, Athens, TX 75751 www.winnieandtululas.blogspot.com

Central Texas

Dove's Nest, 105 West Jefferson Street, Waxahachie, TX 75165 www.thedovesnestrestaurant.com

Hillsboro Antique Mall, 114 South Waco Street, Hillsboro, TX 76645

www.thehillsboroantiquemall.com

Leftovers, 3900 Hwy 290W @Windy Acres Drive, Brenham, TX 77833 www.leftoversantiques.net

The Antique Gypsy, 204 West Alamo, Brenham, TX 77833, www.theantiquegypsy.com

French Market, 108 West Washington, Navasota, TX 77868

Girls @ Rusted Gingham Barn Sale, Gonzales, TX www.rustedgingham.com

Gatherings, 1009 South Austin Avenue, Georgetown, TX 78626 www.gatherinsgeorgetown.blogspot.com

City-Wide Garage Sale @ Palmer Events Center, Austin, TX www.cwgs.com

Uncommon Objects, 1512 South Congress Avenue, Austin, TX 78704 www.uncommonobjects.com

Antiques Week @ Round Top every spring and fall. Here's links to the big shows, but there are many, many more to explore as well! www.roundtop-marburger.com

www.RoundTopTexasAntiques.com
www.zapphall.com

Junk Gypsy Company, 1215 South Hwy 237, Round Top, TX 78954 www.gypsyville.com

Whimseys, 305 Bessemer Avenue, Llano, TX 78643

Binky La Faye, 303 Bessemer Avenue, Llano, TX 78648 www.binkylafaye.blogspot.com

West Texas

Petticoats on the Prairie--The Premier Vintage Market www.petticoatsontheprairie.blogspot.com

The Dragonfly, 118 Walnut Street, Colorado City, TX 79512 www.thedragonflyccity.com

Washington

The Farm Chicks Antique Show, Spokane County Fair & Expo Center, 404 N. Havana Street, Spokane Valley, WA www.thefarmchicks.com

JuNk, 802 4th Avenue, Coeur d'Alene, ID 83816 www.funkyjunksisters.com

Junk Salvation Vintage Market, various locations, www.funkyjunksisters.com

Clayson Farms Antique Show, www.claysonfarm.blogspot.com

2nd Saturdayz Vintage Market, every second Saturday at Warren G. Magnuson Park, 7400 Sand Point Way N.E. Seattle, WA 98115 www.2ndSaturdayz.blogspot.com

Ruffles & Rust—A Vintage Market to Inspire, held twice a year, Monroe, WA www.comejunkwithus.com

Ruffles & Rust Square, 1234 First Street, Snohomish, WA 98290 www.rufflesandrustsquare.com

Annie's on First, 1122 First Street, Snohomish, WA 98290 www.anniesinsnohomish.blogspot.com

Faded Elegance, 1116 First Street, Snohomish, WA 98290 www.fadedelegancestyle.blogspot.com

Joyworks, 1002 First Street, Snohomish, WA 98290, www.joyworks-shopgirl.blogspot.com

M&M Anitques & Collectibles, 119 West Main, Monroe, WA 98272 www.mandmantiques.blogspot.com

The Golden Mean, 115 ½ Main Street, Monroe, WA 98272

Bountiful Home, 122 4th Avenue South, Edmonds, WA 98020 www.bountifulhomeedmonds.blogspot.com

Town Hall Antiques, Located in County Village, 802 237th St. S.E., Suite A, Bothell, WA 98021 www.townhallantiquemallbothell.com

Cranberry Cottage, 23716 8th Avenue S.E., Suite E, Bothell, WA 98021 www.cranberrycottagebothell.com

Common Folk Co., 15600 N.E. 8th Street (A5), Bellevue, WA 98008

Today's Country Store, 1008 Main Street, Sumner, WA 98390

Camas Antiques, 305 N.E. 4th Avenue, Camas, WA 98607

Abundance Vintage, 109 North Tower Avenue, Centralia, WA 98532

Barn House—A Vintage Country Market Place, Battleground, WA 98604 www.barnhousemarket.com

The SHed ANtiques, Arlington, WA

Re-Feather Your Nest, 121 Freeway Drive, #A, Mount Vernon, WA 98273

www.re-featheryournest.com

Seabold Vintage Market, Bainbridge Island, WA 98110 www.seaboldvintagemarket.com

The Quiet Nest, 1231 Griffin Avenue, Enumclaw, WA 98022 www.thequietnest.blogspot.com

About the Author

Lisa Love Harris is a vintage journalist and gypsy spirit who juggles domestic goddessing with her passion for writing and collecting treasures.

She's traveled many of the same blacktops as Jimmie Rae. Although thankfully there have been no dead bodies, there have been plenty of flea markets, road food, Texas blues, quirky characters, and fabulous friends.

Lisa loves junking and setting up her antique business, Garden Cat, at vintage markets around Texas and the Pacific Northwest.

She lives with her 1981 prom date and husband of 30 years, their two teenagers, a slightly spoiled, but sweet dog, and a spunky old cat.

Join Lisa on her adventures down the blacktop at: www.peaceloveandallthegoodstuff.blogspot.com.

Her Facebook author page is Lisa-Love-Harris. She's also on Facebook as The Garden Cat. She can be contacted at www.jimmieraefmm@gmail.com.

14318127R00151

Made in the USA
Lexington, KY
21 March 2012